The Accidental Lives of Julian Landon

A Novel

I0683387

David Thomas Dozier

2015 © David Thomas Dozier

ISBN
978-0-692-37050-6

FIC009010 FICTION/Fantasy/Contemporary

Printed in the United States of America
by
CreateSpace, An Amazon.com Company

for my parents

Acknowledgments

I would like to thank my parents, my remote but loved siblings, my bouts of depression and lesser insanities, my odd wanderings in life, my dreams and awakenings, my unstoppable youth and all my corrected misperceptions of reality. All of it makes perfect sense now.

Special dedication is made to the strength and courage of people living with Alzheimer's disease and those who care for them. For more information please visit the Alzheimer's Association at www.alz.org.

Last but not least, love to Marie, my wife, editor and best friend.

Author's Note

This book is a work of fiction. All characters and events are imaginings of the author. Any similarity to real people or events is coincidental. While geographic locations may be real, fictional events occurring in those venues did not take place as depicted.

Poetry quotations are listed along with their authors. Other quoted material used as sectional headings belong to their authors.

Introduction

One fine spring evening in Boston when Professor Julian Landon packs up all of his belongings in his office and prepares to leave academia at Boston University after a forty-year career, he can only imagine what kind of future awaits him. He hugs Tenley, his young, attractive assistant professor and friend, and exits the University. He intends to make a good start of retirement, planning to ride out his years by writing and not worrying about the encroaching forgetfulness that has been hindering his teaching during the past year.

But the future has other plans for Julian. And youth is one of them. Adventures abound in Julian's unraveling lives, which are filled with passionate loves, mishaps, dreams, flying and foreign places.

The Accidental Lives of Julian Landon is a story of romance, illusions, fractured reality, tragedy and the quirks of mystery and irony that make less tedious the pathways and shadows of our human journeys.

It is a tale of fantasy and reality, interwoven in a visionary way that lays bare the mind's tension between hopes and realness, truths and near-truths, and the logical and illogical.

And it is love that abounds and makes sense of it all.

Prologue

The woman sat in her cell. She was pretty, young and seemed wholly out of place in her cramped confines. She had books to read, magazines and an unsolicited copy of Gideon's Bible.

A small television set sat on a platform that extended from the wall, protected by a fiberglass cover. A toilet, a single bed and a small card table were the only furnishings in the cell.

It was on this day in late spring sunny outside but the woman would never know for there were no windows in her cell, only the artificial luminescence from the only light source: two bare fluorescent bulbs on the ceiling that flickered sporadically, sometimes at lengthy intervals so that no prediction could be made as to when the stuttering light would begin its annoying display. When it did, objects in the room seem to acquire eerie motion, their shadows shuddering in the artificial light.

The lights were turned off without warning at ten o'clock each evening as was the power to the television set. During this time the woman would trade in half of her sleep for interrupted ruminations and an imaginings of freedom. Almost as if flying she would travel through the gardens and meadows of her childhood, alighting in fanciful venues where everything was pristine and innocent and where freedom abounded.

She was sustained by these nocturnal escapes; they refreshed her trust that in time she would be released from her confinement, that the day would come when she would walk out of the prison gates and enjoy her well-earned freedom.

While she blamed no one but herself for her predicament, she held mild contempt for what she believed was an unjust fate. The punishment exceeded the severity of the crime she had committed. She knew other inmates who had served less time for equal or worse crimes. The prosecutor in her case was a woman who held stricter standards for the distaff side.

She hadn't expected communication from friends and co-workers. Except for two trusted friends who were providing her invaluable help, there had been no contact from others. No one in her family knew of her whereabouts.

She did have one friend in her cell, a cockroach she'd named "Belladonna." She sustained their relationship by giving the beetle-like creature morsels of bread from her plate late at night during its scavenging hours. The creature was always waiting for her perched on one of her slippers by the bed. Over the last few months it had grown to trust the woman, even allowing her to brush its back with her finger.

She became fascinated with the small creature. She watched how it ate, delicately maneuvering a small morsel of bread with its labial and maxillary palps, turning the crumb as it slowly devoured it. The creature had been around for millions of years and the woman envied its incredible resilience and adaptability. And its freedom.

She would imagine it scooting down the cell block floor, effortlessly slipping through cracks and under doors and making its way at will out of the prison confines. She imagined it in the lush grass around the confines, its black exoskeleton glowing under the light of the moon. It became for her a strange image of freedom.

The woman became so absorbed by the insect and its ability to survive even during the most challenging times, she began to experience dreams in which she transformed into a cockroach. She would conduct daring escapes from the prison walls, slithering past guards and in and out of other inmate cells effortlessly, as though she was totally invisible.

One morning she opened her eyes, thinking she was fully awake, and was mortified by what she saw. Gazing down at her body, she realized that she had become a cockroach.

At once her new body repulsed her. Gone were her long attractive legs, her supple skin and her once appealing feet. She was lying on the crust of her back, her wings tightly folded beneath, her thorax and abdomen visible, along with three pair of thistle-like legs. She looked in horror as her vision fractured into multiple facets, creating a plethora of view points. In one facet a menacing antenna came into view, plunging into magnified clarity as it alighted on one of her lenses.

She struggled to turn over, wriggling with one pair of legs to maneuver onto her side. Time after time she tried but each time rolled back helplessly on her back. She soon realized what was limiting her mobility. Examining her lower abdomen, she was horrified to see that she was partially eviscerated, a yellow sticky fluid pinning her to the floor.

Her antennae suddenly sensed on oncoming motion, a dreadful and ominous draft of disrupted air. She tried to overturn herself one last time. And then, convincing herself that it was just a dream, she struggled to escape from the nightmare back to the safety of reality. But she couldn't make it happen in time.

The prison guard's boot came down swiftly. She felt the crunch and the blackness as one.

PART I

"For last year's words belong to last year's language
And next year's words await another voice.
And to make an end is to make a beginning."
-- T.S. Eliot

Chapter One

The mood had settled upon him a few weeks before during his final lecture as he looked out upon the sea of faces of the young men and women, many of whom would be starting their chosen professional lives, still young and idealistic, and some for whom the passion of learning would lead them to graduate work and beyond. He saw the future in their eyes not as destinations but as open doors, portals to unknown opportunities and experiences. Statistically, he knew that not all would achieve their aspirations as they traveled on their disparate roads in life. For some there would be glories and exultant successes, and for others less fortunate, tragedies, disillusionment and tribulations based upon chance or poor choices. The young doctoral student in the third row of the lecture room, a quick-witted girl with olive skin, narrow green eyes and a sheen of black hair was a person whose life had been predestined. Curious as to what she planned to accomplish with her advanced degree, he approached the student after his final lecture and asked about her future plans. "Professor," she had said, "Now that my education is complete, I plan to return to Radhanpur in India and tend to my ailing father. It is my calling."

On this late Saturday in spring Professor Julian Landon stood at the casement window in his office and realized for the first time in his academic life that he no longer had a calling. For some retirement might have felt like a rite of passage, an earned future, but to Landon it was as an intellectual dead end. He feared what it would be like not having his students and the ability to experience stimulating discourse with them. He found in their heady youth a partly selfish connection, not of the paternal sort but one of camaraderie with youth and the new generation.

He wondered what would become of his mind and his ability to indulge in the analysis and calculation of formulas. Although he did not fear death, he felt at disadvantage with the process of aging, which during the past year had begun to affect his memory. They were irritating experiences more than anything else, like forgetting a student's name or parts of his lectures or words he used in everyday conversation. They were inconsistent impediments that seem to vacillate between fugues and short lapses of memory and purely lucid periods with fecund recall. He didn't know whether they indicated the normal deficits of aging or were symptoms of serious senility, but he certainly did not wish to share his signs of decline with anyone, especially his students.

Landon rubbed at his beard and looked down at the small courtyard below. The hedge maple tree was in spring fashion, and as the late afternoon sunlight settled, one side of the tree was suited in bright emerald hue. How many years had he looked out the same window and observed the colorful transformation of the maple from spring green to the fiery reds of autumn? And the shades in between?

So too the shades of Julian Landon's professional life: the early days of graduate school, adjunct and then assistant professor and finally distinguished professor, an academic rank he'd held for the past twenty years. They had all been both challenging and rewarding years at the University. He considered himself a lucky man. He'd had opportunities and always good luck, the twin fortunes of any successful path in life. He'd worked hard all of his life, having earned the lauded title of professor emeritus. Landon felt fully accomplished and proud of his life's mission. Someone had told him that retirement should never be looked upon as an ending but rather as a genesis of deeper wisdom and new experience.

There was a knock at the door and then Tenley Harrington opened it, poking her head cautiously into the bare surroundings of the small office.

"You okay?" the charming assistant professor inquired.

Landon smiled and walked across the room to give her a hug. "Of course," he said. "Fine as a fiddle."

This was the fourth time she had popped into his office today, earlier having helped him with the packing of books. She was a strong young woman with a good back, not to mention her bright golden hair, slim body and an absolutely delicious mind full of intellect and insatiable curiosity.

"You must be worn out, Julian," she said, kissing him lightly on the cheek.

"Ready for the pasture, I guess."

"Oh Julian, nothing of the sort. You are at the doorstep to unknown adventures and opportunities. You will be starting a new, wonderful life."

Tenley smelled of fresh lilacs and he imagined she had washed her hair recently. Tall and slender, she felt both fragile and fierce, capable of surrender or amazing strength. As she released and turned, her right arm went up his back, her hand settling on the shoulder of his corduroy jacket.

"We're really going to miss you," Tenley said, adding, "not that you won't be coming back for a visit or two?"

"Of course," Julian lied.

"Harvey's moving into this office next week," Tenley said, sighing. "It's going to be hard to walk in here and not see you huddled over your desk immersed in your charming mathematical theories. Are you still going to teach somewhere?"

Julian smiled thinly and shook his head. "No, today I decided that I'm just going to retire. Maybe start on a memoir, or work on a novel. I'll keep myself busy."

"But you had plans, remember?"

He closed his eyes for a moment. "Don't remind me, please."

"Let's see...well, there was the ocean cruise, buying an island in Greece on the Mediterranean. And then, if I remember correctly, you once mentioned you were going to learn to sail and then take your boat around the world."

"They were just wistful statements. When you turn my age, you'll understand. Perspectives change and, well, possibilities become less appropriate."

"You old codfish!" Tenley said.

Landon's outlook on life had been affected by social stereotypes and more so by the physical and cognitive limitations associated with aging. He would be turning seventy soon. Everywhere he went people would always refer to him as *sir* and the checkout person at the supermarket regularly inquired as to whether he needed assistance taking his grocery bags to the car. They meant well, but sometimes their good intentions made him feel decrepit, if not physically handicapped.

"Take me with you wherever you're going!" Tenley said facetiously, quickly adding, "Seriously, keep me posted on what's happening in your life. We must keep in contact. You have my number."

"Promise," Julian said, "and cross my heart."

"We must do lunch every now and then and share our adventures."

"Yes, of course," Julian said.

Tenley stood at the door and said, "I know you think you're old, but you're far from it. This will be the beginning of a new life."

He watched Tenley gently close the door behind her, and then stared at it, wondering if this *was* the beginning of a new life or just the ending of a completed one.

He would miss Tenley. He could not deny that when she had been his student years ago he'd felt an attraction for her, perhaps more than just a casual one. He'd watched her rise through the ranks of academia and had no doubt that one day she would tenure and earn full professorship. He saw her almost every day when she was between classes and would invite herself into his office, coffee cup in hand, ready for philosophical parlay, literature discussion and sometime just to share parts of her personal life.

He walked back to the window and looked down at a couple of students seated on the stone bench beside the tree. Edifice shadows now cropped part of the courtyard, slanting over the sunlit portion of the tree as if slashed by a painter's brush. The students didn't appear to be engaged in the least; each sat as if the other one didn't exist, not reading books or notes but simply staring into some nebulous distance. Their motionless stares strangely disheartened Landon. Perhaps they were having a spat. Or maybe they just didn't care and were lacking missions in their young lives.

The telephone rang and Landon picked up the receiver to hear a familiar voice. He immediately put it on speakerphone.

"Daddy, I've been thinking about you all day. Are you surviving?"

Carolyn's voice at once lifted him out of his musing. His daughter, a fashion-wear executive with an adventuresome life, was his only child. He rarely heard from her due to her work and travels and was surprised that she had remembered.

"It's been a long day, but it's almost over," Julian said. "I thought you were at the conference in...."

"Geneva," Carolyn completed the sentence. "I'm still here. I'm tucking myself into bed as we speak. My flight leaves early tomorrow. And back to work on Monday. Are you sure you're okay, Daddy?"

"Vacating my office has not been without difficulty," Landon told his daughter. "Both physically and emotionally," he added.

"Was Tenley there to help?"

"Yes, she's been my moral support. She's such a busy girl. I'm going to miss her."

"Then take her with you," Carolyn said, almost sounding serious.

"Tenley's so committed to her work," Julian said. "I don't think she has ever taken a proper vacation."

Carolyn laughed. "Reminds me of someone I know. What's with you academicians? All work, no play. You know me, Daddy. I work very hard but I cherish my free time, being with friends, traveling, going to concerts and always opera. I planned my life in that way."

"You certainly did," Julian said admiringly. He could hear her yawn into the phone. He realized that it was almost midnight in Geneva, and he didn't want to keep her up any longer than he had to.

"Well, now, Daddy, it's your time to play. Go do something daring. Get out of that dungeon of an apartment and consider some traveling or maybe buying an island in the tropics."

Julian laughed. "Oh God, you sound like Tenley."

"No, I mean it. I really mean it," Carolyn said insistently. "It's time for you to fly again. If I were you, I'd pile all those books in a trash bin and set them afire. Not the literature, of course, but all that academic stuff you no longer need in your life. You are still young, Daddy, and there are people to meet out there."

"I think I know enough people," Julian replied. "I rather cherish the thought of privacy…real privacy."

Carolyn yawned again. "I don't mean those kinds of people, my silly old father. You're still dashing and have an intellect certain women would die to be around. You need to find yourself someone who will take care of you..."

"Oh God," Julian laughed again.

"And make you breakfast with champagne. And make wild love to you."

"Carolyn!"

"No, I mean it. You think you're so old but you're not. You look at least ten years younger than you are. You play a mean hand of tennis, you eat properly and have always taken care of yourself. And it wouldn't surprise me in the least if you meet up with some dashing woman who will sweep you off your feet and into her bed."

"Yes," Landon said, somewhat beleaguered by his daughter's comments. But that was Carolyn in true form. Well into her mid-thirties, she had never married but seemed to have a boyfriend in every port, some of them very affluent. To his dismay, she had not settled down with the Greek millionaire who promised to give her an island if she married him. And then there was the up-and-coming congressman from New York whom she had met at a party on Fifth Avenue. No, his daughter wasn't in the least ready to settle down. He would have loved a grandchild, especially a boy, and long ago had been enticed by grandfatherly notions of fishing trips, readings and having arms cling to him with adoring affection. But, alas, this wasn't to be, at least not in the foreseeable future, probably not in his lifetime.

"Promise me one thing, my darling Daddy, and that is that you will never give in to the callous cultural notion of old age. Let the corny proclaim: *You are only as old as you feel!*"

"Well today I do feel old," Julian said, and then not wanting to belabor the point, he added, "It's time for you to go to sleep. I don't want you to miss your flight. Call me when you get home and let me know you are safe and sound."

"I love you," Carolyn whispered.

"Me too," Julian said and switched off the conference phone. It was an unfair assumption but he wondered if his daughter would ever call again. It was customary for Julian to call her, which he did every month or so, but he always felt as though he was imposing or interrupting her busy schedule. Often times she would say that she was in the middle of something important and would promise to call him back, which she rarely did. It wasn't entirely her fault, he reasoned, for she followed a very busy, hectic schedule.

Carolyn was nothing like her mother Elizabeth, who had been a doting mother and a devoted, caring wife. Their daughter had been a spoiled child and had in adolescence developed a temperament of entitlement. She had high expectations of herself and more so of others, which had landed her in mostly vertical relationships with catastrophic endings.

Beyond the grieving period and the acceptance of something he couldn't change, Julian committed himself to always loving Elizabeth. Until five years ago, he'd still worn his wedding ring and had kept framed pictures of his beloved wife on his desk at work and in his apartment. He still loved her today, but the years of her absence had chastened the meaning of that word. He felt strong fondness and respect, and while that fondness would slightly intensify when he looked at his young wife in photos, with her devilish emerald eyes and her attractive face, he had long since alienated himself from that irrevocable past.

He'd last stood at her grave many years past, at a time when he knew she would want Julian to move on with his life. That emotional parting had lasted a year as Julian struggled with the last vestiges of Elizabeth's persona and the escaping bond of their relationship.

Despite his daughter's early insinuations that he needed to seek out personal relationships outside of work, to allow romance back in his life, Julian Landon thought of them as silly, if not inappropriate pursuits. Instead, he'd plunged into his work, working long days, often filling in for colleagues.

People at work knew and respected his rather strict persona and had long since abandoned attempts to include him in social overtures: cocktail parties, nighttime outings and those horrible academic picnics. He had worn a sturdy suit of armor for so long, and now he was taking it with him out through the doors of academic life.

Landon closed the blinds and the curtains in front. The shallow darkness of the room surrounded him in. He turned on the lamp at his desk and sorted through the last piles of papers, most of which he fed into the shredder. The important documents he'd already transferred to his apartment study. He began placing mementos, coffee cups, the mahogany nameplate that read *Professor Julian T. Landon* in gold stencil, the onyx paperweight, pictures of his late wife and the ubiquitous photos of Carolyn's adventurous life into an open cardboard box he'd already labeled with black magic marker: *STUDY.*

Soon there was nothing left to do but depart. He'd planned his escape from the university to occur on the weekend when he knew there would be few staffers about. He knew Tenley would be there because she had promised him; but save for a few devoted graduate students he knew, there were few left to bid him adieu. This was not a day meant for celebrations or the pomp and ceremony of retirement. His obligatory attendance at such events had taken place last week.

There was only one last thing to do. Dixon, the indefatigable custodian who had worked nights and weekends at the university for almost as long as Landon had, would be there at the grand foyer polishing the railings or mopping the massive stone floor. He had always tipped Dixon on those weekends he had reason to stop by the University. The self-effacing man was the epitome of hard work, dedication and success. Landon admired him immensely. His gratuities were not meant as handouts-and Dixon of all people would know that-but rather as tributes for his dedicated hard work. He planned on sending the man a $200 check every month. He owed it to him. Although he probably didn't know it, Dixon had shaped a great part of Landon's own work ethic and his outlook on life. He had been a model of diligence and hard work. He was a role model and an inspiration, and in many ways as much a teacher as Landon.

Having tipped the man handsomely, Landon exited the University holding two boxes at his side, and walked across the street to his car.

The late afternoon had turned chilly and festive. That was Boston in spring. The air was full of blossoms and blossoming events with the innumerable festivities marking the end of winter and its telltale reminders: the encircling gray crusts at the base of lampposts and trees that looked like dirty socks and the salty grit still visible in street gutters, soon to be washed away for the season by the next good rain.

Julian Landon loved Boston. He had lived here all of his life. He liked the solid character of Bostonians, their show-off resilience, their well-endowed sense of pride and their respect for its historical insurgency. Boston was the heart of the country, Landon believed. He had been born here and certainly planned to die in this charming but ever teeming metropolis.

Landon stopped in the parking area and looked at his faithful sportster, an old Austin Healey Mark III he had been driving for over forty years. It had been last repainted two years ago with the original factory paint, a forest green, and sported a tan convertible top, which sometimes Landon replaced with a matching tan tonneau cover when the weather was warm and he was feeling intrepid. It was a cramped midget of a car compared to the monsters currently rolling off assembly lines today. Curiously, it seemed to have shrunk in size over the passing years, and although Landon was of average height, he found it increasingly difficult to squeeze his frame into the narrow confines of the car.

Sitting in the worn leather seat, he wrapped his fingers around the mahogany steering wheel and let his eyes move across the posh dashboard, also a polished mahogany, with its analogue instrument panel. If it were possible to have a relationship with a car, it could be said that Landon had a love affair with this antique beauty. Despite that long-lasting affair, Landon sensed that in the near future he might have to part with the vehicle. The original manufacturer had long since gone out of business and replacement parts from specialty shops in California were outrageously expensive. While he had not made arrangements to sell it, recent offers had been increasingly enticing. Material possessions were becoming less important to Landon.

The furniture from the house had been in storage for decades, although Carolyn had taken many pieces over the years. He planned to sell the remaining furniture as well as the enormous dining set he had transferred to his apartment. He hadn't taken his meals in the dining room for years, preferring instead the small Norwegian-wood breakfast table in an alcove off the kitchen.

"I must divest myself of clutter," Julian Landon said out-loud, as he drove east along Storrow Drive toward his apartment building, a longer but more scenic route. Flecks of silver and gold shimmered on the expansive Charles River Basin to his left, the widest part of the river before it emptied into Boston Harbor and farther out into the Atlantic.

It had been a clear, still day and now the shallow rays of the sun lent foreboding shadows to objects below: lampposts, buildings, benches and vehicles. Shadows like these tricked the senses, especially depth perception, and Landon took seriously that his eyesight was not to be trusted without his glasses, which were in his jacket pocket in the cramped back seat. Too late to rummage for them now.

Waiting for the light to change at the crossroads of Exeter and Marlborough streets, he heard emergency sirens behind him. They were still far away, but their shifting tones were amplified by the transparent evening as they echoed off nearby buildings. It was clear, though, that they were coming his way. Soon he noticed a blur of red and white flashing lights in his rearview mirror.

There were no cars behind him. He advanced a few feet and pulled the sportster against the right curb just to make sure there was ample clearance. If the light changed before then, Landon planned to turn right off his planned route to allow the vehicles clear path. He had always been a cautious and defensive driver and didn't plan to start his retirement with any harrowing experience.

A police car appeared suddenly, screeching into view on the other side of the street. Another, behind it, did the same. For one fantastic moment Landon thought he was the object of their pursuit, and his hands froze on the wheel.

The impact and sudden acceleration drove Landon into the back of his seat so forcefully that he could feel the compressed coils drill into his back. The acceleration seemed to last forever and only ceased when the malevolent force behind spun his car halfway around and careened off at an angle before Julian heard it crash into another vehicle.

It was obvious that he had hit his head on the windshield. Stunned and unable to move, Julian Landon felt imprisoned in a chasm of silence. His heart was beating furiously, as if striving to exit his chest, and his legs, wedged against the floorboard, were igniting with sharp throbs of pain, a pain only equaled by what was surely a broken neck.

The silence imploded as the wail of sirens rushed in. Men's voices were issuing commands. People were running about, pounding the pavement as if they were wearing heavy workmen's boots. A gunshot cracked nearby. And then another.

Dismally, Landon thought it was a case of mistaken identity. He knew he had been shot and envisioned that an officer's car had crashed into him. *What a horrible way to die, an innocent victim of such cruel circumstances.* He closed his eyes and waited to be effaced by death.

The driver's side door swung open with a crunch. "Bud, you'll be okay?" a sturdy voice announced. "I don't want you to move at all. Do you understand?"

The thick arms of a Boston firefighter reached into the car and gently placed a cervical collar around Julian's neck. Questions were firing at him at a staccato pace: *Where do you hurt? Can you feel your toes? Trouble breathing?*

Expecting that the Healey would have to be dismantled for him to exit, Landon was surprised at how easily he was extracted once the fabric of the convertible roof had been slashed open.

The soft, angelic face of an EMT leaned over the gurney to which Landon had been transferred. She had a pixy face with freckles on her brow and cheeks. Her breath smelled of peppermint. "Sir," she said, "I need to know your next of kin. We need to call them."

"Am I dying?" Landon asked.

"No," she said. "Not at the moment."

"What about my car?"

"I'm pretty sure it's dead," the young woman replied.

As he was being loaded into the ambulance, Landon scanned his surroundings, as much as his stiff collar allowed him. Police cars were everywhere, lights flashing harshly in the waning evening light. At least two hook-and-ladder fire trucks were scattered about the scene. One officer still had his gun in his hand. All of it blurred into the evening as the ambulance doors were shut and the vehicle sped away, soon turning on its own siren.

His head wound bound with thick gauze, Landon watched the ambulance medics go about their duties, one having placed a pillow under his legs and the girl starting an intravenous feed. "It's just saline," she said apologetically. "I know you're in pain but I'm not authorized to give you medication. They will do that at the hospital after they've run their tests. You'll be okay, sir."

"Have I been shot?" Landon said in a thick voice.

"I don't think so," the girl said and then ran her hand over Landon's brow and held it there quite firmly. She pressed harder and began moving her lips silently. Her concern for her patient was overbearing. He could see it in her eyes. It was almost as if she was anointing him or perhaps giving last rights.

When he could stand it no longer Landon said, "Please. You're making the pain worse!"

She snapped her hand off his brow suddenly as if she had been burned by a hot plate. "I'm sorry," she said dryly, obviously taking offense to his remark.

Landon regretted the silence that followed and now the brusqueness of the girl's interaction with him. She took his blood pressure again, re-checked the collar and then shined a light into each eye. She called in the information to the hospital.

He tried to sit up but the chest pain flattened him. The girl admonished him for his efforts and then made sure the collar hadn't shifted. "I'm sorry," Landon told her. "You were just trying to comfort me. I didn't mean to offend you."

Landon watched her hardened expression slowly transform. A cataract of emotion swelled in her eyes. Her hands began to tremble. She wiped back the tears with her forearm.

"Are you okay?" he asked.

She shook her head silently.

He apologized again.

"If you really want to know," she said finally, "last night I had a patient die on me. My first DOA."

Landon gently touched her arm. "I'm so sorry. It must have felt horrible. Well, I vow not to be another DOA. So don't worry."

The girl smiled weakly and then a guarded look came to her face. She looked like she had just given away a national secret. "I shouldn't have told you that. It wasn't professional."

"It's quite alright," Landon said. "I understand completely."

The ambulance driver was cutting sharp corners, causing the vehicle to groan and its contents to rattle. Landon gasped as they hit a bump. He grabbed at the frame of the gurney.

"Where am I going?" he asked with slight desperation in his voice.

"Mass General," the girl replied. "It has one of the best trauma units in the city."

"What is your name?"

"Angel," she said.

"You have a good heart, Angel, and you are an expert paramedic."

The ambulance lurched sideways as it took the corner of the ramp and sped through the entrance toward the emergency area of the hospital. Landon could feel the vehicle backing up slightly, and then the rear doors parted to reveal several nurses in faded green scrubs bustling about, unlocking the restraints of the gurney and soon sliding him out under the soft evening sky.

Angel slid a metallic clipboard under his feet. She bent down. "Good luck, Sir. Thank you for keeping your word."

"I always do," Landon said, trying to get the girl to smile again.

Faces swarmed over him. People turned him on his side and palpated and poked, and then
portable scanning machines were brought into the bay. He watched dizzily as tubes of blood were drawn from the catheter on his arm. He was asked to take a deep breath and hold it. Someone pushed so hard on his stomach a vile taste came to his mouth.

A nurse's voice filled his left ear: "Are you allergic to anything?"

"No. I don't believe so."

"Do you know where you are?"

"At the hospital," Landon said.

"What hospital?"

"Mass General, I believe."

"What day is it?"

Landon closed his eyes. "The worst day of my life."

Soon the urgency of the inquisition and the frantic probing of his body stopped and he was swept away to an emergency room bay. Time seemed to slow to a stall. Exhausted, he fell asleep.

The next time he opened his eyes a bespectacled male nurse with a reddish Ginsberg beard was leaning over him, inspecting his blood catheter. The expansive beard appeared to have no boundaries, as though it were an extension of the man's halo of matching frizzy hair.

"What are you doing..?" Landon mumbled.

"I'm going to give you some pain medication."

"Are you sure?" Landon protested.

"You were very lucky," the man said. "Probably a mild concussion but no serious head trauma. You broke some ribs and bruised your pelvis. Other than the pain you're feeling, you're going to be just fine."

"I haven't been shot?"

The man shook his head.

"Thank God," Landon said.

"Delaudid, good stuff," the man said, parting his beard with one hand. Two over-sized front teeth peeled into view as he smiled.

Landon thought absurdly that he was about to be bitten by the nurse. He was watching the Ginsberg beard carefully for any sign of that intent when suddenly, with a deafening silence, the lights went out.

He drifted in and out of an artificial slumber the likes he had never experienced before.

Sirens wailed in his head and then flashing lights, which became towering beams piercing through a very dark sky. He felt little people scurrying about his body, Lilliputian hands tickling his chin and poking at his eyes. He had a vague dream of Carolyn when she was about five, sitting opposite him on a seesaw, her dimpled legs flinging in the air as he propelled her high above the playground. And then he saw the Healey being lowered into the ground, a huge dugout that was obviously meant as her grave. He heard himself argue in a mumbling slur of nonsensical words.

Out of the dwindling of senses and memory emerged a solitary beam of light so brilliant and inquiring, it commanded a response. The light faded not with intensity but as if squeezed into a portal, splinters of brilliance shooting from the door frame as it slowly closed, soon expunging all of the escaping light.

The vague and ironic notion that he had survived a car crash only now to face death again drifted through the waning moments of his consciousness. This time he knew for certain that he was dying. He tried to submit himself to the process.

But then death became a glaring choice.

Julian Landon fidgeted with this dilemma, experiencing it with a fluttering of resentment and excitement. It didn't seem fair. Death wasn't supposed to work this way and, although he felt on the verge of it, Julian felt cheated. *Take me! Take me!* he screamed in the last bleak moments of awareness.

It had come to this. No wrong choices. But a choice had to be made.

Chapter Two

The lights going on and off, chilled fingers feeling for a pulse and the repetitive noise of a pump turning on and then evacuating its air. These sensations had come upon him gradually, drawing him in and out of that profound darkness. He was on the edge between light and dark, a liquid tension, the dark now a drowning pool, the light the brimming surface of life, and he in between, gulping for air.

Although the slumber had been deep, he was becoming aware of exhaustive travels through the night. Vague perceptions of arrival and departure and states of altered awareness fluttered through his gaining consciousness. Although his body felt rested, his mind was exhausted as if he had finished a night of complicated calculations, working with implausible formulas. Suddenly, he yearned for more sleep, even deeper sleep where his imagination and thoughts could take silent refuge.

He yearned but yet he struggled to stay conscious. He didn't want to go back there for fear that he would never return. Suddenly he rose, as if propelled by a great force beneath him. The hospital room met him with a brilliant explosion of presence.

"I am not dead!" he blurted out in an exhalation of anguish.

This got the attention of a nurse seated a small computer station next to the open door. She arose and came to Julian's side and began taking his pulse. She looked down at him with a fixed resolute smile.

Landon wondered for a second whether she had heard his words or only his gasp. He realized that he was wearing an oxygen mask, each breath clouding the inside of the plastic shroud. He struggled to remove it.

The nurse looked up at the monitor and then unfastened the mask. "Professor Landon, you are doing just fine. You had a serious reaction to the medication they gave you. At one point we thought we might lose you. In fact, you stopped breathing several times."

"Dilaudid," Julian Landon muttered, recalling the man with the Ginsberg beard.

He rose slightly from his pillow and gazed about the small room. A casement window much like the one in his office allowed a slice of pale sunlight to fall across the room, laying itself like a faintly-lit blanket over the foot of his bed.

Slowly he remembered what had happened the evening before, not the details but enough to discern that he had been in an accident. It wasn't as much troubling as it was revelatory. Being able to remember something, he assumed, meant that his brain was still working.

Julian struggled to say something but his words were suddenly garbled. For a second he thought he'd uttered a profanity.

"May I have your name?" he finally managed through dry lips.

"Nurse Claxton," she said. "You will be under my care until your doctors decide what to do with you."

Julian rubbed at his eyes. "I hope they have good plans," he said.

Claxton said nothing. She was a stout middle-aged woman with recently-dyed brown hair cut short with thick bangs. She appeared to be of German stock, big boned and strong, a person, Julian fancied, whose capabilities were not to be taken lightly.

An attractive Polynesian woman swept into the room with a bright smile and a cheery countenance that would have vacated a dungeon of devils.

"Breakfast, sir," she said politely and set down the tray on the moveable table beside his bed.

Nurse Claxton gave the young woman a tense look, not exactly ill-willed but as a moral caution that she was not to be fooled by the motives of young people, especially attractive young girls.

Seeing the nurse's expression, the young woman threw Julian a wink.

Nurse Claxton moved in like a dark tide, forcing the girl to hurry her exit. She swung the table so that it was above Julian's waist and then pressed a blue button on the railing to raise him into an eating position. She removed the cover to the tray and examined the meal.

Finally, she said, "I have taken a personal interest in you as a patient because we are connected, so to speak."

"Do I know you?" Julian asked, considering the possibility that he'd left behind at least some portion of his memory.

"My father was one of your students," Claxton said. "He admired you immensely and always made a point to select one of your classes. He always talked about you and your brave theories. You ignited his intellect and curiosity."

"Oh," Julian said. "What was his name?"

"Charles Claxton. My father was a missionary and although he never used his academic credentials in his work, I think he was inspired by you, Professor, to take on a life of dedicated missionary work."

Claxton repositioned the pillow behind Julian's head. He didn't know what to say because the name escaped him entirely. Finally he said, "I'm honored to know that I inspired your father. Where is he now?"

Without a shift of expression, Claxton said, "He died in a plane crash flying over Nairobi...about five years ago. But he died doing what he loved to do."

"I'm so sorry," Julian said. "I'm sure I would recall your father had it not been for the accident. You see, my memory right now seems somewhat compromised."

"Understandable," Claxton said. "But he probably won't stand out in your mind. My father always had a quiet, unassuming character."

"Well, I'll do my best," Julian said as Claxton left the room with her charts.

He looked down at his meal: scrambled eggs, toast and a strip of bacon, along with milk and a cup of juice. He poked at the eggs, ate half of the bacon and then pushed the tray away.

He glanced at the clock above the door and saw that it was barely seven. He struggled for the button on the railing, found it and began lowering the head of the bed. At first he strove to find a face for Charles Claxton. He had taught many hundreds of students over the years and he couldn't possibly remember all of their faces and names, he comforted himself. Nevertheless, he tried to focus, but the advancing bank of what was surely amnesia rolled in like a gray fog. He was soon fast asleep for the effort.

◆

He was awakened abruptly by Tenley's voice at the doorway, and then Claxton's stern voice. They seemed to be arguing.

Tenley was then leaning over his bedside. She kissed him on the forehead. "Oh God, Julian," she said. "Are you okay?"

Julian tried to smile. "They say I'm a miracle case...be out of here tomorrow."

"That's not exactly what *Nurse Ratched* said." Tenley sat down on the edge of the bed. "I'm afraid it's going to be up to the old battle axe when and if you are going to be released."

"How did you know I was here?" Julian said.

"Oh, Julian, didn't you know that I'm your *next of kin*?"

"God. I'm sorry," Julian said. "They were so insistent at the accident scene. I couldn't think of anyone else. You don't mind, do you?"

"I'm honored, my dear Julian. But you know that you have a very loving daughter who should be with you now."

"Carolyn's in Geneva," Julian said, and then realizing the time difference and the day's passage, he added, "Well, in fact, I don't know where she is at the moment."

"You must call her."

"No," Julian protested. "I don't want to upset her travels. She is such a busy young woman. If I were at death's bed, it would be a different matter. She's due back in Chicago by mid-week, so I'll just wait and call her then. Please don't call her yourself."

There was a hard knock at the door and Tenley stood up from the bed. Two suited men walked in and approached Julian, Claxton in tow. "Fifteen minutes," she said. "That's all!"

They introduced themselves as detectives from the Boston Police Department. One took a seat in a chair near the bed, the other on the edge of the vacant bed. Tenley moved off to the window.

"I'm Lieutenant Cowley," said the larger of the two men, inching his chair closer to the bed. He had a gray handlebar mustache and a cavernous dimple on his chin.

"Lieutenant Bowles," the other said blandly, sounding as if the words rose involuntarily from deep melancholy. He wore an equally bland expression.

"Professor Landon," Cowley went on, "I wanted you to know the details of your accident yesterday evening. First off, quite clearly it wasn't your fault, and the police report reflects that. You were in the wrong place at the wrong time. Police were chasing the getaway car, which unfortunately back-sided your vehicle at the intersection of Exeter and Marlborough."

"Getaway car?"

"From a bank robbery at the Citizen's Bank in East Cambridge," Cowley continued. "The fugitive led us on a wild chase before he slammed into your vehicle. You're very lucky your gas tank didn't ignite, Professor."

"God, yes."

"I'm afraid your vehicle was totaled, but I'm sure your insurance company will replace it once you've made the claim."

"I don't think so, detective," Julian said sadly. "It was an antique, beyond replacement, I assure you. But it doesn't matter. I'm just glad to be alive.

"Yes sir," the detective nodded. "You were very lucky."

"But I remember hearing gunshots," Julian said.

Cowley and his partner stood up simultaneously, the lead detective pushing the chair back from the bed. "I'm afraid the case is under investigation. All I can tell you is that the fugitive was shot. I have a statement you need to complete. There's no rush, Professor, so I'll just leave it with the head nurse."

"*Nurse Ratchet,*" Tenley whispered from the window.

Julian smiled and then waited for the detectives to exit. When they did, Tenley rushed over and took her seat on the edge of the bed. She was wearing an ecru pants suit with a flowery blouse and her hair was damp as if she'd recently stepped out of the shower.

"Well, you *are* a troublemaker," she said.

"No," Julian said. "Like the detective said, it's being at the wrong place at the wrong time."

"I didn't mean it seriously," Tenley said. "Now, I'll need your apartment keys. You'll have to tell me your favorites and what else I should bring."

"Favorites?"

"Your clothes, Julian. Pajamas, underwear, shirts and slacks. And of course shoes."

Julian sighed. "I'll wear what I had on. Please don't bother."

Tenley laughed. "Then you'll be going home in the buff. They cut everything off when you were in trauma. You must have left your shoes in the Healey. No one has reported seeming them.

Julian closed his eyes. "Better to be buried with the car," he said, for a moment relishing in the memory of the sportster and the expensive Fluevog wingtips he'd owned almost as long as the car. He looked up at Tenley. "The place is a mess. Just bring whatever you think I'll need. Slippers would probably be more comfortable than shoes. I have a laptop in the den, so if you wouldn't mind, bring that too."

"Consider it done," Tenley said, leaning over again to kiss him on the forehead. "And if you can think of anything else, just give me a call. I know I'm in your address book but I don't see the phone, so I'll leave my number here beside the bed. Back in a jiffy, as they say."

Julian watched as the young professor walked swiftly to the door. She had an air of proprietary attractiveness, good looks that left no doubt that she was equally educated, intelligent and assertive. He had heard over the past year that Tenley had caught the gaze of many wandering eyes, in not but a few cases attracting offers of assignations from some of her more eager male students.

Suddenly, Julian missed the university. The feeling hit him so suddenly and deeply, he felt a slight aching in his throat.

What was he thinking? It was over, a done deal, the first pension check already deposited in his bank. It was far too late to reverse his decision.

But it wasn't academia or the university he would miss, he soon admitted. It was Tenley.

◆

Landon awakened again, this time to the sound of a curtain being drawn over a rod. He opened his eyes to a white canvass backdrop, now recognizable as privacy curtain around his bed. He heard Nurse Claxton's voice, a bit muffled, giving instructions. Other people were present as well, as Julian watched silhouettes move across the partition. There were several loud clicks.

An intruding hand parted the curtain, and the head nurse leaned in. "You're awake," she said. "Just wanted to let you know that you have a roommate."

"I thought this was a private room," Julian said, not quite irritatingly but with enough of emphasis to indicate his displeasure.

"Only as long as we have enough beds," Nurse Claxton said.

"I'm sorry, I don't mean to complain," Julian said.

"Well, we wouldn't want you to complain, Professor. It's the reality in hospitals these days. We can't ship patients onto the street when there are extra beds in unfilled rooms. It's not like the old days."

"I understand," Julian said, regretting now that he had ever mentioned the comment.

Claxton said firmly, "When you have visitors please make sure they stay inside the curtain. It'll only be until the morning when we hope to have a free room for our *visitor*."

"Yes, it's quite alright," Julian said apologetically.

For the next half an hour, Julian drifted in and out a fugue state, not sleep but a shallow awkward day-dreaming that seemed to incorporate external noises around him, so that a door opening or footsteps or what sounded like metallic rattling became like theatrical sound effects.

Drawing out of that vague state, Julian began piecing together fragments of memory about the accident. Now he remembered getting into the sportster, his hands firmly planted on the steering wheel. It repeated to him like a short video clip, starting and rewinding, as if it held enormous importance in the slow recollection of events. He remembered starting the Healey and feeling its rough idle as he allowed the engine to warm up. Then the sequence stopped altogether, leaving a palpable blankness in its place.

Julian shut his eyes, pressing them closed for several moments as if that effort would bring it all back: the drive toward his home, the thoughts in his mind and the accident. The more earnestly he tried, the less he could recall. He remembered Tenley but wasn't sure now when he'd last seen her. He didn't think she had come to the hospital yet.

His mind was playing cruel tricks once again. The confusion worsened as he struggled to put the clipped scenes of memory together. The concussion must have exacerbated his memory loss, which had come upon him now so suddenly. An anxious tremor in his brain, a vague recollection of struggles and fear, all swelled in his mind as significance neared.

It had been occurring for the entirety of a year. Names, even people he had known for ages, slipped his mind. He had compensated for it in lectures by resorting to detailed outlines, which he arranged in chronological order at his lecturing desk. Remembering his students' names didn't pose a threat, as he always asked the students to introduce themselves in a roll call manner. Landon simply wrote in their names on the classroom seating chart. Now these troubling thoughts arranged themselves in Landon's mind not as accurate events but rather as annoying probabilities.

Had this been the real reason he had decided to retire? As if attempting to dismiss this conclusion, Landon's memory suddenly emerged as if the muscles of dementia had released his captive recall, as a clam shell would its shining pearl. He grabbed at it and began experiencing exquisite recollections.

"Sara Thornton," he whispered brightly, recalling the moon-faced senior seated in front row of the lecture room. And then, "Bailey and Pete," the two pre-law showoffs who possessed the finesse to transform a mathematical theory into a legal case.

Julian further tested his memory by recalling the faces of people he'd encountered in the hospital. "Ginsberg!" he erupted, remembering the male nurse in the trauma bay. He laughed when he recalled the man's teeth.

"Tenley," he said. Of course he had seen her that day. She was at his apartment.

At least for now his memory was fine.

There was a rattling at the nearby bed. "Shut up, old man!"

Embarrassed, Julian made a short apology.

"I've got to go," the man grumbled insistently. Julian didn't know if the statement was directed to him.

Another man's voice responded unintelligibly. And then the metallic rattling ensued. His roommate obviously got up from his bed. "How do you expect me to piss with these on!?"

Realizing the situation, Julian tensed. *Good God!* he said to himself, considering that the man might be a murderer or at least a felon having committed some terrible crime. Indignation swept over him. He planned to submit his complaint to hospital authorities. Full or not, the hospital had no right to put him in with a handcuffed criminal. He planned to complain to Nurse Claxton directly, as well. He didn't like feeling this way, but this was over the top.

Lying anxiously in his bed for several minutes, Julian heard the man return and the sounds of handcuffs being put on and locked to the railing. Remembering what Claxton had said about a shortage of beds in the hospital took the edge off his resentment. Why bother to formally complain? It would change nothing, he rationalized. Anyway, he would probably be released tomorrow.

Julian turned on the overhead television and skipped through the channels, stopping on NBC news, where they were discussing the latest congressman's fall from grace. The junior member had apparently fondled himself in the chambers of Congress.

After following the story for a while, Julian turned the television off. What in God's name was happening to his government, the very seeds of which were sown right here in his beloved Boston. All of it was out of control, the malfeasance, the corruption and the radical divisiveness between parties. At least he didn't have to deal with it. He paid his taxes with regularity but he'd long ago stopped his contributions to his party of choice. Cynicism was called for in cynical times.

He lay there for several more minutes and then Julian felt a wave of curiosity wash over him. Soon it nagged at him, as well as the obligation he felt to be neighborly. The man was just a few away and for better or worse, he *was* his roommate.

"Excuse me, sir," Landon began, suddenly realizing that he was sounding much too formal for the occasion. "My name is Julian. Julian Landon."

"So?" the man answered immediately. He sounded young, perhaps a man in his late twenties.

"I apologize for my earlier rambling. I was half dreaming and I didn't mean to disturb you."

"Yeah," the young man responded. "I guess I overreacted. They've got me in four-point restraints, not the hospital kind but regular old cuffs, and they hurt like hell, even more than the gunshot wound."

"You were shot?" Julian said.

"In the back, upper left shoulder. Bastards. I'm going to sue them for this. How could I be a danger to those cops if they shot me in the back. I was retreating, not confronting them."

"I'm sure it was an accident," Julian offered lamely and abruptly realized that was not what he meant to say. Quickly, he added, "No, in the back, that wouldn't be an accident at all. I hope you have a good attorney."

The man laughed. "I'm hardly in a position for hiring a lawyer. I haven't even been allowed my first call. The gunshot wound was superficial, they say, and I should be out of here tomorrow. If I have to rob another, I'll find the money to get me lawyered-up and then sue the bastards!"

"You should," Landon said, "but please don't rob another bank. Listen, I know some very good attorneys in town. Perhaps I could help."

"You would do that?" the young man said, perplexed.

"I don't pose idle offers, Mr.---"

"Golf," the man said. "Jerry Golf. It's nice to be talking to a good guy for a change."

They lay there together, Landon and Golf, separated by a few feet, a flimsy curtain and by, Julian thought, the diverse consequences of their situations. A car accident and an attempted robbery had resulted in consequences that felt vaguely and strangely connected. Life, Julian surmised, was like that: a series of unintended consequences in a drama of connections and non-connections, of serendipity, destiny and chance.

Golf rattled the handcuffs and cleared his throat forcefully. "If you don't already know," he said, "I guess I'm the reason you're here. I rammed your car but I didn't exactly have a choice. The cops had me boxed in. What was that car? It looked like an antique."

A first stunned, Julian was just beginning to accept the cruel irony of his situation. "It was a 1968 Austin Healey Mark III sportster. I'd owned it for a long time."

"Man, I'm sorry." Golf said, adding in a quite different tone, "Your taillights were out."

Julian struggled with the irony for a few minutes and then with a trained mathematical mind calculated the odds of something like this happening. He had a better chance of winning the lottery or being hit by lightning. Was it planned by some merciless higher power or was it just fate, this curious turn of events that had landed him in the same room with the very person responsible for his accident?

Perhaps hospital officials weren't even aware of this strange and uncomfortable juxtaposition. But again, Julian thought, it didn't merit rocking the boat, causing a fuss, when he knew it would be over with tomorrow. But a perpetrator and his victim only a few feet away in the same room? It seemed radically absurd to Julian.

"You're still going to help me get a lawyer, aren't you?" Golf asked.

"That was before I knew you were the cause of my accident," Julian said.

"But I didn't mean to hit your car," Golf lightly protested and then added, "I guess I don't blame you. I'd be pissed off too."

"I'm not pissed off," Julian said.

"Maybe if I explained what really happened...?"

"What do you do for a living, Mr. Golf? I mean besides robbing banks," Julian said.

"Actually, I'm a master carpenter...well, almost," Golf said proudly. "I'm a year short of my construction management degree.

I'm really good at what I do. I plan to return to trade school after all this has been taken care of. Did you know that Jesus was a carpenter?"

"He didn't rob banks."

"I didn't really rob that bank," Golf said. "I went there to get a loan."

Julian rolled his eyes. *Now that's one for the books*, he thought.

Golf continued. "I was sitting at Ms. Lerner's desk...she's the senior loan officer and had just finished the application...when I had a spell. From there it went south pretty quickly."

"A spell?" Julian said.

"I have a rare form of Tourette's syndrome. I've suffered from it since I was a kid. At first it was a bunch of involuntary tics and then sudden cursing. It went away for a few years and then about ten months ago it came back.

"I was saying something to Ms. Lerner when it happened. Just like that, through no fault of my own. I guess I cursed at the lady and picked up a letter-opener on her desk and I must have blurted out something about a robbery."

Julian was sitting forward, captured by the absurdity of Golf's account. "Have you been diagnosed with...Tourette's?"

"Oh yeah, when I was about 12 years-old. I took medication for it a long time. But when the tics stopped, I took myself off the meds."

"So, you're telling me that you took no money from the bank?" Julian said.

"Well, not exactly," Golf said, almost ruefully. "I snapped out of the Tourette's but by then everyone was freaking out, especially Ms. Lerner, and then without thinking about it, I just went to the teller's window and she started shelling out wads of money. I wanted to stop it right then and there, but it was irreversible, I mean, the course of events I had gotten myself into. Have you ever been in a situation like that, you know, when something you do seems fated and there's no escaping it?"

"You really expect me to believe this?" Landon said.

"I'm just telling you the truth, the way it happened," Golf said, sounding genuine.

Stranger than strange, Julian thought. He decided to leave it at that. He would never know if Golf was telling the whole truth.

But there was no such thing as absolute truth, he reminded himself. It was all relative, wasn't it? To Golf, it may very well be the truth. Certainly the police had another, more contrasting story to tell.

Nurse Claxton parted the curtain and peered in. "How are we doing? Lunch will be served shortly."

"Why didn't you inform me that I would be sharing my room with a convict?" Julian said in a sour whisper.

Claxton said nothing at first and then told Julian that it wasn't planned that way, that she was sorry for any inconvenience it was causing.

"What exactly do you know about the man?" Julian said.

Nurse Claxton shook her head. "I'm afraid Federal law prevents me from discussing any patient details. I'm sure you know that, Professor."

"He caused my accident," Julian said and then intently watched for any sign of reaction on the head nurse's face. "You allowed the perpetrator and his victim to be housed in the same room together. If there isn't a Federal law about that, there should be!"

"Professor, it really wasn't planned this way," Claxton said. "I wasn't aware that he was the cause of your misfortune." Lowering her voice, she added, "If it's really upsetting you, I can talk to hospital officials."

Julian realized he'd led himself down a road he really didn't want to follow. His emotions were getting the worst of him again. He really didn't want to make a fuss about the situation. It wasn't his character. For a brief moment he thought about what Golf had said about a course of events being irreversible, fated.

He apologized to the nurse, adding, "I just don't do well in hospitals. Emotionally I'm not up to par at the moment. Quite a lot has happened to me in such a short period of time."

"Understandable," Claxton said. "I'll speak with the officers and see what can be done."

Julian ate his lunch somberly, feeling dreadfully out of character for having complained. He also felt suddenly guilty for how his grievance might affect Golf. Would they transfer him to a prison infirmary or just let him sit in a jail with his wound? He had just as much right to be in this hospital as Julian did.

He'd only pecked at the broiled chicken leg with his fork, and sampled the green beans and mashed potatoes. It wasn't that the food was bad. Julian just lacked appetite. He turned on the television to see if there was anything new on the news. There wasn't, and he clicked the remote off. He saw a folded copy of the Boston Herald on the edge of the bed table and opened it. The page was a blur, and soon Julian fumbled about the table looking for his glasses. In the process of realizing that they weren't there and instead lay crumbled somewhere in the ruins of the Healey, he knocked over a cup of fresh water, which pooled into a wet spot just below his stomach. "Shit!" he hissed and grabbed a handful of Kleenex to mop up the spill.

It occurred to him then that he had nothing on but a faded paisley gown and what felt to be socks on his feet. He felt for his alumnus ring and discovered that missing, which only added to his sense of stark nakedness. All of his possessions were gone.

Julian threw his head back on the pillow and then rubbed at his eyes. This was worst than incarceration, he thought glumly. Suddenly he missed his apartment with such a deep feeling of longing he began to visualize the antique brass bed with its stuffed linen comforter and firm pillows, the matching brass bed tables with Eden glass lamps, all gifts from Carolyn on his 50th birthday. He yearned to open his chest of drawers and find his socks, undershirts and shorts piled in neat rows. His ring would by lying atop, somewhere among the tie clips, cufflinks and the two photos of his daughter, one when she had graduated from college and the other, more recent, on a recent trip to Milan.

What he would give to sit down at his writing table, his glasses on, and begin to write a letter to a friend, perhaps William, his brother, or Judith, an elder colleague who had retired five years ago and with whom he occasionally corresponded.

Just to be back in familiar and friendly surroundings, with his furniture, his books and his new routine.

A commotion began behind the curtain. They must be letting his roommate use the toilet, Julian surmised, hearing the officers' voices and the clinking of cuffs and a few obscenities from the prisoner. This time Golf was giving them resistance. Men were shouting for him to calm down. Obscenities rose from both parties until finally there appeared to be a truce.

"I guess farewell, Professor," Golf said with dramatic flair. "I'm headed for the dungeon."

"No," Julian said, almost in protest. "Where are they moving you to?"

"To the Suffolk County jail. I'm being arraigned on Monday," Golf said. "I guess they'll put me in the infirmary."

"Do you have a telephone number?" Julian asked and then, realizing the absurdity of the question, he added, "He will find you at the jail."

"Who?" Golf said.

"Jacob Pearson. He's one of the best criminal defense attorneys in the city, if not the entire Commonwealth. He's an old friend who owes me a good deed. I can't assure you that he will take the case, but at least it's worth a try. You can find me in the telephone book...that's Julian F. Landon."

Golf laughed.

"What?"

"Nothing," Golf said, adding, "I didn't think they made phonebooks anymore."

Not bemused, Julian said, "I'm sure you will find one."

"Why are you doing this for me? I mean, I'm the guy responsible for what happened to you."

"Because I've given you my word, and that's in short commodity these days. I'm old fashioned, Mr. Golf. In the end, I stand by my convictions."

"Does that mean you believe my story? Golf said.

"It doesn't matter whether or not I do. If that's what you believe happened at the bank then so be it. As a professor of mathematics, Mr. Golf, I'd say it's a sixty-forty roll of the dice. That is, the odds are slightly against your veracity. I don't mean to offend you."

"You haven't, Julian. Can I still call you Julian...or should I say 'Professor'?"

"Julian is fine. When are you leaving?"

There was a slight scuffling sound and then the stern orders from the officers: "One smart-ass move and we'll have to shackle you, understand?"

Golf let out a growl of pain. "That's where I was shot, damn it!"

Julian could tell that they were all at the door.

"Adieu," Golf said. "And thank you for offering to help."

The abrupt silence assaulted Julian as he sat for a few seconds searching for the clinking of handcuffs, Golf's voice and the sounds of the officers. He was alone. Absurdly he thought, *they've taken everything from me, my clothes, my personal effects and now my roommate.* He immediately chastised himself for being so childlike, so selfish and petty. He had pretty much ordered Golf out of his room. It couldn't be reversed. It was a done deal.

Ten minutes later Nurse Claxton's face appeared as she swung upon the privacy curtain. "Well, that's that," she said, a little too triumphantly. "Professor Landon, the doctor will be making his rounds within the next hour. You might have questions for him, so I suggest that you jot them down now, before he arrives. Do you need a pencil and paper?"

"No, I do not," Julian said irritably. "Believe it or not, I've committed them to memory. I still have a memory, Ms. Claxton."

"Of course you do, Professor."

The insinuation swelled in Julian's mind, and just for a second or two he thought about an escape plan from this horrible place. He would need an accomplice, though.

And then the telephone rang.

Chapter Three

When Tenley had parked her car in a visitor's space near the entrance to the Garrison Square Apartments, it came to her with mild panic that she had forgotten to obtain Julian's apartment keys.

Now she stood at the concierge's front desk, having telephoned Julian for permission to have his apartment opened.

"I'm so sorry, Julian," she said, "but I'm in a bit of a fix here. I forgot to get your keys before I left. Mr. Leighton, your concierge, has agreed to open the apartment for me upon your approval."

She apologized to Julian again and then handed the phone to Mr. Leighton.

"Yes, no problem, Professor," Leighton said, nodding his head.

Tenley had driven past this historic building before and had been intrigued by its 19th century brownstone architecture, it's lavish landscaping, brick walkways, fountained courtyards and tall, elegant windows. The lobby was something out of a Dickens' novel, royal, with two marbled columns rising from a mosaic tile floor, volute capitols and modillion crown moldings. A luxurious staircase led to the first floor.

They took the elevator to the third level. Leighton said, "Professor Landon said he was in the hospital. Is he alright?"

"I'm afraid he's had an accident," Tenley said, quickly adding, "but he's fine."

Leighton turned, looking at Tenley over his glasses. "Not the Healey?"

"Yes, unfortunately. But the professor is taking it quite well, I think."

Leighton led his visitor down a short hallway to the door to Julian's condo. He unlocked it, opened it in a grand way, as if showing the interior to a prospective buyer. He told Tenley to make sure the door was locked when she left.

"Wow!" Tenley said as the door closed behind her. The foyer was small but elegantly furnished, with a Louis IV marbled half-table, a gilded mirror and Persian rug. Copies of Renoir and Matisse paintings hung on the soft blue walls.

She went straight to the first door on the left, Julian's bedroom, and stood there, entranced by the stark brass bed and end tables. An old wood trunk lay at the foot of the bed made with leather straps, faded brass holders and key lock plate. A dark rusted key was set inside the lock.

Tenley was tempted to open the trunk, imagining a treasure trove of some sort, perhaps diamonds and jade necklaces, gold coins and gypsy clothing, a pirate's hoard. Or just the residuals of Julian's life.

She found his underwear and socks in the top drawer his chest, shirts and pants hung well-ordered in the closet, along with a pair of moccasins and business shoes at the bottom of the closet. She grabbed the light L.L. Bean jacket and a few linen handkerchiefs. She put them on the bed and then on the top shelf of the closet found a suitcase, in which she neatly packed all items. In the bathroom she found a brown leather toilet bag packed with razor, cream, toothpaste and brush, and small bottle of Mennen Skin Bracer. It was packed and ready to go, as if Julian had already prepared it for an upcoming trip.

With her duties almost accomplished, Tenley entered Julian's small office and found the laptop, an old Dell that had seen better days. He was right: the office was cluttered and probably hadn't been cleaned in years. An old Remington portable sat open in its case on a studio couch. A large poster of Einstein with his tongue sticking out hung on one wall, on the other an arrangement of black and white photos: children's faces in half-light, an old man's veined hands clasped together, the profile of a man's face Tenley didn't recognize and a daguerreotype of an American Indian in full headpiece.

There were boxes stacked upon boxes in one corner of the room and a file cabinet on which were piled stacks of typewritten paper. Intrigued, Tenley grabbed a few pages and put them on the desk. The top one was title of a novel: *Odessa's Feud by Julian Landon*. She read the first pages, intrigued by the opening to what appeared to be a romantic work. It read just as Julian would speak, rich in description and narrative. She was captivated by the words he had chosen to describe Odessa, obviously his main character.

"Julian Landon!" Tenley spoke out loud, "You old codger, you've never once mentioned that you were a writer, a novelist at that."

She noticed yellow sticky notes all along the edge of his desk and a few stuck to the wall beside the desk. At first they hadn't stood out as anything particularly unusual to find in an office, probably notes to himself or telephone numbers. She pulled one off the wall and saw that Julian had scribbled down the phrase, *wake up 7:OO a.m.*, followed by a formula she recognized as the *Schrödinger* equation. Another had someone's name, this one with a notation of the Pythagoras theorem it. One said, *keys*, with an arrow pointing downward toward the desk with two summation symbols.

Tenley found more inside the drawer, dozens of them, some with formulas, others with names and household items like *can opener, doorbell, shoes, blue socks.* One had her own name on it with a smiley face, and more with the names of fellow colleagues, many of whom she recognized.

She tried not to give these peculiar notations any more significance than simply a man managing problems with early memory loss, but when she went to use the toilet and found the wall next to her covered with notes, she considered this might be something more serious. Julian may be suffering from early dementia.

She'd never noticed anything amiss during several years of conversations with Julian, even when she had been one of Julian's students. He had a great memory. A man who could work complicated formulas in his head certainly was not someone suffering from dementia. But why the scribbled notes? Perhaps it was merely an exaggerated reaction to normal forgetfulness. It was not unusual for a person his age to forget things every now and then.

"Poor Julian, we'll get you fixed up," she said, trying to remember the name of a good neurologist in town. Testing would tell whether this was something serious or a symptom of normal aging.

Not overly concerned, Tenley began to dismiss the curious arrangement of notes as an idiosyncrasy, not unusual for a man with a brilliant mind. She would never say anything about her discovery to Julian, although she would pay more attention when they talked. Just in case.

Tenley went back to the bedroom and lay down flat on the bed, its mattress coils squeaking as she did. The feel was so lumpy and uncomfortable, she couldn't imagine how Julian managed a good night's sleep. The mattress sagged deeply in the middle, causing a slight crevasse under her back. It was amazing that Julian could stand up straight, much less walk without back pain. She considered purchasing a new set of box springs and mattress and have them delivered on Julian's upcoming birthday. It was the least she could do.

◆

Tenley drove her bright yellow Volkswagen Beetle GSR north along Storrow Drive as the sun set to her left beyond the Charles River, setting in motion rivulets of gold on the surface of the fast-moving water. The edge of evening lay ahead, cool and draped in obscure cityscape shadows.

She used her cell to call her best friend Julia who lived in the Roxbury area of the city. They had scheduled lunch on Monday and Tenley realized that Julian might need her to be there at the hospital when he was released that same day. After all, he no longer had transportation and would need a drive home. They rescheduled for Friday at a Mediterranean grill on Beacon Street.

Dusk in Boston came a good hour before official twilight, a shadowy urban darkness that was peculiar to the city, with its crowded brownstone buildings and its overlap of shadows. There was still a glow of sky between buildings and on the Charles River, where the surface glimmered with a strange shifting grayness.

Tenley had unintentionally taken the long route north through Science Park and was now coming down Charles Street, the last stretch to the hospital. It was prime visiting time and most of the metered parking spaces were filled. She drove down toward the emergency end of the hospital and found someone pulling out of a space, in which she immediately parked. She fed the meter with as many quarters she could find at the bottom of her purse and then, heavy suitcase in hand, made the distance to the main entrance.

The elevator was filled, and Tenley was squeezed against the side wall, a portly man with offensive odor pressing her against the hard railing. A child was wailing on the other side, its mother obviously attempting to quiet the child with demonstrative whispers. Arriving at her floor, she had to ask the large man to move as she wiggled her way out of the elevator, toting the weighty suitcase.

When Tenley opened the door to Julian's room and walked inside, she was startled to find a much younger man lying in the hospital bed.

"Oh, I'm so sorry," she said, explaining to the handsome man that she'd entered the wrong room. She looked up at the door number as she quickly exited, certain that was indeed the room in which she last saw Julian.

Looking about the nurse's station, she found Nurse Claxton and asked her the obvious question.

Claxton smiled thinly and said, "Professor Landon has been moved." She said this with a strange flair of authority and accomplishment, as if her patient had just been promoted. "He's been moved to the Phillips House, room 620," Claxton said and then added rather mysteriously, "I think he's earned it."

Tenley took the crossway to Phillips and noticed right way that this was obviously an affluent section of the hospital. She was able to peer into some of the rooms, which appeared more like private bedrooms then regular hospital rooms. There was carpeting and furniture, with elegant table lamps and chandelier lighting.

She had to use a second set of elevators to reach the sixth floor. The door numbered 620 was down a short hallway from the elevators. Exhausted from the haul, her arms aching from the weight of the suitcase, she paused before knocking at the door, which had Julian's name posted on it.

The room was twice the size of the previous room and possessed the amenities of a fancy hotel room, with plush brown carpeting, a pair of Queen Anne wingbacks, writing table and a light blue paisley overnight sofa against one wall.

Tenley found Julian neatly tucked into a fancy hospital bed, with a comforter and thick pillows. He was squinting at an unfolded copy of the *Globe*.

"You'll never guess what happened," he said, rather triumphantly, and quickly filled her in on the details of the ill-fated Golf.

"Dear God!" Tenley said, trying to imagine how it had felt to be in a room with someone who had caused you harm. Relieved that the troubling event was over for Julian, she asked how he had ended up here, in this posh and coveted section of the hospital.

"I'd like to think they are being decent about my misfortune and compensating me for my ordeal," Julian said. "But I have a feeling they checked with my private insurance and realized that the obscene cost of this room would be covered. Can you imagine what the nightly rate is here?"

"Exceedingly overpriced," Tenley said.

She removed the items from his suitcase, placing the shirts, jacket and dress pants on wood hangers in the cedar closet. She put the shoes at the bottom of the closet and the moccasins beside Julian's bed.

The toilet bag in hand, she asked Julian if he wanted the case by his bed or in the bathroom. She noticed that he was wearing a set of blue-striped silk pajamas, no doubt another perk that came with the expensive room.

"They've been so good to me here," Julian said with a sigh.

"I bet they have," Tenley said. "I would hate to see the final hospital invoice."

"For dinner I was served grilled lamb chops, asparagus, rice pilaf and a half bottle of fine Syrah. I declined dessert because I was thoroughly stuffed."

"I bet you were," Tenley said, adding, "but they shouldn't be giving you alcohol with whatever medications you are taking. Are they still taking your vitals?"

"Yes, dear," Julian said, amused that Tenley was taking unusual interest in his care.

"Who is your charge nurse?"

"A marvelous young nurse named Ashley. She took her nursing degree right here at BU and plans to become a physician's assistant. She said that I should be released sometime tomorrow, barring any complications.

Tenley turned to face Julian. "I'll take you home, of course."

Julian made light of the moment and said, "Actually they said it would be fine if I jogged my way home." The comment, meant to be humorous, fell on deaf ears. "Really, don't bother. It may be late in the afternoon. I'll have someone call a cab."

"Absolutely not," Tenley said.

"I need to rent a car until things are worked out with the insurance, so it makes sense that I do that right away."

"It's out of the question," Tenley said, standing firm ground.

"Tenley," Julian said calmly, "You're rightfully exhausted, my dear. Go home, pour yourself a glassful and then get some good sleep. Tomorrow is no big deal. If you want me to, I'll telephone you when they give me a time."

Not wishing to further the disagreement, she began rearranging items on the bedside table. She refilled his glass with fresh water, and then kissed him on the cheek. "Absolutely promise to call me?"

Julian smiled. "On my honor," he said.

Chapter Four

In the morning Julian enjoyed a late breakfast: croissants and two eggs over easy with parsley sprouts and fine Boston ham.

The doctor made early rounds and told Julian he could stay another day if he wished or be released within the next hour or so. Julian chose the latter. He took a shower, damped dry his beard and put on the slacks and shirt Tenley had brought. He was packed and ready to go by noon.

He'd arranged for Enterprise to pick him up at the hospital entrance. He rented a new gray Toyota Corolla and was amazed by its interior size. He drove to his apartment complex, feeling renewed and excited to settle in at his apartment. He was now officially retired.

Later that day Julian called Tenley on her cell and explained that he had been released earlier than expected and had already rented a car. He had expected her to be upset, at least mildly argumentative, but she wasn't, just relieved that he had made it home. She made him promise to call her if there was anything he needed and asked him if they could have lunch in a few weeks just to keep in touch. Tenley said that her class was about to begin and had to go.

Looking at himself in the foyer mirror after he had hung up the phone, Julian saw a man who looked his age, a person deserving of retirement. His beard was well-trimmed and where his skin showed there was a hint of high cheekbones and a sharply-receding hairline. He had a moderately-aquiline nose and faded blue eyes. The handsomeness of youth and middle age had long since departed, leaving him with a hardening of features and yet a rather dignified look.

Julian made it a point to stick to a schedule. He arose early every morning but slept until ten on Sundays. He took almost daily walks when the weather permitted and committed himself to engage in conversations with people he met: Ralph at the deli, Eddie, the dog walker and Gary at the newsstand. He commiserated with Leighton, his concierge and confidant at the apartments, about the Healey's demise and not having a job anymore.

Tenley called weekly, as did some of Julian's friends and colleagues. He hadn't heard from Carolyn since the day he left his office but understood that she had a hectic schedule and would contact him when she could.

A few days later he received a call from Jacob Pearson's secretary. "Are you available to speak with Mr. Pearson?"

"Of course," Julian said, remembering his promise to Golf in the hospital.

They exchanged pleasantries and then Pearson said, "Golf's an interesting case, I'll give you that. I initially laughed when I reviewed his case and then had Audrey do some research on Tourette's. We were surprised to discover some legal precedence. There actually have been cases where the disorder has involved strange obsessive-compulsive behaviors, some where patients have amnesia and even forget their aberrant outbursts."

"Really?"

Pearson continued, "I think this may play well to a jury. I believe your Golf fellow might have a fighting chance."

"Really?" Julian repeated. "What did they charge him with?"

"Well, it wasn't simple burglary. I'm afraid he's looking at 25 years to life, if convicted of all charges. He doesn't exactly have a stellar record. We can plea bargain but I don't think that will turn out in your boy's favor. There's a small but reasonable chance we can get an acquittal if it goes to trial."

"Yes, of course."

"Julian, I have to be upfront with you. I don't do pro bono's anymore. I know I should, but the firm has laid out some pretty strict guidelines. Without appeals, a short trial would cost a few thousand, eight at most."

Julian closed his eyes. A gentleman's promise was a true promise, he thought. He couldn't let the kid down, not at this point. "That's fine," he told Pearson, requesting that he be kept apprised of any progress in the case.

Maybe when Golf earned his degree and started a flourishing carpentry business, he would offer to repay his benefactor, Julian thought a bit lamely.

◆

One morning in late June Julian Landon glanced at the bathroom mirror. He'd set the bath going and his image in the mirror was fogged with condensation. Using a hand towel, he cleared a spot. What he saw was revelatory, if not disarming. He looked like a very old man, with his beard unkempt, a froth of overgrown hair in each ear and his eyebrows looking like small untended hedges. Although it had thinned considerably over the years and had turned slightly gray, his hair was mostly full. But his facial skin was pitted and was more wrinkled than he could ever remember, and the small wart aside his nose seemed more prominent.

He sat down on the edge of the tub and looked at his hands; they were veined and loose-skinned, and there was a visible sagging under his upper arms. He looked, he thought, positively ancient, a man ready to lie down in his grave.

It was a Tuesday and he'd overslept, breaking one of his own cardinal rules. There was no point in breakfast as lunchtime was fast approaching.

Yesterday had not been a good day for Julian. He'd concluded the day with full resignation to the fact that he was further descending into senility and the forgetfulness accompanying that condition. He was going to take a spin in his new BMW he had just purchased but couldn't remember where he had placed the keys. He'd plucked all the sticky notes off the walls, desperately looking for clues. After two hours of unsuccessful searching in the apartment, foraging through drawers, cabinets, old boxes of office files and even the old steamer trunk, enraged and wounded, Julian collapsed at his desk.

Now in the bathroom, the gloom transported from yesterday, Julian not only felt senile but fully resigned to the fact that he was suffering from irreversible dementia. Panic set in and Julian's mind raced through the probabilities. It would get worse. Sooner than later he would need a caretaker, someone to bathe him, dress and feed him. He could look forward to forgetting the names and faces of loved ones and friends. Eventually, he wouldn't even recognize his own face.

After the bath, Julian didn't bother to dress. He sat bent over his desk, wearing an old flannel robe and his moccasins, and decided that he would begin a daily diary. The idea had come to him earlier but more in terms of a memoir. But now it was a life ring, tossed at him by the surviving neurons of a logical mind. He decided to always leave the notebook open on his desk with a sticky note attached with an arrow and the words, *Begin here. What happened today?*

This day's entry was terse: *Still can't find keys. Bathed and then moped around all day.*

The telephone rang around one in the afternoon. It was Tenley.

"Well, how do you feel, birthday boy?" she said in a chirpy tone.

Julian didn't say anything, realizing ever more somberly that he had forgotten his own birthday. Finally, he said, "I don't exactly feel in a celebratory mood."

"Well, you should," Tenley said brightly. "You are beginning the best days of your life."

"How would you know?"

"Julian, something is wrong. What is it? You even sound horrible. Are you sick?"

"No," Julian said with somber finality.

"I'll be right over, Jul--"

"You will not!" Julian interrupted and then hung up the phone.

Guilt now fed the morose state of Julian's thoughts. He shut all the blinds in the apartment, closed the curtains in his bedroom and tried to find solace in the darkened room, his head under the thick covers. He tried to sleep but couldn't. He began to panic as horrible considerations flashed through his mind: he had Alzheimer's disease, his brain riddled with plaque; he would eventually lose all of his cognitive ability; he would end up in diapers in a infantile state. Hadn't he feared this all along? Now he was facing the cold truth of his condition. He should never have retired. Intellectual stimulation had kept the disease at bay. He would rather be dead and buried.

Mercifully, Julian drifted into an embryonic sleep. Neither dream nor thought penetrated that cocooned respite. He was awakened two hours later by the sound of someone knocking at the front door. He lay there for a full minute with neither the inclination nor the energy to answer it.

More knocking ensued, and then a man's raised voice. He could hear the door open and then a scuffling of shoes on the foyer floor.

The light was turned on. "Professor Landon?" the concerned concierge said.

"Oh God, Julian," Tenley said and rushed to his side. Leighton backed out of the room with a look of sympathy on his face. Julian heard him shut the front door.

"I'm sorry I hung up on you," Julian said, relieved to get it off his mind.

"Has something happened?" Tenley said, pulling the covers down as if to give him a cursory exam.

"I'm naked," Julian protested.

"Oh," Tenley said in a slightly mischievous tone.

"I know you mean well, but I really want to be left alone."

"But it's your birthday," Tenley protested.

"I'll have another next year," Julian said, covering up his chest.

"I know something isn't right. This is not you, Julian, to be locked in darkness during the middle of the day. Now, get dressed, and I'll go put on a fresh pot of coffee."

Tenley opened the drapes in the living room. A dismal grayness was visible to Julian as he took a seat in the wingbacked chair across from Tenley. Spits of rain ticked at the windowpane.

"It's raining," Julian said in a flat voice.

"Yes. It's been dreary all day. I believe we'll have thunderstorms by evening." Tenley's gaze turned from the window and she looked at Julian. "Now, are you going to tell me what's going on in that brilliant mind of yours?" She noticed more stickies on the edge of the coffee table.

"Oh God. I think I'm loosing my mind," Julian said and had a sudden desire to fall into Tenley's arms. He didn't have to, for Tenley was suddenly at this side, rubbing his hands. She felt his forehead. He thought she was about to burst into tears. The notion terrified him. The last thing he wanted was pity.

"It's nothing that can't be fixed," Tenley said, sounding a bit naive.

All of the gloom, the emotions and the fears erupted from Julian like a fountain. He told her all about the memory loss and when it started almost a year ago. He explained the reason for the yellow stickies and finally ended with yesterday's horrible events when he couldn't find his car keys.

Tenley said, kissing him on the forehead, "You've got to take into account that you've been through quite a lot...retirement, the accident and now finding yourself with loads of time on your hands. I bet you've stopped reading and keeping yourself abreast of current events. You should be working on your memoirs, stimulating your mind as much as you can. What's wrong with taking on a visiting professorship?"

Julian shook his head, realizing that Tenley had missed the gravity of his situation. He looked up at her imploringly. "Dementia, maybe Alzheimer's, he stated gravely.

Tenley stood straight, startled but strangely relieved by his statement. She had heard once that people who think they have Alzheimer's usually aren't suffering from the disease. Awareness is the saving grace.

"I don't think there's any hope for me," Julian said, evermore despondent.

"Don't talk like that, Julian. First of all, you don't know for certain what is causing these symptoms. It could be depression or fatigue or just normal forgetfulness, and you're simply overreacting."

"I am not overreacting. How can you say that? You are trying to minimize what is probably a serious disease."

"I'm sorry, Julian. I didn't mean it that way. Whatever we have to do to find the cause of your symptoms we'll do it. We'll get through it, I promise."

"I should never have retired," Julian said, looking away.

"Have you shared this with Carolyn?"

"God no."

"Anybody else?"

"No. How could I?"

"Good," Tenley said. "I have a plan...I mean if you'll consider it."

◆

Julian was faring a bit better when he drove the BMW to his appointment with Dr. Marlene Farley, a reputable neurologist affiliated with the Brigham & Women's Hospital in south Boston.

In the two weeks since Tenley had visited him, he had escaped from his gloom and decided to take a proactive approach to his situation. He decided to minimize the use of the sticky notes, to unclutter the walls, and only jot down reminders for each day, tearing them up as each reminder was met. The car keys were now always left in plain sight on the foyer table. Organization seemed to be a good facilitator for short term memory.

Tenley had wanted to accompany him to see the specialist but Julian felt it was a personal matter, and he wanted to be the first to hear the truth. The waiting room was crowded and filled primarily with elder people, though he noticed some adolescents sitting with their mothers. One of them was a girl in her mid teens, with a round pallid face and brunette hair that appeared to be cut unevenly, almost hacked off in some places. She had noticed Julian walk in and take a seat and now had him fixed with such an intense stare, it began to irritate him. He put on his new set of glasses and began reading a copy of the Atlantic. The elderly woman across from him with a full head of white hair and lost blue eyes was also starring at him. Julian found himself covering his face with the magazine.

Was it that obvious? Julian wondered, imagining grimly what a leper might feel like in a room of attractive people.

Relieved to hear his named called, Julian followed the nurse to an examining room. She took his pulse, blood pressure and his oxygen level and then began asking him questions pertaining to his medical history. Finally she placed her hands atop the chart and looked up at Julian inquisitively.

"What brings you here, Mr. Landon"

Julian hesitated. "I have an appointment with Dr. Farley."

"Are you not feeling well?"

"I've been having issues with memory," Julian said reluctantly.

The nurse smiled. "No problem," she said, adding that Dr. Farley would be with him shortly.

Julian surveyed the examining room timidly, like a child at his first dental appointment. While there were few medical instruments visible, some of the abstract paintings on the walls, especially the black obelisk with pink background, made Julian feel intensely out of place. There was a model of the human brain atop the small desk, ready to be unhinged for instructional purposes.

Shortly, there was a light rap at the door.

"Are you decent?" a lively voice said. The door opened to reveal a young woman in a gray business suit, with smartly-styled blonde hair and piercing blue eyes. She was tall for a woman and possessed an affable smile. She reminded Julian of Tenley.

"Marlene Farley," she said, reaching over to shake his hand. "Please, Professor, may I call you by your first name?"

"Yes, please do," Julian said, feeling almost instantly comfortable with the woman. He was not surprised to hear that she had graduated from BU before medical college at Harvard. They had mutual friends and colleagues.

"I see that you have just turned seventy, Marlene Farley said, glancing down at the medical chart. "You're worried about memory loss. Is that why you're here?"

"Yes," Julian said.

"Forgetting where you placed your keys, not recalling names, frustration...that sort of thing?"

"Worse," Julian said. He told Farley that it had started long before his retirement and the strange ways he employed to remember students' names and faces, and then about the sticky notes and the mathematical formulas that had helped him initially to remember names and daily tasks. Then he told her about Tenley's plan, how she called twice a day to remind him to take a shower, fix meals and perform needed errands. "I would never have remembered to keep our appointment had it not been for Tenley's reminder," he added soberly.

Dr. Farley looked over at her patient with a new concerned look of appraisal. Finally she said, "I don't think I will give you the standard set of memory tests. I think right now they would only add to your frustration. But I do want to run some other tests, and they can done right here at our facility, most likely today, if you have the time."

"What kind of tests?" Julian said.

"Well, we'll start with a standard MRI, a magnetic imaging X-ray of the brain. And an amyloid PET scan, a new test specific to dementia and Alzheimer's. Blood and urine tests." Marlene Farley continued. "I will also arrange for you to have a special spinal tap, but I'm afraid we'll have to schedule that later."

"Do you think I have dementia, doctor?"

"I think you are dealing with severe memory impairment, Julian. From what you have described, the condition is certainly interfering with your daily activities and it's probably causing some depression. I want you to arrange for a full physical examination so that we can rule out systemic causes like a brain tumor or vascular issues. The important thing now is to ameliorate the worst of your symptoms, and I think I can do that by giving you a new medication that has shown promising results in many dementia cases, and vitamins." She wrote out a prescription and then told Julian to take daily supplements of vitamins E and B12.

Julian nodded.

"Do you take fish oil?"

"I'm basically a vegetarian, some poultry and a little fish."

"The omega-3 fatty acid in fish oil has shown to be a benefit for people suffering from dementia. Let's add that to your vitamin list."

"Would you mind writing all that down for me?" Julian said.

"Of course. At least we have a game plan," Marlene Farley said with an encouraging smile.

◆

It was late when Julian returned to his apartment. He had missed the turn on one of the streets leading out of the physicians' complex, become temporarily lost, and then with great relief found the Blue Hills Parkway leading toward the apartments. Along the way, he stopped at a CVS pharmacy, waited ten minutes for the prescription to be filled and then added the vitamins. Pulling into his apartment space, he examined the navigation system built-in to the dashboard and realized that this was a new fangled instrument he would soon have to rely on. Tenley could teach him.

True to his own plan, Julian dropped the keys on the marble foyer table, checked for phone messages and then examined all of the notes he'd left himself that morning. He had forgotten lunch, but that was a reasonable omission, given his long appointment that day.

He opened a can of tomato soup, along with a packet of saltine crackers. He wasn't very hungry, although he felt tired in a positive sort of way. It had been good to get out of the apartment and drive on his own. His talks with Marlene Farley, despite the gloomy prospects of his condition, made him feel reconnected with the world. He had a comrade-in-arms, a sensitive and skilled doctor with whom he could share his symptoms and feelings. A vague but comforting sense of direction eased his mind.

Tenley called and they talked about the doctor's visit and then she quizzed him about what his schedule would be tomorrow: no appointments, breakfast, a twenty-minute walk before lunch, reading his mail and then she would call in the early afternoon. She asked him if he would be interested in joining her and some friends at Nantasket Beach on Saturday, that it was going to be a splendid day weather-wise.

Julian said he would think about it, that it sounded tempting, and immediately felt good about himself for having the courage to consider the offer.

He popped the green capsule out of its packet and swallowed it with a glass of water. Concerned that the vitamins might interfere with his sleep, Julian wrote on a note that they be taken with breakfast.

It was past eleven when he switched off the bedside lamp. He suddenly felt very encouraged, considering the gloomy events of the day. He had made progress. He had followed a plan that might very well lessen his memory problems. He had solid support from his new doctor and, of course, Tenley.

Farley had told him that the new medication might take a couple of weeks before any effects would be felt. Julian doubted that it would take that long because, he sensed, he was already experiencing some positive effects. He felt encouraged, for a change. He could recall more names and faces of colleagues at the university, and even remembered both his and Tenley's telephone numbers. Maybe it wasn't the pill but a pleasant placebo effect. What did it matter?

Julian fell asleep, immediately swept into a dream in which he was flying, his feet hovering over the ground and with a strange tensing of his arms being able to fly high over trees and farm houses in a bucolic countryside of, perhaps, his youth.

He awoke from the curious dream, went to the bathroom and back to bed, where he pulled the covers over his head. He couldn't wait to continue his dream.

He fell asleep almost instantly and found himself in a long narrow room with only a slit of light at one end. Slowly he drifted toward the light, which blossomed into an open door, through which he passed almost effortlessly and began rising into the whiteness.

Julian Landon was flying again.

Chapter Five

Saturday morning arrived quickly. Tenley had called earlier to remind Julian of the beach trip. She would be picking him up at ten.

Standing at the mirror in the bathroom, he washed the basin clean of the hair and shaving cream, took a hand towel to pat his face and then proudly gazed at himself. "Well, done, Julian," he said out loud. He'd shaved all of it off, trimmed his eyebrows and cleared his ears of hair growth. He thought he looked ten years younger.

He put on a pair of old tennis shorts, old chronologically but rarely worn. He knew they didn't meet the fashion of the day. Younger men preferred the baggy sort, which hung loosely over the knees. He found a pale yellow Gingham short-sleeve shirt ordered from Neiman Marcus by Carolyn. He wanted to wear sandals but couldn't find a pair that suited him. Instead, he settled for a pair of white tennis shoes with calf-length socks.

The day before he'd ordered a delivery from the grocery store: loads of fresh fruit and vegetables, milk and two boxes of Cheerios.

He'd cut up slices of banana into a bowl of the breakfast cereal and consumed his breakfast with the vigor of a youngster off to school.

Tenley had told him not to pack a lunch as the girls had prepared a picnic basket with enough food to feed a college tennis team. She also reminded him to take his medication and vitamins, which he had already done.

Expecting to see Tenley's VW Bug, Julian was led to a pink 1959 Cadillac convertible doubled-parked on Garrison Street. He first noticed the four young women inside and then his eyes fell on the lavish relic with its double chrome grill and the three sets of headlights. Chrome-trimmed pink tailfins rose from the rear carriage like a sculpture's masterpiece. It had full whitewalls polished to a dull gleam.

"Gorgeous!" Julian said as he squeezed into place in the backseat next to two blondes and a brunette.

Tenley took a seat on the passenger side, smiled back at Julian and said, "The car or my friends?"

They roared off under a warm bright sun and cloudless sky. Tenley's friends chatted on like they were on a couch in a quiet sitting room. Julian couldn't make out a word, their voices muffled by the rush of wind and the dull whistle of tires on asphalt. The cool air blew through his hair and made his cheeks tingle. He felt almost as if he was flying again.

On a clear area just below the rocks, opening to a long stretch of white-sanded beach, Tenley and the girls spread out two enormous blankets and unfolded a capacious pink-and-white striped umbrella. A large wicker picnic basket was set under the umbrella's shade, a cooler beside it.

They had brought a beach chair for Julian and a little plastic table for food and drinks. He sat down under the shade and felt absolutely regal. *A throne and his own little harem*, he mused in a delightful sort of way.

One of the young women, a blonde with long black eyelashes, introduced herself as Claudia.

"Can I get you something to drink, Professor Landon?"

He asked what she planned to drink and said he'd have the same, a wine cooler. When she returned with the ice-chilled bottles, Claudia sat down beside Julian on the blanket, her arms thrown back, looking up, her long blonde hair flowing over her shoulders. He couldn't recall if he'd ever seen a more beautiful woman.

"We still have a ways to low tide," she said, pointing down toward the low bubbling surf. "Are you going for a dip, Professor Landon?"

"Please call me Julian. Are you still in college?" he said.

Claudia laughed deeply. "College? I haven't set a foot in a classroom in ten years. No, Prof..., I mean Julian. I'm a vice president of a consulting firm in town. I've been there for five years."

"Ah," Julian said. "What kind of consulting, if you don't mind my asking?"

"Investment technologies."

She threw her head back again. Julian noticed that her hair wasn't all blonde, subtle undertones of black at the crown of her head, feeding out a quarter inch under the fan of blonde mane. She was wearing a one-piece, white, with gold trim on the shoulder straps. Her legs were tanned even this early in the summer, and she bore a small tattoo just on the inside crease of her left thigh. Julian struggled to make it out without appearing obvious.

"It's a scorpion."

"Ah," Julian said, and then added, "Friend or foe?"

"Friend to me, foe to many," Claudia said.

One of the girls yelled out and Claudia jumped to her feet and ran down the beach with the others.

The water must have been cold for Julian heard shrieks and cursing as two of them plunged into the water head-first. Claudia must have been one of them as he heard her say, leaping out of the water, "Fucking cold!"

The other three young women were named Sue, Bentley and Lillian, all good-looking and about the same ages. Claudia was the owner of the vintage Cadillac, a gift from her father, who collected antique automobiles.

He looked down at the girls with a curious fondness, as though they might be part of his family. He took a few sips of the cooler and then lay his head back. This is what Tenley and Carolyn were talking about when they'd advised him to be adventuresome, out of the old apartment, and taking on a new lifestyle. Lying there, he felt invigorated, younger and youthfully playful. He took off his shirt and laid it neatly across his lap. The scruff of gray-white hair on his chest tingled in the fresh beach air. He noticed that his chest and arms were unusually pale, an inadvertent result of donning too many business suits over the years.

For lunch, Tenley and the girls brought out the ham-and-cheese sandwiches and cylinders of Pringles chips. Claudia opened a large jar of pickles and lay one on each paper plate, along with a paper napkin. Julian noticed that she was on her third wine cooler. She was acting a bit giddy and her constant laughter was deep-throated and a bit distracting to Julian.

They had collected two young men from the beach, a tall gangly one with red hair and a well-toned fellow with dark, deep-set eyes, perhaps of Latin descent. His name was Arturo, and it became obvious to Julian that Claudia had selected him as *Beau-de-Jour*. They took lunch together at the end of the blanket, Claudia laughing almost hysterically at times, draping her long arms across the young man's muscular neck. Before long they kissed, Arturo laying her down on the blanket with romantic flair.

Tenley came over with another of the girls and asked him if he wanted another wine cooler.

"Bentley!" Julian said triumphantly and grabbed for the girl's hand. She obliged him rather cautiously as she and Tenley took seats in front of him. He had remembered her name without even trying. Tenley must have noticed the significance as she smiled back at Julian.

Bentley had short-cropped auburn-colored hair and a long pointed nose, not something, Julian thought, she wanted to accentuate. Her eyes were soft, almost doe-like. Her voice lent the impression that she was used to consoling people, perhaps a social worker or psychologist. She began telling Julian of the long struggle with her mother, who was apparently in the very late stages of brain disease. Bentley said she'd had to drop out of graduate school to care for her mother.

"I'd rather have someone shoot me than be a burden on others," Julian said.

"It's altogether different when you're caring for someone you love dearly."

Bentley explained that she'd hired a live-in nurse but still had to drive her mother around to appointments. She'd moved into her mother's bedroom at night and would watch the woman breathing, concentrating on the shallow breaths and the almost imperceptible rising of her chest under her floral nightgown.

"Sometimes I think she's gone and rush to take a pulse," Bentley said solemnly. "They've done just about everything for her as far as medication, aggressive treatment, experimental drugs. Hospice is out of the question. So, we just support her in every way we can."

"I admire your outpouring of love and your obvious stamina in this situation," Julian offered, gulping down another mouthful of wine. His eyes felt heavy, his body so relaxed, for a second he thought he might not be able to get up.

He closed his eyes, thinking of how he could change the subject. When he opened them, Bentley was gone, having joined her friends down by the water.

Claudia and her beau lay intertwined on the edge of the blanket, her hair fanned out over the sand, sparkling with wetness and trinkets of sand. They were obviously dead to the world, for neither was moving. Julian wondered whether the couple had had the audacity to do it right here in full view of God and humanity. Had the scorpion been a tad too friendly?

Though giddy and ever so relaxed from the wine, Julian arose from the chair and stood there looking down at the beach where the girls were standing, ankle-deep in water, sipping their wine coolers. He lay his shirt across the back of the chair, adjusted his shorts and then began taking off his tennis shoes. He pounded lightly on his chest and then ran his fingers through his hair, massaging the back of his neck as he did.

He felt young, brave and adventuresome. There was a bounce in his stride as he headed down to the water. Halfway there he stopped. Tenley and soon the others noticed him and began waving. He started to jog, stumbled a few feet, regained his balance, and burst into a full sprint during the last twenty yards.

Tenley appeared to be in an awkward stance, arms outstretched and a bit low to the ground as if she was prepared to catch him should he fall again. The other girls were cheering him on, at least one calling out, "Go, Professor, go!"

Julian felt like he was *really* flying now. He was surprised at the strength in his legs and the way his arms were pulling him forward, faster and faster, like a professional sprinter dashing for the finish line, which in this case was a spot past the girls farther out in the water.

He galloped forward through the chilly water, feeling the rocky sand beneath his feet. The water was shallow, enabling him to maintain speed as he passed the girls. *He must be impressing them*, he thought gallantly when suddenly the bottom fell away. Julian twisted forward and began lurching at the water with his arms, moving his legs as if he were in a race for his life. He was swimming and making progress, planning to go another fifty yards before turning around.

Soon his legs became entangled with what felt like seaweed. He struggled to break free, kicking furiously when he suddenly realized that he had lost his shorts. He stopped and struggled to free himself, soon rolling into an awkward summersault as he attempted to clutch at his departing apparel. He was suddenly free, fully naked, dangling in the dark, icy grips of the water. Realizing that he was sinking, Julian flailed with his arms, sputtering the words, "Help...help me!"

Farther he sank, as if being pulled down by some merciless weight. Carolyn's face flashed before his eyes and then Tenley's and then a glimpse of flesh where the scorpion hid.

It was the last he remembered when the flooding whiteness arrived.

◆

Tenley had found him, about three feet down. She and the others had pulled his lifeless body to shore, taking the lead as she performed mouth-to-mouth resuscitation, finding a strong pulse and then turning him on his side to evacuate the water from his lungs. She'd watched him cough back to life.

They'd pulled him up the beach to his chair and laid a beach towel over his body, now rubbing at his skin, drying his hair, Tenley crying and trembling in her efforts to warm his body.

Claudia came over with her pink blanket and draped it over his head and shoulders. She leaned her body forward, embracing Julian's body with her heat. He was shivering so much that it made her own body tremble.

Soon Julian settled down under this warming, wonderful contact. "My shorts," he managed, as Claudia pulled away and Tenley's face came into view.

"Your shorts? Julian, you almost killed yourself. What were you thinking?"

A beach patrol four-wheeler pulled up and a stout man with sun-bleached hair leaned out of his window. "Is he okay? EMS should be here shortly. This is quite a ways out of their jurisdiction. I have O_2 if he needs it."

"No!" Julian blurted out. "I need neither. If an ambulance arrives I will refuse to go...do you hear? I'll refuse to be transported to a hospital. I have that right."

"You do," the man said calmly. "But what harm would it do to have yourself checked out?"

Julian stiffened forward in his chair. "Absolutely not. I shall never go to a hospital again."

Tenley and the girls tried to argue with him but soon yielded when it was obvious that Julian might make a scene. They shrugged their shoulders and then thanked the man in the truck.

"It's my fault," Tenley said. "I should never have left you alone."

Bentley patted her on the back. Claudia lit a cigarette and stood there as if she were examining the scene of a crime. Her boyfriend must have fled during all the commotion.

"I must have something to wear," Julian said, looking at Tenley.

"Perhaps you could drive back to the apartment."

"It's almost four o'clock, Julian. I'd never make it back in time in the traffic, and besides I don't think I could manage to drive a car that big."

"Try these," Claudia said after rummaging through her pink beach bag and dropping a pair of white shorts in Julian's lap. "They're too large for me now since I've lost weight. If they don't button, just pull your shirt down over your waist."

He cringed at the thought of wearing women's clothing and being seen in public in such very short shorts. Of course, no one would really notice until he had to walk from the car to his apartment.

The girls stood at all four sides, their backs to Julian, who struggled frantically to wiggle the shorts to his waist. They were far too short for a man and he had to pull them down to accommodate his decency. The shirt was long and amply covered his waist and the top of the shorts.

Claudia turned when he'd finished. "Sex-xy," she said, smiling.

"Please..." Julian said, sounding offended but feeling rather different, like a younger man taunted by youthful play.

They all ate the rest of the sandwiches and washed them down with the remaining coolers. The girls brushed their hair and threw on various colored jogging pants over their suits. Claudia's was pink, of course.

Julian watched the still brilliant sun lowering to the west, highlighting sparkling jewels across the sand. Tall shadows leaned from the people still on the beach, resembling stick figures as they lingered in the last warming sunglow.

Claudia refused to close the convertible top on the Cadillac, and as they drove away from the beach, Julian hunkered down, now in the passenger seat, shivering in the cool early evening air. The radio was blaring. Not but a few times, Claudia swerved slightly on the highway, catching herself and jerking the steering wheel to center position. Julian shut his eyes at the prospect of being stopped by the police, of being forced from the car in his obscene attire and having to explain himself to the officer. And what if they arrested the crazy blonde and impounded the car?

The mood traveled with Julian until they finally arrived at the apartment complex. Pulling into a space on Studio Place, Claudia threw up her hands. "Hooray, Professor Landon. We made it!" she cried out. "And all in one piece," she added, obviously referring to her inebriation.

The radio was still blasting and as Julian reached to turn the volume down, he noticed a couple of passersby approaching the vehicle. They looked to be teenagers or at least boys in their early twenties. "Man, what kind of a cool car is that?!" one of them said, swinging onto the hood and quickly lighting a cigarette. "Hey, you girls from around here?"

Tenley said, "Please get off the car."

The other boy looked down at Julian. "Gramps and his harem, huh?" he said, patting Julian's shoulder.

They were obviously drunk and steeped in bravado. The boy on the hood drew up his leg and somewhat pensively rested his chin on his knee.

"Get off the fucking car!" Claudia said.

The drunk on the hood flashed a set of keys at Claudia, obviously threatening to scratch the paint.

Incensed, Julian rose from his seat. "You'll do nothing of the sort," he said, clearing his throat and then attempting to open the passenger door.

The boys taunted him for several seconds until Julian collapsed back in his seat, realizing his predicament with the shorts.

It happened in a blur. Claudia leapt out of the driver's seat without opening the door. She had the boy in a chokehold and as he thrashed about a set of keys fell to the pavement. She let him go as he gasped for air, kicking his rear-side, landing him, now coughing, on all fours. She picked up the keys.

The other boy cautiously backed away from the Caddy, his hands slightly raised, obviously not wanting to tangle with Claudia or to upset her anymore than she was. "Sorry, Ma'am," he said in a mousy voice.

When the two had fled the scene, Claudia went over to inspect the hood and then, with a wild pitch, flung the keys into the distance. "Punks!" she said.

"That was quite a show," Julian said, meaning to compliment Claudia's efforts.

"I should have gutted him with his own keys," she said, now a bit wobbly on her feet.

The event had caught the eyes of a few people across the street who had paused but were now moving on. Julian hoped no one had called the police.

Arriving at the apartments, Julian stood up, pulling his shirt as far down his waist as he could. He asked Tenley if he could use one of the beach blankets to cover him during the dash for the apartments. Claudia opened the enormous trunk and pulled out her pink beach blanket. "I have a plan," she said in a low mischievous voice.

Crowded together they hobbled across the street like a pink blob, only Julian's head appearing, the girls crouched at his side, the bottoms of their bare legs visible under the large towel. Claudia stumbled several times, cursing and laughing as she did. She had a stranglehold about Julian's waist, which, he thought, helped to hold his shorts in place.

"Thirty feet dead-on, girls!" Julian roared as if commanding a small troop into battle.

Leighton met them in the foyer, looking a little alarmed until he recognized the professor. Nevertheless, there was a concerned look on his face as he escorted them safely to the elevators.

Once inside, Julian darted for the bedroom. He heard Claudia say, "Let's all have a bath." He quickly locked the door.

Rinsing himself off and putting on a decent set of clothes, Julian combed his hair in the fogged mirror, rubbed his fingers across his teeth, tested his breath with a cupped palm and then opened the bedroom door. He thought he looked dashing for his age.

Lillian and the girl Julian now recognized as Sue, the two quiet ones at the beach, were seated in the living room in the pair of Queen Anne chairs. Tenley was straddled on an old Moroccan foot rest Carolyn had returned with following one of her adventures. Claudia, barely awake, lay across the sofa, her arms outstretched, one leg on the floor.

"Shall we have a drink?" Julian said confidently, feeling at last secure in his own milieu.

"What do you have?" Claudia mumbled from the sofa.

"Whiskey...and of good stock," Julian said gallantly.

After pouring rounds for the ladies, Julian took a seat on the floor in front of Sue, his own glass tinkling with ice. "I don't think we talked much at the beach," he said, trying to startup a conversation with the pretty brunette. She looked vulnerable and alone, almost, Julian thought, like a lost little girl.

"I don't...speak...English...very good," the young woman said in a thick French accent.

Julian's face brightened. "*Julien Landon. Je suis enchanté de faire votre connaissance.*"

"*Qui, Julien. Suzanne Belgard ici.*"

"Actually, your English is very good," Julian said.

"*Merci, Julien.* I study English in...the night. *Très difficile.*"

"Goodness, when do you sleep?" Julian said, trying to be humorous.

"*Merci, Julien,*" the young woman replied, obviously not comprehending Julian's question.

He watched her sip daintily from her glass, which Julian could tell was heavily diluted with water. Now here was a reserved young woman, he thought, very much wanting to befriend her.

"*Tu es très belle,*" he said with a smile.

Claudia slid off the sofa and came over, her glass empty. "You have to speak English *all* of the time," she said to Sue, almost with parental censure. "That was the deal. *Comprendre*?" She looked at Julian. "That's damn good stuff," she said with a slight slur.

"Another?" Julian asked.

"Of course, another...and another after that," she said with almost hysterical laughter.

"I don't think so," Tenley said and tried to stand up, wobbling a bit as she joined them in the kitchen. Despite Tenley's opinion, Claudia let Julian pour herself another glass of Chivas Regal, pressing the neck of the bottle to her glass as it filled to the top.

"I think....we'll need to...crash here," Claudia announced, fumbling her way back to the sofa.

Julian was ready to party and have a grand old time. The idea of having the girls sleep over, while at first a sensational thought, soon turned into a threatening notion. They would probably want his king-sized bed and he'd end up sleeping on the couch with just a blanket thrown over.

An hour later, the mess cleaned up in the kitchen and living room, Julian dried his hands on the hand towel and surveyed the sleeping girls in the living room. He'd tucked them in with extra blankets and a few pillows and then turned off the lights.

Settling in his own bed with one less pillow than customary, Julian took a last sip of whiskey from the glass he'd taken to the bedroom and set it firmly on the nightstand. He felt curiously proud and quite paternal for having taken care of the girls. Carolyn would be proud of him, he thought as he closed his eyes.

Drifting off, Julian's eyes popped open. Something was happening. Embarrassed at first, he stared at the ceiling and then yielded to the giddy feeling with calm and sensual surrender.

Chapter Six

One morning after a long and refreshing sleep, Julian Landon awoke to a morning brightness that seemed to emanate from a lightness within. For the first time in years he felt revived, as if a thick and merciless cloud had been lifted from his shoulders.

He could remember everything now.

The worries of his failing memory seemed insignificant, like a passing affliction. He could not explain how, beyond the medication and vitamins, he had experienced such a miraculous reversal of symptoms.

He began reciting poems he had memorized as a younger man and then historical passages from Gibbon, all without error. He detailed out loud some of his more complicated formulas and computations.

Nothing about him physically had changed. He looked at himself in the bathroom mirror: some wrinkling of the brow, slight jowls and all moles in their proper configuration. Age, apparently, had not been affected by this remarkable cognitive transformation. His eyes, though, looked brighter, more youthful.

Without telling Tenley, he went back to his neurologist and passed all of Farley's memory tests. She told him to keep on the medication, that it was doing wonders for him. She didn't seem as astounded by his recovery as he expected she would. It was almost as if she knew it beforehand.

Sitting at a table in Abe & Louie's restaurant on Boylston Street, Julian shared his miraculous transformation with Tenley. He'd quickly memorized the menu and began reciting the entrées and the entire wine list to her. He recited a poem by Tennyson and then another by her favorite poet Dickinson.

"Julian, this is amazing!" she said, cupping a hand to her mouth.

"I feel rather accomplished at this point," he said, his tone hinting that there might be more miracles to come.

Tenley raised a glassful of wine and they toasted the grand occasion. "What are you going to do now?" she asked.

Julian shook his head. "I don't really know at this point. I suppose I could return to teaching. I could un-retire."

Tenley laughed. "Or sail around the world. This is wonderful, Julian. I'm so happy for you."

They ordered another round of the good wine before the meals were served. Julian reached across the table and held Tenley's hand for a little too long. She smiled and slowly pulled it away. "You have a whole new life ahead of you, Julian. And you must make the best of it," she said.

And Julian did. He took longer walks about the city and could be seen dining at some of the best restaurants in town. He went to the theater at least once a week. He met new people by attending social events.

His appetite increased and he indulged in ample servings at the restaurants he frequented. He went off his vegetarian diet and desired only gourmet steaks and potatoes, along with rich desserts. He drank less whiskey, preferring expensive vintage wines.

Julian joined a health club on Dartmouth Street and began working out, at first taking laps in the large pool and then lifting weights with the guidance of Mel, a thirtyish transplant from Brooklyn, where he was once a metropolitan firefighter. After a month of training, Julian's shoulders had broadened and his biceps and calves took on a sculptured look. He'd put on a few pounds, which Mel advised was only normal as he gained new muscle. His waistline had shrunk to 33 inches.

Although it was late autumn now, Julian left the top down on his BMW and preferred to drive around with the brisk air in his face, his hair wafting in the crosswinds. He liked to visit the shopping malls, to be out with the crowds, and was given to spontaneous purchases: the latest style clothing, a gold necklace and a smart-looking brown leather flight jacket. To his delight, he noticed that young ladies would turn their eyes in his direction when he passed them. He hadn't quite figured out an appropriate reaction to these inviting glances, so he just winked.

Although Julian was not fond of cocktail parties, he allowed himself to go to one hosted by one of the more influential Boston families. There he met up with a woman about twenty years his junior, Celeste Birmingham of Cambridge. She was a prominent obstetrician and had several practices around town.

They stood in a far corner of the spacious sitting room, around the improvised bar, away from the noisy chatter, where a man in a white jacket was diligently filling requests from guests.

Celeste was on her third Manhattan, by Julian's count, and had an annoying twitch in her right eye that caused her eyebrow to spontaneously arch when she spoke. Julian noticed that the condition had worsened with each cocktail.

"Professor," she said, drawing slightly forward, "do you know how many screaming brats I've brought into this world?"

Julian's eyes turned toward the entranceway for a moment as he noticed a beautiful woman make entry, soon surrounded by the hosts. She reminded him of Dorothy Lamour in her heyday, tall and glamorous and star-like. A bevy of eligible bachelors (and probably husbands) followed the starlet across the room.

"Over seven thousand," Celeste said, with a subdued tone of triumph in her voice.

"Astounding," Julian said.

"And you, Professor? What have you brought into this world?"

Julian thought the question was arrogant. "Abstract formulas," he said at last. "Some of them screaming brats."

Celeste broke into raucous laughter, shriek-like and annoying and out of character for a woman of her professional stature.

Julian backed away as the good doctor leaned forward again, losing her balance and falling into his arms, an action that only exacerbated her manic laughter. She continued to advance as both of them fell into an awkward, shuffling dance. She grabbed for the sheer window curtain and suddenly spun about, landing hard on her bottom, the curtain enshrouding her like an enormous bridal veil.

Julian called for help, telling the woman who'd come to his rescue that he thought the doctor needed to use the powder room. He heard her still laughing as she was escorted away.

Determined, he didn't want to let the starlet get away. He found her ringed by several middle-aged men and a very young man who, Julian surmised, couldn't have been more than twenty-five. Dressed to a T in a morning dress with coattails and white ascot, the boy had a freckled face and large teeth, which only accentuated his immature, flamboyant appearance. His small head made him look like a grasshopper, Julian thought.

Julian stood around and let the boy make a fool of himself and then watched the others make their determined advances. During this time their eyes met, Julian's and this glamorous woman, and she smiled politely with a subdued look of desperation in her eyes.

It was right out of a movie script. Julian grabbed her hand and led her toward the door, saying only, "I have a better place in mind."

They drove to a quiet upscale bar on Exeter Street. They took a table in the corner of the fashionable lounge, well away from the serving bar. She ordered a gin and tonic and he a half-bottle of Perrier-Jouët.

"I'm sorry," he said reaching for her hand across the small table. "I'm Julian. Julian Landon. And I deplore cocktail parties."

She laughed. "Me too. I'm Dorothy Berkshire. Good to make your acquaintance." She had a firm but sensual handshake.

Julian was going to make a remark about her first name and how she looked like a certain movie star of ages past, but he decided that would foolishly date him and would probably make no sense to this young woman.

They ordered Reuben sandwiches with the best coleslaw Julian had ever tasted.

Dorothy reminded him of a girl from his youth. Her soft brown hair was swept to one side, held in place by a diamond brooch. Her green eyes sparkled under the small chandelier light. She spoke in a soft affluent tone.

"You know," she said after biting into her sandwich and neatly tapping her napkin to her lips, "that was tantamount to kidnapping back there. I could have you arrested."

"But you looked so helpless and about to be taken advantage of," Julian said, sounding a bit too serious. "I thought they would snatch you and take you off somewhere never to be found."

"So you are my savior, Julian dear, my knight in shining armor." She reached for his hand, squeezed it gently. "You are one of the nicest men I have ever met."

Soon they were sharing their stories. She came from an equestrian family in Virginia, graduated from Bryn Mawr with a masters degree in English and then an MBA from Harvard. She was in-between jobs following what she called a *nasty divorce* from a lawyer who took her to town with an alimony suit. The divorce and subsequent loss of her position at her husband's firm had left her disillusioned and ready to make a change in her life.

"I'm thinking of joining the Peace Corps," she said matter-of-factly.

"Good God, no," Julian said. "These aren't the best of times for that noble organization, what with wars, sectarian violence and all the new terrorist activity."

"I was thinking about some safe sector, perhaps in Indonesia. I'd like to teach English."

Julian said that he planned to talk her out of it, that perhaps he could find her a comfortable position at an accounting firm. He knew people, he said.

She thanked him and then veered from the subject by asking about his life and his work at the University. With great impulsiveness, Julian wanted to share with Dorothy his recent and magnificent transformation, from an old man with little memory to a person now of full wit and new-found youth. He didn't, realizing the story would place him in a precarious situation: either she would find it ludicrous or perhaps question Julian's state of mind. He decided to limit his conversation to his scholarly work. He talked about Carolyn and her successful career, mentioning too that his wife had died many years ago.

"But you're fully retired now," Dorothy said in a leading manner. "You've lived a challenging life and you've achieved so much, Julian. Have you thought about giving back to society?"

"Oh no," Julian said in a skeptical tone. "I have no interest whatsoever in joining the Peace Corps or any other organization that's going to place me in harm's way."

Dorothy smiled. "I plan to talk you into it. I have some brochures and videos to share with you. You might have a different viewpoint after reviewing them. There is so much suffering in the world, mostly the young and innocent, and here we are riding in our BMWs, wearing our diamonds and expensive attire." She looked squarely at Julian. "It's time to give back. Don't you feel that, Julian? Or at least have you considered it?"

"I give to charity on a regular basis."

"That's entirely different," Dorothy said, shaking her head. "Please consider it, Julian, and perhaps after we get to know each other better, you might share my viewpoint."

They ordered cheesecake and Vienna coffee, sharing some jovial moments, and then Julian said he would drive her back to her car. Dorothy said that she didn't drive, that she'd taken a taxi to the party.

They arrived at her townhouse, a large two-story brownstone Dorothy said her father had purchased for her while she was at Harvard. The inside was very Victorian with capacious ceilings and obviously priceless furniture.

Julian stood in the foyer and took Dorothy's hand. "This has been marvelous," he said. "We must do it again soon."

It might have been a flick of his imagination, a snippet of fantasy, but he soon realized it wasn't. Dorothy was leading him up the spiral staircase, her hand warm and moist, a faint fragrance of perfume wafting his way.

Upstairs on a heart-shaped bed, in a room with soft coral walls, Dorothy made love to Julian.

◆

Taking a full weekend to accomplish it, Julian began clearing out his office at home. He replaced the old mahogany roll-top desk with a large modern-style one, with two large sets of drawers and a spacious top to accommodate the flat-screen computer monitor he'd recently ordered. He moved the ugly old file cabinet into one of the two closets in the room. Gone were the dingy prints on the walls, along with his framed academic degrees. He shoved the massive green corkboard into the closet, wedging it against the cabinet, and filled two large garbage bags with papers, including old letters, ready to be thrown into the dumpsters.

Although he did little to change the living room, Julian had an enormous flat-screen television mounted to one wall. He had taken an interest in sports lately, everything from baseball to boxing, and enjoyed lying long ways on the sofa, his feet propped on one armrest, eating popcorn and drinking sodas.

There were a few other additions to the apartment. Julian had ordered a new king-size bed with a high tufted cream leather headboard and matching leather side tables, and curved black wrought-iron lamps. The bedroom, too, had been recently installed with flat-screen television. A large print of Goya's *La Maja Desnuda* hung above the bed.

Julian and Dorothy maintained a largely unromantic relationship. They made love a second time in Julian's new bed but otherwise continued with a platonic alliance, meeting up for lunch and enjoying the latest action-thriller movies at the theaters. Julian realized that she was dead serious about joining the Peace Corps.

She had sent in her application and sat through one interview. They had an opening in Tandag in the southern Philippines but Dorothy said it wasn't a teaching position. She had given up on her efforts to interest Julian, although he had viewed the video and several brochures. He had begun to admire her noble and compassionate interest in helping people in need, but this was not an interest he could honestly share at this time in his life.

Carolyn was back in Chicago, following trips to Milan, Sidney, Paris and Dubai. Her business was flourishing. She never called but occasionally sent Julian postcards. For reasons he couldn't quite understand, he had no desire to share any of his good fortune with her. The less she knew the less complicated their relationship.

Tenley and Julian remained close friends. They talked weekly and often took lunch together. She was worried that he was overdoing his exercise regimen, commenting that too much strain might be damaging his heart and putting him in jeopardy for stroke. She continued to be enthusiastic about his memory recovery.

One inclement afternoon, after watching a movie together in the living room, Julian mentioned something that had been on his mind for months. "Tenley," he said, "I've never seen you with someone and you've never mentioned a relationship. Is there a boyfriend in your life?"

"My, we are getting personal now," Tenley said.

"But you know everything about me. Well, almost everything."

She broached the subject tenderly, starting off with her childhood and then her first years at college. She said she knew it for sure during her first year at the University when she met someone very special.

"Oh, Julian...didn't you know that I am bisexual?"

"Oh my God," Julian blurted out, truly shocked by the admission. It had never crossed his mind. He always thought that she worked too much and just never had the social opportunities for developing a serious relationship with a man.

"It's not a disease," Tenley said, laughing.

"How often are you one or the other?"

"Julian, why are you asking such personal things?"

He was silent for a few moments. "I'm sorry. It really isn't any of my business."

"No, it isn't your business in the way your affair with Dorothy isn't any of mine."

Julian could feel his face flushing. "How did you know that?" he said, almost in a demanding manner.

Tenley smiled, reached for his hand and said, "Word travels. I am so happy for you, Julian. It's what you should have been doing years ago. Close relationships are so important in life."

"Yes," Julian said, wishing the topic were over. It seemed so out of his character to ask such questions of his good friend, and he felt somewhat ashamed of himself. He apologized, hoping that his inappropriate curiosity hadn't affected in any way their relationship.

"I want you to know, Julian, that you are the dearest friend I have," Tenley said.

Before leaving she hugged her friend and then gave him a kiss on the cheek. "Let's do this again next week," she said. "I hear there's a new indie thriller coming out on Netflix."

Julian cleaned up the living room and then went to the window and stared out into the gloomy weather. Thunderstorms had been forecasted. The sky was gray and tumescent, a ridge of threatening clouds rolling in from the west. It had been a perfect day for watching movies, but now the weather matched Julian's souring disposition. The conversation with Tenley had left him feeling foolish, and vulnerable in a way he had only experienced when Elizabeth had died.

But soon thoughts of his miraculous recovery and the new way of life he had chosen lifted his mood. Something of extraordinary good fortune had come his way.

And he was determined not to let it go.

◆

Tenley drove home as the first spits of rain hit the windshield. The initial sweeps of the windshield wipers made the glass smear with the autumn residue. For a second, Tenley couldn't even see the street. She pushed the washer button and was relieved when all came into clarity.

By the time she arrived at her apartment, Tenley was already feeling a bit guilty but she didn't know why. Her life was her own. She had chosen not to tell Julian about her affair. She was seeing someone, a girl in her twenties from California, with whom she had fallen in love almost instantly. Jennie was one of her students, a young woman who was attractive intellectually as she was physically. The relationship had just begun and was a little past the flirting stage. They shared coffee together in the staff cafeteria and when the weather was right they walked about the campus, indulging in existential musings. They both adored the works of Ayn Rand, most especially the novel "The Fountainhead".

She had no aspirations about the relationship but just knew it was right at this time in her life. Sensing Julian's possessiveness earlier that afternoon, Tenley wondered how long he had felt that way and if, in the future, it would threaten their friendship.

That night she fell into a dream, not one of Jennie or any of her other friends but of Julian. The change in the man worried her. Though he looked better physically than he had in recent years, the changes he'd made in the apartment seemed odd and out-of-place and suggested a man frantically avoiding his advancing age. She was relieved that he had finally purchased a new bed and that he enjoyed watching television, a past-time he wouldn't have considered even a year ago. He was definitely emerging from his retirement shell, and she was happy for him.

In the dream she saw a boy's bedroom, with luminescent Star Trek stickers on the ceiling and walls, action figures atop the small chest of drawers and a large Rubik's Cube dangling over the head of the small bed. It vaguely reminded her of an old photograph of her father's bedroom when he was seven or eight.

She stood at the foot of the bed for what seemed like an exaggerated period of time. As she did, more details of the boy's room became apparent to her: a Farah Fawcett poster along one side of the closet, boy's clothing overflowing the tall wicker hamper and an old stuffed toy in the shape of monkey, partially visible from underneath the bed. She noticed the figure of a boy beneath the covers, motionless and obviously fast asleep.

The dream lay suspended like that for the longest time and at one point Tenley desired to end it, as if the stagnation bored her, like a video stuck in its playing.

Suddenly, the small form underneath the cover moved and out sprang Julian, this time with his old beard and weathered face, eyes wide, his tongue sticking out at her.

Tenley startled herself awake and lay there glaring up at the ceiling, Julian's visage still fresh in her mind. Finally the image faded as she grew more conscious of her own familiar surroundings. It occurred to her that the dream may have been a sign, a premonition of some sort.

Maybe Julian was in danger. Had he fallen or suffered a stroke? Was this Julian calling out for help?

Tenley looked over at the bedside alarm clock. It was only one in the morning. She had been asleep barely an hour. She reached for her cell phone and called Julian's number. He answered on the third ring.

"Julian here," he said brightly. The sound of a movie playing made his voice fade.

Relieved but feeling guilty for calling him this late, she asked if he was alright.

He began to answer her but the background noise obscured his words. She heard him turn down the blaring television. "Tenley, is that you?"

"I'm sorry but I had nightmare and I just wanted to check that you were okay."

"Why wouldn't I be?" Julian asked, obviously perplexed by his friend's inquiry. "Of course, I'm okay. I'm up late watching a rerun of the Star Trek series, one of my favorites. Were you dreaming of me?"

"I just had a strange dream, not *really* bad but enough to startle me awake. When I have those kinds of dreams sometimes I think they're portentous."

"And what did this one portend? You *must* have been dreaming about me, darling," Julian said.

They said goodnight and as Tenley was shaking her head at her clumsy effort to show concern for Julian's welfare, fragments of the dream revisited and began to congeal. Soon she was reliving all of the details.

It was almost three o'clock before she slept again.

Chapter Seven

Julian had a hard time keeping up with his appetite. Now bound to the television as though it was a new and fantastic invention, he found himself ordering pizzas and fried chicken from the deli, along with cream soda, now his preferred beverage. Besides watching his favorite shows and movies, Julian had installed X Box One and spent hours playing video games, which lay stacked in their cases on top of the coffee table; several were scattered on the floor.

He decided to share a mounting predicament with Mel one day when he'd finished his workout. He seemed like a guy he could trust with manly imperatives.

Mel was wiping down the seat of one of the bench press machines when Julian asked him if he was still aroused around women.

Appearing blasé about it, Mel said, "I'm only forty, man. Of course chicks still turn me on, especially some of the ones who come here in their sexy workout suits. And you?"

Julian shook his head. "It's unrelenting. Sometimes I feel like a teenager unable to contain himself." He added that although a pleasurable feeling, it was causing him to stare at young women, even searching out for pretty blondes on his jogs through the parks.

"You're jogging now?" Mel said. "That's great, Professor! You really amaze me."

"Well, that's the reason I have to jog. It's away of releasing sexual energy."

"Testosterone," Mel said. "You'd be surprised how many older men mention that. You see, muscle-building requires testosterone. That's why most women don't have muscles. It's absolutely normal." He looked up at Julian with a grin. "You don't want to hold it in too long or you'll burst. I'm sure there's a good-looking woman in your life, eh?"

Julian said he'd had one or two and soon realized it would prove impossible for Mel to really understand his situation. Mel was relatively young and with his good looks and muscular frame probably had no problem attracting women.

"If you're really hard up," he said quietly, almost conspiratorially, "just give me a call. I'll share my book. Or if you need something underneath the table, I'm your man." He gave Julian one of his personal cards and then punched him lightly in the arm.

Julian decided to stop by the mall on the way back to his apartment. He didn't intend to purchase anything. He just thought it would be good to be around others for a change. He did some window browsing and then looked at some watches at Ross-Simons Jewelry, where his eye was caught by a gold and silver Rolex, a sports type with timers and buttons, a chronograph of immaculate workmanship. He asked the saleswoman to show it to him, which she did with a charming smile. "Never owned a Rolex before?" she said.

"Does it tell time?" he asked facetiously.

The saleswoman laughed and looked seriously at Julian. "You look like a man who takes care of himself...I mean, physically. You probably run and belong to a gym. This would be a perfect watch for you."

"Yes," Julian said.

"Rolexes are pieces of jewelry, like a diamond necklace is for a woman. This watch will make a statement about who you are and where you are going."

She started to explain the watch's capabilities in detail, but Julian's mind was elsewhere. He interrupted her by saying that he wanted to buy the expensive watch.

"Wonderful choice," she said, looking a little startled for having made such a quick sale.

Julian carried the small dainty shopping bag with gold-tasseled handles firmly in his hand. Shopping malls or any areas where large crowds congregated were not safe these days. He ate a taco at the food court and then decided to open the box and put the Rolex on. It fit perfectly and sparkled in the bright fluorescent light of the mall. It made him feel young and newly successful.

Weaving his way through a strand of kiosks, occasionally looking at his watch and admiring it, Julian came face-to-face with a tall woman of Asian descent with sparkling green eyes, matching eye shadow and a smile that was wide and quite appealing. She smelled of Jasmine and her skin was smooth, her dangly black hair held up by an emerald side brooch.

"Now, you are a fine gentleman," she said, taking his arm. "What is your name?" She spoke in proper English, no doubt, Julian surmised, educated abroad.

"I don't want to buy anything," Julian said, feeling assailed by the young woman. He had seen them before in this section of the mall, preying on older gentlemen to peddle off their goods.

"I believe," she whispered into his ear, "that it begins with the letter J, perhaps Jason or Justin... No, it's *Julien*." She exaggerated the French pronunciation by drawing out the name so that it sounded like *jOO-lee-uhn*.

Surprised by not baffled by the woman's feat, Julian watched her seductive smile as she led him to her kiosk. "My name is Zelda."

"Really, Zelda, how did you guess my name? It's a trick, isn't it?"

"Feminine intuition," Zelda said, still smiling.

Julian noticed two Asian young men dressed in gray suits, their arms folded, standing to the side of the kiosk. One of them was holding a two-way radio. *Accomplices*, he thought. Perhaps they would drag him into a side room if he decided not to purchase anything. The thought became suddenly absurd.

"You have a lady?" Zelda asked.

"Well, actually I don't," Julian said, hoping that that would end the conversation.

"Then, I have just the perfect solution for you, *jOO-lee-uhn*. I have oils made from the minerals of the Black Sea, a solvent that when applied correctly works as an aphrodisiac, a fragrant oil that women cannot resist." She opened the small bottle and slowly rubbed a drop on the underside of Julian's wrist. She bent over and kissed the spot. "Ooh-la-la," she whispered as Julian fumbled in his pocket for some cash.

Julian stuffed the bottle in his coat pocket, not bothering to receive change from the purchase. He hurried off, feeling duped and assailed.

"You bought a fine Rolex," Zelda called after him.

Realizing the scam, Julian decided not to let it interfere with his good mood. Obviously accomplices in the jewelry store had seen him purchase the watch. They had probably tipped off the two men near Zelda's kiosk.

Once at home he frantically dialed Dorothy's number. He let it ring until the answering machine came on. He left a message, saying that something had come up and would she please return his call.

When she didn't call back after half an hour, Julian put on his jogging suit and headed for Lederman Park overlooking the Charles

River, barely a two mile jaunt from the apartment. It was one of Julian's favorite places to visit, and he hoped to take a short rest there and then proceed on a five-mile run, using Boston's fine biking paths.

Expecting Dorothy's name to come up on his cell, he saw that it was Tenley. He found a bench at the park and with labored breathing, answered the call.

"Julian! Something...horrible...has happened," she said, gasping, hardly able to release the words from her mouth.

Chapter Eight

By the time Julian arrived at Tenley's apartment, the police were gone. A maintenance man had just finished replacing the front door locks. He handed the new keys to Tenley, who sat on the sofa beside Julian, wiping the tears from her eyes with a tissue.

"How damn foolish of me," Tenley said. "That's never happened before. I was only gone for fifteen minutes." She explained that she was walking Beverly's dog because her neighbor had gone out for day. She hadn't bothered to lock the door.

"Did they take anything besides your purse and keys?" Julian asked.

"Some jewelry from the bedroom and...some of my underclothes.

"Good God!" Julian said. "Perverts."

"I feel like I've been raped," Tenley sobbed.

Julian said that they would have to cancel all of her credit cards and notify DMV first thing in the morning. He worried about identity theft but did not want to overburden Tenley at the moment. He asked if the police had checked all the other doors and windows.

"Yes, they went in with their guns drawn and looked everywhere, even the small attic. They assured me that all was secure." She stopped, startled. "All the keys to the University were in my purse. I've got to notify them."

"We can do that tomorrow," Julian said, massaging the back of Tenley's neck. He noticed that she was still shaking.

"Oh Julian, what if I had been in the apartment? I might be dead now!"

Julian pulled her toward him. "It's not important what could have happened but that you are fine now. Everything lost can be replaced. In a month you'll have forgotten the matter. You have insurance?"

She nodded and said, "They have my car keys...but I suppose the door locks can be changed, if they don't steal the car first." Julian could feel her shudder again. "They know everything about me, where I work, where I shop, my class schedule. I feel so vulnerable, so exposed. At least they left me my phone; it was in the bathroom, on the edge of the tub, where I left it after my morning soak."

"This happens all the time," Julian said, realizing at once that it was a feeble remark. "I mean, nine out of ten times the police find the culprits and everything returns to normal. You'll see."

"Are you just saying that to console me?"

"There are video cameras everywhere in this city and probably a few in this complex. I'm sure the police will check into all that," Julian said convincingly.

Later, they ate in the kitchen at a round glass table, sipping from hot mugs of tomato soup and eating leftover sandwiches. They watched the news on a portable flat-screen but offered few comments.

Tenley developed a headache, one that didn't respond to the several Tylenol capsules she had taken. On the sofa again, this time outstretched, with Julian sitting helplessly in the floral wingback chair across from her, she said, "I can't take this anymore."

Julian offered to take her to the emergency room but she declined emphatically. "Five hours sitting around a roomful of sick people," she said, "I truly think would do me in."

She said that she would try another hot bath to see if it would calm her nerves and the resulting headache.

"Do you want me to stay around?" Julian asked.

"Please don't leave, not now," Tenley said and then asked if Julian would mind drawing her bath.

The bathroom was off the bedroom and was spacious, with coral tiles and an antique-white claw foot tub with brass water faucets. It was deep enough to drown in, Julian thought as he began filling the tub.

Tenley came in from the bedroom, wrapped tightly in a fluffy coral towel and wearing furry white slippers. She poured an ample amount of strawberry bubble soap into the steamy water, swished it around and then asked if Julian wouldn't mind waiting for her in the bedroom. Leaving the door ajar, he settled himself in a blue tufted chaise lounge, his heart beating just a little faster than usual.

The image of Tenley, naked but for the towel, her long smooth legs and bare shoulders alarmingly visible, was still vibrant in his mind. It soon became overwhelming, and Julian decided he better wait in the living room.

"Julian, are you still there?" she called, and Julian rushed over and put an ear to the door.

"Yes," he said. "Is everything alright?"

Tenley asked him to come in. She was fully submerged in pink bubbles and lathering soap, only an oval of face and a surrounding swirl of wet hair visible. She rose slightly as Julian approached so that her shoulders and back emerged from the frothy water. "Would you mind scrubbing my back," she asked, quite matter-of-factly, as if she was asking him to pass the sugar.

She produced a back brush from somewhere near her feet, bending forward and exposing the soft nubs of her backbone.

As Julian went to work, briskly working the brush, Tenley said, "My father used to do this for me, even when I was a teenager. I know he felt embarrassed at first, but soon it became a family ritual." She laughed. "He became the designated back brusher in the family and did the same for my mother and younger brother." She dropped her head forward, sweeping her hair from her neck. "Oh Julian," she said, "that feels so good. You must be experienced at this."

His heart pounding every more swiftly, Julian thought he was going to pass out. Suddenly he dropped the brush and hurried to the door, excusing himself by telling Tenley that he was light-headed, probably from the run, and needed some fresh air.

"Don't leave me," he heard Tenley say as he left the bedroom and headed for the foyer. He opened the front door and took deep breaths of chilly Boston air. He shook his head, feeling a mixture of relief, embarrassment and failed denouement.

Later that evening Tenley made him promise not to leave her alone for the night. That had been his own thought earlier when they were discussing the details of the break-in but now seemed exceedingly rational and imperative. Even with the new locks, the robbers posed a danger to Tenley. They knew everything about her.

She asked him if he wouldn't mind sleeping on the lounge in her bedroom. She said she had pillows and a large comforter and that he was welcomed to use the portable flat-screen. She said that she slept like a log.

Yet in his jogging suit, Julian washed up in the bathroom, which still smelled of strawberry and jasmine. He looked into the mirror and saw that his face was flushed.

Tenley was obviously exhausted. After fixing up the lounge chair, she kissed Julian on the cheek and then heaved into bed, pulling the comforter almost over her head. She tossed a few times and then peered out of the covers

"Julian, you are my knight in shining armor," she said not entirely whimsically. "I don't know what I would do without you. You are so dear to me. I love you."

The words sank in slowly, like a mesmerizing truth he had already known in some other time and place, a remembrance of both arousal and peace and generosity. It was as if a princess had kissed him.

Unable to sleep, Julian lay curled up on the chaise, listening to Tenley's soft snoring. Thankful that she was out of the real world, with all of its harshness, fears and threats, he imagined her dreaming. *What do princesses dream of ?* he asked himself. *Bubbles, jewels and princes.*

Once when she coughed, he went over to the bed and put his wrist on her forehead, hoping she hadn't developed a fever with the headache. She felt normal. He was walking away when he heard her mumbling unintelligibly. He thought she was trying to say his name. He returned and leaned his ear to her mouth. She stopped suddenly and said, obviously awakened by his efforts, "Julian, for God's sake, go to sleep!

◆

They awoke late in the morning. Tenley had found some dried croissants in the breadbox and popped them in the microwave, which re-moisturized the pastry so that it was warm, fluffy and delicious. She fixed Julian a soft-boiled egg, which she placed in a silver holder and then lopped off the top of the shell. She put a drop or two of butter on the top. Tomato juice and a slice of good ham completed the brunch.

She called the police to see if their investigation had turned up some clues, if not the thieves themselves. They said they would call her, reminding her that the theft had occurred only the evening before.

Julian helped her call the credit card companies to have them put an immediate hold on her accounts and issue new cards. She called the DMV and asked if she could come down and replace her driver's license. She was told to bring both her passport and her birth certificate. She said that the passport had been in her stolen purse but that she had proper identification from Boston University.

She called her insurance company to keep them apprised in case the car went missing. She called the car dealer to make sure the locks could be replaced and a new set of keys issued.

Those tasks completed, Julian said that he would jog back to his apartment and return with the car, for Tenley feared her second set of keys was locked in the glove compartment.

"No, wait," she said, grabbing at Julian's arm. "You can't leave me here like this."

They finally devised a plan that felt suitable to Tenley. She would walk down to the DMV, which was only two blocks away, and he would pick her up there after retrieving his car.

Before he left she called the car dealer and arranged for her car to be towed there as soon as possible.

At the door, Julian turned and said, "I am so glad you've got your nerves back. You've thought of everything. I'm so proud of you."

Tenley smiled back. "Not without your help. Thank you, Julian, thank you so much."

After meeting her at the DMV, Julian returned Tenley to her apartment. She was more confident now and told him that she would be fine by herself. Julian made her promise to call him whenever she felt the need to.

The next day after another refreshing jog, Julian was back in his apartment. He didn't want to waste any time, so he quickly changed into slacks and polo shirt and a pair of Nordstrom leather sandals. He put on his new Rolex, grabbed his wallet and keys and was out the door in under ten minutes. He needed to be around other people again , especially young crowds.

There was mystery, excitement and urgency to the day, feelings that gave Julian even more energy and a rush of robustness. He felt as if he could run a marathon, hurl a pitch to out the batter and, even better yet, to cause miracles to happen.

As if some amazing miracles hadn't already happened.

Chapter Nine

Two weeks after the incident, Tenley called Julian with the exciting news that the thieves had been caught, the purse and car keys returned. The two boys involved, in their early twenties, had tried to use her debit card at an ATM and clear photos had been taken during the attempted transaction. They were in the county jail awaiting arraignment. The prosecutor had told her they would get several years as their records indicated a history of criminal activity. As she had not witnessed the crime, she would only have to provide the prosecutor a formal written statement, that her appearance in court was not needed.

Relieved in more ways than one, Julian accepted the case as closed. He congratulated Tenley again on her bravery and tenacity.

"You sound different," Tenley said as they were closing the conversation.

"How?"

"I don't know, Julian...I guess your voice. Are you okay?

"Just getting over a cold, some congestion," Julian offered, wondering what Tenley would think if she saw just how much he had changed. He knew he would have to avoid her from now on.

The realization that a strange metamorphosis was occurring, that he was actually getting younger by the week, was at first perplexing but soon accepted as yet another turn of good fortune. Ironically, it reminded Julian of the feeling of achievement he'd once experienced when able to grow his first beard. It was a process of nature he couldn't tamper with.

His hair had grown thicker and slightly curly and had taken a chestnut tone. His face was smooth and his ears more compact. His jawline was more pronounced and slight dimples creased his cheeks. His hands were smooth and firm, his eyes intense and seeking.

He tried to operate under the cover of darkness, sneaking out at night for social escapades. He met up with Dorothy on two occasions, both in her place in her heart-shaped bed, with the lights turned down. She seemed not to have noticed his physical transformation, which puzzled Julian. They had been passionate affairs, Julian wanting more and more until Dorothy gasped with exhaustion. "My God, Julian, what's got into you?" she'd said, falling back in the bed.

The third time he asked to come over, Dorothy told him she had other plans, that she had met up with another man. It didn't surprise Julian and in a way he was glad. Dorothy seemed older, more puritan in her sexual predilections. The realization that he was now attracted to much younger women seemed a natural part of his miraculous metamorphosis.

One day, a month after last seeing Tenley, he realized that he couldn't pass for himself anymore. For two weeks he didn't dare venture outside the apartment. No one would know who he was. He had lost his age in the most peculiar way.

With a great idea in mind he called Leighton and in a forced nasal voice explained that his nephew would be using his place while he was in France for at least two months, maybe more. He would have *Brad* introduce himself, and asked Leighton to let the young man have full reign of the place and to oblige him when he had requests.

"Brilliant!" Julian said after completing the call, breaking into boisterous laughter, holding his fists up in victory. And *Brad* was a perfect pseudonym.

Weren't these the best of times? Was he ever this dashing, this brash and debonair?

◆

Julian soon got bored with his video games. His taste for music had turned from baroque to hard rock and then rap. He loved LL Cool J and Jay-Z and Niki Minaj and would often mimic the lyrics to his favorite songs. They blared through the apartment at all hours.

His taste for soda stopped, now craving cold milk, which he drank with chocolate-chip cookies or peanut butter sandwiches. As he hadn't been out in weeks, deli deliveries were daily and sometimes at all hours of the night. Barbequed chicken wings and coleslaw were frequent orders.

He noticed his first pimple on his forehead just below his hairline and broke out in triumphant laughter. He craved to pop it but new it was best to leave it alone, so he covered it with a small oval Band Aid.

One day he slipped outside and found Leighton helping an old lady into the foyer. He walked over to the man and introduced himself as Brad Hartwood.

"Yes, Mr. Hartwood," Leighton said. "Your uncle called me a while back. He said you were to have the run of the place but I'm quite sure he meant for you to follow the rules and not entertain wild parties in the apartment. Are you in school, young man?"

"BU," Julian said, feeling such intrepid irony in his words he could hardly keep a straight face.

"Mr. Hartwood, about the loud music, I just want you to know that several guests have started to complain. I would suggest that you keep it down past eleven o'clock. I think your uncle would agree."

"Sure," Julian said, realizing that he would have been the first to complain of a noisy neighbor in earlier times.

"You will be driving the BMW?" Leighton asked cautiously.

"Of course," he said. "Unless I decide to sell it."

Leighton gave him an odd look that at once turned into a minatory glance of disapproval.

Julian drove to the mall and purchased a new wardrobe of clothes: Wrangler jeans, tee-shirts, a pair of Nike basketball sneakers, close-fitted sweaters and a Red Sox cap. As soon as he paid for his purchases, he slipped into a men's restroom stall in the mall and switched his clothing, dumping the old ones in the trash bin. He wet his hands and ran them through his hair, noticing yet another small pimple on the side of his face. He thought he looked like a teenage Matt Damon.

He had a milkshake at the food gallery, ate a pretzel and stared at a pretty young woman across the court. She was with two other girls and it looked like they had just finished their lunch. They noticed him and all three smiled.

Walking down the mall together, Julian and the young women introduced themselves, he, of course, as Brad. The prettiest was named Heather, the other two, Brenda and Jill. They were probably in their very early twenties, somewhere around Julian's new age. Their meeting had been so refreshingly casual, so natural, drawn together by the magnetic powers of good looks and youth and curiosity. By the time they all exited the mall, they'd made plans to meet up at Tunnel on Stuart Street, a popular night lounge.

Julian asked if he should dress up, and the girls burst into laughter.

"Exactly what you're wearing," Heather said. "Just come as you are. Promise not to forget, Brad. Friday at seven, okay?" She gave him her number, which he effortlessly memorized.

With the top down, the radio blaring one of his favorite songs by Niki Minaj, Julian drove to the Verizon store on Boylston Street. He swung out of the BMW without opening the door. Inside he tried to trade his old flip phone for a fancier smartphone.

The young man serving him looked at Julian as if he was crazy. He told him the phone had to be ten years old and had absolutely no value. Shown several of the newest smartphones on the market, Julian picked out the latest iPhone. All the girls at the beach had owned one and he was confident that this smartphone would be trendy enough. The young man transferred all of the numbers from the old phone to the iPhone.

As Julian waited, he glanced over at the other counter and recognized Claudia from the beach. He was startled by her appearance because she looked much older than she had clad in her one-piece bathing suit, her blondish hair loose and flowing in the breeze. Now she wore a chain print flounce skirt, white blouse and black mid-heels. Her hair had been dyed a rich brunette and was cut short in a retro 50s hairstyle. Julian couldn't stop staring at her, and when she finally looked over Claudia gave him a nose-up look of dismissal.

"Damn," Julian said as the assistant returned with the programmed phone. He signed the two-year contract. The iPhone was re-boxed and placed in a small shopping bag, along with the papers. The man asked how he wished to pay for the purchase, and Julian said, "Debit card."

The young man scrutinized the bank card and then told Julian that he would need a driver's license as an ID. Julian reached for his back pocket and froze.

"Wait just a moment," he said with a touch of old formality. "This is a debit card and I have its PIN number. That's all that's needed." He looked sternly at the man. "Is this some form of profiling? Do you ask everyone with a debit card for their ID?!"

The assistance manager came over, listened to the young man's explanation and then to Julian's account. "I have a solution, Mr. Landon. We'll just give the bank a call to make sure the card is legit."

Julian could hardly contain his anger. This had never happened to him before. And then the anger turned inward as he realized that he should have anticipated such as situation. Some old geezer's face was on his driver's license. It had come to this, an untenable predicament. He would forget the purchase and get the cash at an ATM.

Five minutes later, the assistant manager returned. "You've obviously had an account there for some time," he said, adding, "and they've cleared the purchase, Mr. Landon."

As Julian was finishing the transaction, a small ringing sound came from the boxed phone. He thought it might be Tenley and quickly unpackaged the phone and answered the call. Realizing who it was, he smiled, thanked the voice on the other end and held up the phone, waving it in front of the men.

"My bank," Julian said triumphantly.

As he drove off, Julian considered the more pragmatic aspects of living a life of sudden youth. He had been smart enough to anticipate identity problems with Leighton but now unforeseeable complications loomed in his mind. How would he get into the nightclub? Certainly they would ask for an ID. What if he got stopped by the police? He considered doctoring his license but soon realized that he would probably end up destroying the card.

And then he had an idea.

Tenley hadn't seen Julian in over a month. He had not returned any of her calls, and she worried. They had spoken last a couple of weeks after the break-in. He seemed fine then, in good spirit and health. She had sent him a special thank you card for all he had done, it's greeting, in bold script, *My Knight in Shining Armor*.

Evermore concerned, Tenley got in her car and drove to his place. She found Leighton and asked if the professor was in.

"He's in France for a few months."

"Oh," Tenley said with a slight gasp. She asked Leighton where in France he might be.

"No, I'm sorry. He never told me, but his nephew might know."

"Nephew? I didn't know he had a nephew," Tenley said.

"He's apartment-sitting while the professor is away. A young man named Brad, a rather arrogant boy if you don't mind my saying."

Tenley asked if he was in and Leighton replied that he had taken off in the professor's BMW earlier in the day. She thanked the man and, walking back to her car, she paused, then headed back to the apartments.

Leighton closed the door behind him as Tenley looked at the place in utter horror. What had this nephew done to Julian's quaint apartment? He'd left it a mess: soda cans strewn about the living room floor, candy boxes, crumpled deli bags and chewing gum wrappers scattered everywhere. A hideous-looking game box lay in front of the television in a tangle of control wires.

She called Julian immediately but it went to voicemail after two rings. He certainly wouldn't approve of this mess.

As far as Tenley could see at least the boy hadn't damaged the apartment. She checked the other rooms and, except for the bathroom, which had clumps of towels and washcloths on the floor, everything seemed in good shape.

Admiring his new bed again, Tenley noticed the card she had sent him sitting on the nightstand. She picked it up, read it and then pressed it to her chest.

"I miss you Julian," she whispered.

She returned the card to the table and considered calling Carolyn to see if she knew of her father's whereabouts, but remembered her promise to Julian.

Somehow she would track Julian down. She would find his nephew; surely he would know the details of his strange escape.

◆

Julian wasn't sure exactly how he would approach the man.

"Yeah, kid, what can I do for you?" Mel said with enough indifference to indicate that he was too busy to make conversation.

"You're Mel," Julian said with a smile and introduced himself as Brad, Professor Landon's nephew.

"Great," Mel said, asking how the professor was doing. Julian explained that his uncle had found a very young woman in Paris and had moved into her pied-à-terre on the Left Bank.

"Now that's a man with youth in his blood," Mel laughed. "I'd like to borrow *his* little black book."

"Well, actually that's why I'm here," Julian said, stepping closer. "My uncle told me before he left that if I should ever need a favor, I should see you, Mel. He said you could work little miracles."

When Mel saw the wad of hundred dollar bills, he said, "No problema, kid. But we'll need a current photo. I suppose you want to be 21. I have a man who is a genius at making fake IDs."

They shook hands in a gentleman's agreement. Julian handed over the two thousand dollars, asking again if the license would be ready before Friday. Mel assured him it would.

He drove back to the apartment, parked the car and made his way into the grand foyer.

"Brad," he heard Leighton say. "I'm sure you don't mind but I opened the apartment for a very good friend of your Uncle. She's been here many times. I think she's worried about the professor's whereabouts."

Julian froze in his tracts. "Oh, yes," he said, trying to sound matter-of-fact about it. "She told me she might be stopping by one of these days to collect some of Uncle Julian's papers."

"She did, eh?" Leighton said, not attempting to conceal his skeptical look.

Julian's heart was pounding when the elevator door opened to his floor. He looked to his right, where the apartment was. "Geez," he said under his breath. It wasn't that he was afraid to meet up with Tenley--in fact, he held a strange desire to do just that--but he knew she wouldn't believe him, no matter what he told her. He hardly sounded or looked like himself anymore. Knowing Tenley, she would probably call the police and that would arouse the suspicion that he was an imposter, that perhaps he had done something to the old professor. He would be arrested and placed in jail.

Julian began to walk casually down the hallway away from his apartment. He heard a door open and soon after, Tenley's voice.

"Brad?" she said, hurrying toward him.

He turned around with a puzzled look on his face.

"Are you Brad, Professor Landon's nephew?" Tenley's face looked deeply concerned, her eyes imploring. She had been crying, her cheeks flushed. That she appeared older to Julian came with a mixture of alarm and melancholia.

"Excuse me?"

Tenley repeated her question, searching deeply into Julian's eyes.

"No," he said. "Do I look like him?"

"No, of course not...I mean I don't think so..." Tenley suddenly looked like a vacuum had sucked all the air from her lungs. She gasped, her face deathly pale, and collapsed full-weight into Julian's arms.

He lay her down on the carpet, her head in his lap, and began fanning air to her face. For a few seconds he thought she might have had a heart attack, and he reached for his phone to call 911. Just as he did, color rushed back to her face and she began mumbling some words. Soon she was struggling to stand up.

"I'm...so...sorry," she said, leaning heavily against Julian's arm. "I don't know what happened. I skipped lunch...and I guess my body's paying me back."

"Ma'am," Julian said. "Are you sure you're okay? I was about to call 911."

Tenley stiffened at the suggestion, releasing her grip of Julian's arm. "Of course," she said curtly as if he had made some untoward advance. "I'm fine, just fine." She thanked him and hurried back to the elevator.

Julian had waited a reasonable period of time at the end of the hallway near the emergency stairs, ready to make an escape if either Tenley or Leighton returned. Now inside his apartment he lay collapsed on the sofa, shaking his head.

"Damn!" he said. "That was close." He warned himself again for having overlooked potentially-perilous situations where, to his disadvantage, his true identity would be revealed. He had to be more careful, even if he was just a kid having the time of his life.

For the first time in forty years he lit a cigarette from a pack he'd purchased at the mall. He inhaled deeply, causing a stuttering cough, inhaled again and let the cigarette dangle from his lips. His thoughts dwelled on Tenley, not so much on the dangerous encounter now, but from a growing despair that he had lost her to her generation. He was probably fifteen years her junior and perhaps growing younger. It was an odd juxtaposition, his youth now against what was the beginning of her middle-age years. She was once the luster of youth and beauty and he had always been attracted by those qualities as an older man. *It doesn't seem fair*, he thought.

◆

Thursday afternoon Julian picked up the package from Mel, who seemed more than indifferent, almost aloof, as Julian opened it and inspected the new license. The selfie he'd instagrammed Mel was perfect, although Julian thought it made him appear too young to be twenty-one.

Later, he called the girl from the mall. "Heather? It's Brad. Are we still on for Friday?"

Music blared in the background and Heather had to shout into the phone.

She told him to hold on, that she had to go somewhere where she could talk. "Cool, Brad," she said as the background noise faded. "I'm really glad you called. I've been thinking about you."

"Oh," Julian said, not quite sure how to respond.

"You know what I mean," Heather said. "You left quite an impression. Maybe we could go somewhere special afterwards."

Not wanting to commit himself, Julian said, "Sounds cool. We can talk about it."

"Do you do coke?" she asked.

Realizing that she meant cocaine, he quickly said no, that he wasn't into drugs of any kind.

"Are you sure? How about weed?"

Julian insisted that he didn't, that it wasn't his scene, sounding, he thought, like a staunch church boy.

"Thank God," Heather said. "I drink some wine but that's all I do. I don't like to be around people who are high that way."

Julian asked about the nightspot they were going to tomorrow. He tried to warn Heather that he wasn't a very good dancer and that she could expect him to be a bit clumsy.

"Oh don't worry, Julian. "It's a great place. Just go with the music and your body will follow."

"Sure," Julian said.

"Can't wait to see you, Brad," Heather said. "I like the beginning of relationships, don't you?"

"Sure. I do too," Julian said.

"It's like opening a new novel. It's full of intrigue and mystery," Heather said wistfully.

Chapter Ten

There was a small line in front of Tunnel. Heather was waiting for him at the door. She kissed Julian lightly on the lips and they held hands. Her friends at the mall were not present, and Julian assumed they had gone inside or had decided not to come.

Julian watched as a man wearing a black polo shirt, light green khakis and Turkish leather-braded sandals greeted the guests. *A bouncer*, Julian surmised quickly enough and felt for his wallet. Astonished that he was let inside without showing his ID, Julian quickly met up with a young woman with purple streaks in her hair. She asked for his ID, requesting that he remove it from the clear plastic holder in his wallet. She looked at his face then at the photo and then back at Julian. "Nice watch," she said, handing the license back with a glittery smile.

The lounge was far smaller than he had expected it to be. The decor was surprisingly handsome, with blue lounge sofas, large red cushions and racks of blue-and-white lights on the ceiling. There was a small dance area, a bar and several tables. The DJ had just put on *Va Va Voom*, one of Julian's favorite songs by Nicki Minaj.

Heather led Julian straight to the crowded dance floor. She was a good dancer, with fluid moves in perfect beat to Nicki's song. She was dressed in a bright pink blouse with black slacks and stylish suspenders. Her blonde hair was combed up over the crown of her head with ringlets dangling down her neck and sides.

She looks like a movie star, Julian thought and soon found himself in perfect sync with the music. They danced another song and when they sat down on one of the lounge sofas, he noticed the tiny beads of perspiration on her forehead. It mingled with her perfume, making a fragrance of its own, full of energy, youth and the precipice of the unknown.

Heather ordered champagne in a tall silver-rimmed glass and he a cranberry spritzer.

"You're a fantastic dancer, Heather. And you look gorgeous."

Heather reached for his hand, hers soft and delicate, and rubbed it gently. "And you look great, a handsome young lad."

Julian didn't know how to take the statement. It seemed anachronistic for this time and age and suddenly reminded him of how his father used to address his young son. He must have looked puzzled.

Heather burst into laughter. "I don't know why I said that...it just slipped out." She looked genuinely apologetic. "You are a handsome man, Brad. You know, I dreamed about you last night."

"A nightmare?" Julian said.

Heather shook her head. "No, not like that at all. It was a romantic dream. We were on a voyage, I think on a ship, and stars were glittering above, the night air warm. You kissed me and said you were taking me to a magical place. It was such a neat dream."

Julian smiled. They held hands and Heather talked of her love for animals, especially dogs. She had two chocolate Cocker Spaniels and a yellow cockatiel that could recite the Pledge of Allegiance. She had an apartment on Mount Vernon Street near Old Harbor that she shared with two other girls. She worked at an upscale boutique, where she'd been employed for over a year. She said rather mysteriously that she was saving for a great adventure. Heather seemed full of hope and aspiration and a carefree *joie de vivre*.

"And you, Brad Hartwood? How did you come to be here, now, at this moment with me?"

"Well, I was actually picked up at the mall and, *voila*, here I am."

Heather laughed. "No. I told you pretty much of my life history. Now I want to know all about you, what you do, where you came from. I bet you have a college degree because you look very intelligent."

Julian said yes, that he'd graduated from BU two years ago. He had a wealthy uncle who had been taking care of him since his parents were killed in car crash nearly ten years ago.

"Brad. I'm sorry," Heather said and squeezed his hand.

Julian continued with the story, amazed at how facilely the lies fit into place. It was like writing a story, a improvisational talent not appreciated until now. He didn't feel guilty at first but by the time he'd finished he could barely look into Heather's eyes. The monologue had flowed too smoothly, lie upon lie, and it looked like Heather believed every word of it. She had probably never told a serious lie in her life.

There was an unintentional omission in Julian's account, and Heather picked up on it right away. "Do you have a job?" she asked.

Julian was about to say that he was about to start a doctoral program in advance mathematics at the University, hoping to insert some semblance of truth in his story, but decided against it. That irony seemed fraught with problems.

"Family wealth and good fortune," he said, "have given me just about everything on a silver platter. I feel I have taken so much and now it's time to give in return. I'm thinking of joining the Peace Corps."

Heather looked startled, her eyes widening. "Brad," she said, "that's absolutely amazing! I never imagined you were going to say that...I mean, that is epic. You're so *chivalrous*!"

Julian wondered for a few seconds about Heather's use of the word *chivalrous* and then reminded himself that he wasn't all that familiar with trendy, young expressions. He tried to minimize the details of his commitment, saying only that he had just recently started reading Peace Corp material.

Heather said, "You're so modest about this, Brad. I am so proud of you, but I am not going to allow you to leave me until we've gotten to know each other better."

They danced to two more songs, one a slow dance, with Heather draping her arms over Julian's shoulders, her head down, he holding her close, barely moving his feet. She smelled of innocence, girlish sweat and of the moist heat of youth.

There was a beach where Heather wanted to take him. It was a starry night and she wanted to catch some falling stars. They took his car, the top down, the radio tuned to an oldies station, which Heather said was one of her favorites. That she hadn't even been born when the songs were released seemed a bit ironic to Julian.

It took them just over an hour to reach White Horse Beach on Cape Cod Bay, a cozy cove of a beach Julian had never heard of before. There were few people on the beach at that hour, most of them young lovers holding hands as they strolled along the water's edge.

Heather had taken along a blanket from her car and now she smoothed it out on the sand on her hands and knees. She'd taken her shoes off and pulled a light sweater over her shoulders.

Julian took his sneakers off and sat beside her, looking up at the diamond sky, which seemed to pulsate in quadrants of irregular glitter, like Christmas lights not quite in unison.

"There's one!" Heather said, pointing up to her left.

"Missed it," Julian said.

"They'll be more. Just keep watching."

And there were, at least a dozen in the next half hour. Heather had made Julian promise to make a wish for each falling star, and that they should save their wishes for unhappy days.

"I won't have any," Julian said, smiling boyishly. "So they're all saved for you, Heather."

They talked about their young lives, their aspirations and beliefs in destiny. Julian spoke freely, honestly and with an open heart about the wonders of life. They shared their interests, which Julian didn't have to lie about. She loved to read philosophers, her favorite, Descartes. And he shared his taste for baroque music. She talked about sailing and her days of living with her parents aboard a 40-foot ketch and how she dreamed of owning her own boat and sailing it around the world.

"How much do they cost?" Julian said extemporaneously.

"You'd need at least a 30-foot sloop with full keel. With all the navigational equipment, a new one could run into several hundred thousand dollars. Well under a hundred for a used one."

Heather talked about her dream to sail around the world taking the southern route starting in California, rounding Cape Horn and Cape Point and then stopping in western Australia before returning to California.

"Do you think you could do it?" Julian asked, amazed.

"Besides the boat, it would take about a year to prepare for. I soloed to Bimini when I was thirteen, so I know I can do it." She looked down at Julian, who was lying on the blanket, his hands around the back of his head, his legs drawn up, his large flat feet planted on the edge of the blanket. "Some people want to be millionaires before they're thirty. I plan to sail around the world by then. I've got just under nine years to make it happen."

"Wow!" Julian said, with truthful amazement.

"And you, Brad, what do you want to do by the time you reach the ripe old age of thirty?"

"I just want to be happy and be in a position where I can help others."

Heather pouted slightly. "That makes me feel so selfish."

"No, no," Julian said. "We need that kind of courage and adventure in the world. So many fail to go after their dreams." He reached for her hand and held it.

After that they both fell silent. There seemed no need to talk anymore. They walked along the beach by the water's edge, their toes in the gentle slapping surf. It was as if a silent conversation was continuing, and Julian could feel it through their clasped hands, their shared fragrance, their breath and in Heather's eyes and her effortless smile.

This is what it had been like when he was twenty the first time around. No illusions or false promises, just the implacable innocence of youth. He felt privileged and connected to something superior and captivating and secret.

He stopped and kissed her lightly on the lips, tasting her breath and her courage. She placed her head on his shoulders, and they let their clasped hands dangle between them.

Julian felt no urge other than to be near her. He had arrived somewhere totally by accident, a venue beyond sexual urges and the hastening sense of manhood. He loved Tenley, had always loved her, but this was entirely different. He was experiencing the privilege of first love, with its pure, innocent emotions flowering in the moment. The next hour, the next day made no difference, for there was no tomorrow to worry about. He wanted it to go on forever, a suspension in time, a perfect place to reside in for the rest of his life. Despite her daunting aspirations, he knew that Heather felt that way too.

There was a light breeze and the air had turned ever more chilly. They packed up and Julian pressed the button in the car to raise the top. They sat there for a few moments, snuggled in the bucket seats, holding hands. Julian turned on the heater. She kissed him again. He promised to call her tomorrow, and every day after.

◆

When Julian returned home he drank a soda and lay across his bed, his thoughts swirling with memories of the evening. Heather had awakened in him something unremembered but strangely familiar, a naiveté and a wonderful feeling of invincibility.

He was asleep in short time and when he awoke the next morning, the sun cut a swath of light across the floor by the foot of the bed. Full of bright energy, he got out of bed. He shaved, showered and combed his still-wet hair back. It was thicker than ever but was too long, especially for young men's hairstyles he had seen at Tunnel. He admired the muscular physique he had developed earlier during workouts at the gym. He clasped his hands together behind his head and began flexing his chest muscles and biceps. It seemed incredible.

At a hairstylist on Newbury Street, Julian asked the pretty stylist to pick out a cut that would best suit him. She pulled out a photo album and showed him various styles, but he couldn't decide.

"You pick one, Charlene," he said, glancing at her nametag.

"How 'bout a buzz cut?" she said, ruffling his thick brown hair.

"Anything but that," Julian said.

"Well, I have an idea," Charlene said pensively, and then went to work, tucking a towel under his collar, drawing the barber's gown around his neck and then wetting his hair down. Her scissors clicked furiously as she pulled strands of hair through her fingers, causing wads of hair to drop to the floor, some errant strands landing on the top of his gown.

When she had finished and turned the chair around to face the mirror, she said, "Now, this is *you*."

Julian liked the style, his hair short and spiked in spots. It was, he thought, a conservative punk cut, though he didn't like the copious amount of styling gel she had used. Nonetheless, he left her a good tip.

He stopped by Riccardi, a trendy clothing store in the Back Bay area, and completely updated his wardrobe: shirts, pants, shoes, jackets and coats, all very colorful and clearly in vogue. He wanted to purchase a herringbone flat cap, which he had become accustomed to in olden days, but quickly decided against it, even though, he was told, it was considered chic these days. The total purchase was almost $5000.

He called Heather and asked her if she wanted to go out for the day. He picked her up in front of her apartment, swinging the passenger door open from inside. She pecked him on his cheek and, obviously startled by the new look, squealed, "Oh Brad....you look fantastic!" She made a comment about the volume of shopping bags in the back seat and then looked at herself in the vanity mirror, rubbing her lips together and then fiddling with the strands of loose hair dangling along her neck.

He turned the Sirius radio to a sixties channel. They listened to *Positively 4th Street* by Dylan. They sang the ending chorus together:

> *"Yes, I wish that for just one time*
> *You could stand inside my shoes*
> *You'd know what a drag it is*
> *To see you."*

They had lunch at B&G Oysters in South End, sitting at a table in the small outside courtyard. They both ordered *yellowfin tuna tatare* with grapefruit, avocado and sesame tuile, along with glasses of white wine. Julian had frequented the restaurant many times during his working years and knew the chef and several waiters and waitresses, one a dazzling brunette who was taking an order at the table across from theirs. When he caught her attention, he was about to wink but instead smiled warmly at her.

"You're so good to me," Heather said, reaching for his hand across he table. "I wish this could last forever and ever," she added, sounding very auspicious to Julian.

"It will, Heather," he lied.

"I wish I had the money to buy that boat and we could sail together around the world. Just you and me...and my dogs and my cockatiel. We would live our entire lives in an adventure...and never grow old."

Fancifully, Julian imagined the prospect and then wondered whether he could come up with the money for the boat. He decided he probably could, but then realized that he knew nothing whatsoever about sailing.

"I could teach you everything I know," Heather said as if she had read his mind.

Later, they walked about Burroughs Wharf in the harbor and talked about the sailboat she would eventually buy. He asked her specific questions about size, hull, sails and what kind of engine it would need.

She was obviously very knowledgeable and knew exactly what type and model would provide the safest travel in the treacherous waters of the south Indian Ocean. She mentioned that her grandfather had left her a modest inheritance, which she had placed in an investment portfolio. She calculated that enough money would accrue in several more years and that the sum would meet all of the necessarily expenditures for a journey of that kind.

"You can't imagine how cheaply you can live at sea," Heather said. "And imagine all the people and cultures I could visit. I've always wanted to spend time in Johannesburg."

"Isn't that a bit inland?" Julian asked.

"It's not far by train or rental car. Or I could hitch a ride. I'd berth in Durban and then find a hostel in the city."

"You've really got this planned out, Heather. I envy you."

She gripped his hand and squeezed it. "I guess you'll be doing some traveling of your own. You're not going to be leaving soon, are you? You'd break my heart."

Julian squeezed back and kissed her on the cheek. "Not anytime soon. I promise."

◆

It was just past midnight when he got home after dropping Heather off at her apartment. Dreamily, he had a snack and drank a can of soda and then went to bed. Heather called to make sure he'd made it back okay.

Julian fell asleep almost instantly. Just at the cusp of a wonderful dream about Heather, he was awakened by the buzz on the iPhone. He fumbled for the phone, thinking it might be her.

"Daddy, where are you in this magnificent town?"

It didn't seem real or maybe it seemed too real, and Julian had a difficult time focusing on what Carolyn was saying. He lowered his voice. "I'm sorry...I was asleep..."

"At this time of the day?" Carolyn said and then laughed. I telephoned Leighton the other night and he told me you had taken off for Paris. "Oh you mischievous old man. I just landed at Charles de Gaulle, a miserable flight, the AC wasn't working properly and the person next be me had a horrid snore. So, Daddy, I am looking at my *arrondissement* map and I see that the Rive Gauche is in the *quatorze arrondissement*. Where exactly are you?"

Julian's mouth was agape. With apprehension, it all came to him clearly now. Carolyn was in Paris trying to meet up with him. This wasn't going to be easy, but what choice did he have?

"Oh Carolyn, I'm so sorry, but I am visiting with Monique's family in Northern Ireland and won't be leaving for a while."

"Northern Ireland? Monique sounds very French. What on earth is her family doing in Ireland?"

"They moved here five years ago because of the terrorist activity in Paris."

"Oh Daddy...whatever," Carolyn said with insouciance. "Well, at least it won't be a wasted trip. I have an impromptu show here at the Carrousel du Louvre and then will be heading back to Chicago. By the way, you sound fabulous. Your voice has changed a little, but then a lifestyle change like yours will do that. You sound handsome, if that makes any sense. So, when can we meet up?"

"It may be a while. Monique's father is ill and may have to go to the hospital. Eventually we'll return to Boston."

"Are you bringing Monique with you?"

"We're not sure," Julian said carefully.

"You sound so happy."

"Yes," Julian said, "I am very much."

"Well, I love you dearly, Daddy. Please tell Monique hello for me. I'll call. Got to go."

Julian fell back on the bed, half-stunned that his young voice had not given him away. Of all people, Carolyn would have recognized that this was not the voice of her father, a seventy year-old man.

Don't fret over things that haven't happened, he thought, closing his eyes. Soon memories of Heather coaxed him back to sleep.

Chapter Eleven

Julian had awakened later that morning with a terrific idea. It grew on him with such excitement, now, as his eyes rapidly scanned Sunday classified ads of the morning paper, he couldn't wait to share his surprise with Heather.

He jotted down several numbers after circling the ads with black magic marker. He called two numbers and was told that they had already been sold. The next call was very encouraging.

The sailboat was a bit old but was in excellent condition. Julian jotted down the details as the man described them. She was a 37' Endeavour with a fiberglass mono-hull, recently painted, with new rigging and sails.

"What kind of a boat would you call it?" Julian asked.

"A sloop, of course."

"How many masts does it have?"

"If she's a sloop, there's only one."

"Could you navigate the globe with it?" Julian asked excitedly.

"How much experience do you have, young man?"

"Well, actually none," Julian said. "But I'm willing to learn."

"In that case, she won't." the man said, adding, "But I've taken her around twice when I was younger. This may be a bit large for a fellow just learning how to sail."

"Actually," Julian said, "it's not for me. I'm buying it as a gift."

◆

He'd found one of those theater masks at a costume store in the mall on his way to Heather's. He made her put it on and had her promise not to peek. She was wearing white shorts, a yellow midriff blouse and chic white deck shoes. She had on small heart-shaped gold earrings and wore blush pink lipstick. She was holding on to Julian's arm as if they were navigating through a dark room. The car had swerved at times when she tugged a little too hard.

They arrived at Boston Waterboat Marina on the harbor in short time. Julian told Heather that he was going to look for someone he wanted her to meet, and that if she dared to peek while he was away he would drive her back home.

He looked for the old green Toyota Cruiser in which Mr. Farmington said he would be waiting. A man approached him from behind.

"Brad," the man said, shaking hands.

"How did you know it was me?" Julian asked.

"Well, son, it's rather obvious," Farmington said, putting a friendly arm around Julian's shoulders. "I saw you drive in in your red Beemer with that pretty young lady wearing the mask. Quite dramatic. You really are going to surprise her."

They walked to the slip where *Ginger* was berthed, and Julian was startled by the size of the craft. It looked brand new to him, its white hull gleaming along with the teakwood trim and decking. To Julian, it looked ready to sail the globe.

Carefully leading Heather down the pier to the slip, he reached over and slipped the mask off.

There was dead silence and such a look of static astonishment on Heather's face, he thought she would pass out for lack of breath.

"O..M..G!" she said, emphatically pronouncing the letters. "It's an Endeavor, just like the one my parents owned, the one I told you I sailed solo to Bimini."

"Impressive, young lady," Farmington said. "Well, come aboard."

Julian watched as Heather climbed into the cockpit and ran her hand along the trim. Immediately, she climbed forward and tugged at the rigging and then ran her hands along the base of the steel-reinforced mast.

Farmington was about to head down to the cabin when Heather intervened and began asking a flurry of questions, some sounding quite technical to Julian.

Inside, the original redwood was immaculate. Heather pointed out the stove, refrigerator, the head and then the forward sleeping compartments. "It's in incredible condition," she said and then turned and looked squarely at Julian. "I can't believe you're interested in sailboats. This is great...and I can teach you to sail."

"It's for you," Julian said with a smile. "A gift."

"Brad, no, I can't accept this."

"Sure you can. I plan to register this slip so that you'll have a place to keep her. And that will be paid for, along with whatever other accessories you'll need planning for your cruise."

"No..."

"Done deal," Julian said, feeling such a warming sense of generosity he could hardly contain himself.

He wrote Farmington a check and the man looked at it, startled himself that Julian was willing to pay the full amount asked. He wrote down information from Julian's ID and then looked up.

"You live at Garrison Square? You must have affluent parents. You are a lucky young man, Brad."

Julian was going to tell him the fabricated story and then felt no need, as Heather was out of listening range.

"I can't give you ownership until the check clears tomorrow. Is that alright?"

"Of course," Julian said. "Can Heather and I stay aboard for a few hours. I'm sure she has more things to check out."

Farmington agreed, and they drew out the sales contract. He said, "You're not only a lucky young man but a magnanimous one at that."

Inside again, Julian watched as Heather once more toured the main and forward cabins and then came back, sinking into the cushion beside him. Tears were welling in her eyes.

"Brad, I love you," she said.

Julian smiled and then they kissed.

It was more than youth he felt at the moment but a deepening surrender to beauty, benevolence and trust in the moment. It occurred to him, though, that beyond this moment, things would change, that he would grow incrementally younger and Heather older. But he still had time to dwell, to enjoy each cherished moment of this ever-puzzling reversal of fortune.

◆

The next Saturday they were sailing *Ginger* out the wide harbor, over the Ted Williams Tunnel and south towards Quincy Bay. Staying relatively close to shore, Heather pointed out small coves with their rocky beaches and points along the shore that Julian had never seen from this vantage point. He was amazed at Heather's sailing prowess, the way she'd managed the mainsail and forward jib, her knowledge of sailing routes and how natural she appeared at the wheel.

The westerly winds seemed strong to Julian and he was amazed as she tacked effortlessly to show off her skills. She laughed and then came about as the mainsail filled out with the wind.

"She handles beautifully!" she shouted at Julian and then had him come to the wheel. "Take over...just keep a 20-degree heading. I'll manage the sail."

He felt the power and beauty all-in-one as he gripped the magnificent wheel and held the boat on course. Now this was adventure, he thought, his heart slightly racing.

"You're doing great!" Heather repeated a couple of times as some smaller craft navigated across the bow, one a jet-skier that shot a rooster tail over the pulpit railing.

"Let's take her out," Heather said after they traversed Hingham Bay and were making their way through the straights between Hull and the recreational island.

"It's a bit choppy and with this wind..."

If she heard his words she wasn't about to heed them. Once through the straights, she instructed Julian to make for a northeasterly heading and then moved toward the jib, which she lowered effortlessly and replaced with an asymmetrical spinnaker that immediately ballooned out off the port side.

At first unnerved, Julian began to relax as he watched his captain deftly maneuver out to sea, both the mainsail and spinnaker filled, the bow rising and falling against the larger swells, the wind at his back, rustling his hair, spreading the back of his collar.

They spent the next two hours in deep waters, buffeted by the wind and the swells, feeling the salty sea spit against their faces. The farther out they sailed, the larger the rolling waves and the more expansive the seascape. The immensity of the ocean seemed breathtaking and magical and terrifying. Julian imagined what it would be like to sail around the world, as Heather was planning to do, to wake up to horizons of ocean, to be free of the hustle and bustle of cities, their clamor and swallowing landscape, and to be truly at one with the sea and its mercy.

Heather tugged at his life jacket and pulled him close, so that they were sharing the wheel, her head leaning on his shoulder. "I've never been happier in my life," she said in a voice barely audible in the waterfall rush of wind and sea.

Julian squeezed her, feeling the same, hoping this day would never end.

They found a cove north of Deer Island Park on their way back and dropped anchor. Julian helped with the mainsail and then Heather stored the spinnaker. She had brought a lunch of ham sandwiches and coleslaw and he a six-pack of Heineken, and they ate a late lunch below at the polished cherry wood table and talked about sailing. She regaled him with stories of sailing ventures with her parents and more details about her solo to Bimini.

"To be at sea, alone and free, is such an incredible experience," Heather said with such longing he thought that she might leave tomorrow and never return.

"Are your parents still sailing?" Julian asked.

"They were killed in a car crash when I was sixteen."

"Oh my God, I'm sorry."

"It was awful back then, especially at that age, but I've had years to process it and feel totally at peace with what happened. I miss them and love them, but I have let them go. I think we need to learn to do that in life. The past is the past, now is now, and the future doesn't exist."

"Yes," Julian said thoughtfully. "You're right about that."

Heather looked deeply into his eyes. "Brad Hartwood, where have you been all of my life?"

"I don't know," Julian said as if the question was meant to be answered.

"Well, I won't be letting you go anytime soon," she said.

Julian felt the full irony of her question as if an axe blade had kissed the back of his neck, and he shuddered inside, suddenly haunted by what the future would bring. It was the first time he had considered the broader reality of his situation. He felt panicky for a few moments and was suddenly tempted to tell Heather the truth, all of it. But how could it be explained? He could hardly wrap his own mind around it, so how could he expect a young woman with her whole future ahead of her to understand such an implausible predicament?

He reached for Heather's hand and held it tightly, as if the rushing sea would sweep her away.

She kissed him, pulling him up and lead the way to the forward cabin, where they lay down on one of the berths. "And now, Mr. Brad Hartwood, I want to make love to you.

"I can't," Julian said, surprised at his reply. He soon realized that he didn't want to spoil the purity of innocence they were sharing.

"Yes, you can," Heather said, rolling her body atop his, her face flushed with the warmth of sudden passion, her eyes and her earrings twinkling in the shaft of light pouring through the narrow cabin window.

"I.. I have a problem," he said, and then concocted a story about temporary impotence, adding, "It's probably due to the medication I'm taking for allergies."

"Oh," Heather said, not in a tone of disappointment or annoyance but in a thoroughly accepting way. She rolled to his side, kissed him again and then, lying on her back, closed her eyes to the sound of the water lapping at the hull. He did too, and before long they were fast asleep.

◆

Julian awakened to the sound of the anchor rope slapping harshly against the hull and to the sudden realization that the boat was rolling heavily from side to side. And then the rain came and soon after the wind.

"A storm!" he shouted, amazed that Heather hadn't been awakened by all the noise and hard shifting of the boat. He felt panicked but was soon reassured by Heather that it was no big deal. She told him in a calm voice that they would have to use the inboard to navigate back into the harbor, and that they were both going to be soaked to the bones.

They came deck-side and with Julian's help, Heather pulled in and stowed the anchor. As she was raising the jib sail, she said, "Shit!" and hurried sternward toward the cockpit. Worried, Julian followed her and heard the high-pitched whirring of the starter. When it was obvious that the engine wouldn't start, Heather instructed him to drop anchor immediately.

Returning, he found her below, hunched over the exposed engine.

"It was running fine when we left," Julian offered naively.

"And we have a full tank."

"Maybe we should call the Coast Guard." he said.

"We might have to," Heather said soberly. She reached down and appeared to be fidgeting with rubber lines, and then found what she was looking for. She told Julian to go up and hit the starter while she hand-pumped the diesel fuel.

On the third try the engine caught briefly and sputtered out. They tried several more times unsuccessfully and then Heather moved her arms back to support her as she worked her neck muscles by rolling her head. Julian helped, feeling the tenseness in her neck and shoulders. She was shivering slightly from the cold rain.

"I know what it is," Heather said in a defeated tone. "I had a Volvo engine like this in my boat and had one go bad. The fuel pump, I'm afraid."

"But Farmington told us it was recently rebuilt," Julian said, as if protesting would correct their predicament.

The waves were slapping harder against the hull and Julian could feel the boat jerking and stopping as the anchor began slipping against the force of the waves and what was now a strong north-easterly wind. Despite the hatch cover, rain was sluicing down the sides of the ladder, causing a puddle to form next to Julian's feet.

Heather looked more disappointed than concerned by what was surely a hopeless situation. She stood up and tightened the hatch and then sat down next to Julian at the table. "I think we can wait it out; it's probably a passing storm."

"The anchor," Julian said. "We'll be swept out to sea..."

She assured him that the bottom was rocky but as they were pushed out of the cove the anchor would catch in the hard sand. She didn't sound exactly confident but as if it were best to just have faith in the moment.

They finished their beer after nibbling at the remaining sandwiches. Heather found an oldies station on the radio and they listened to Otis Redding's *Sittin' On the Dock of the Bay*, humming softly to the tune.

The rain was pounding the deck and soon lightning flashed, a crack of thunder following seconds later. Larger swells raised the boat and slammed it back into the water as if with a temperament intent on crushing the hull.

The hair raised on the back of Julian's neck just as another bolt of lightning struck, this one probably only a quarter-mile away.

"That's not good," Heather said, collapsing Julian's attempted faith in the moment.

They both grabbed at their bottles and the sliding container of coleslaw and then held firmly to the table as if the next swell would wash them out to sea and certain drowning. It amazed Julian that Heather displayed no outward signs of fear. She was like a veteran sea woman who had supreme confidence in her skills, yet realized the harsh reality of circumstance and bad luck.

"I love you," she said, which brought mortal panic to Julian.

"Are we going down?"

"No," Heather said. "But I think it's time to call the Coast Guard."

Chapter Twelve

Tenley hadn't believed the absurd story that Julian had taken off for Paris and was living there with a girl named Monique. She had quizzed Leighton for more details, and it all seemed very implausible. Recalling her own brush with danger during the break-in, Tenley held firm to the notion that something nefarious had occurred. She considered that Julian had been kidnapped and was being held hostage somewhere. He was a wealthy man and many in Boston knew that. But whom would they contact for a ransom? If not a ransom demand, then had he been harmed or killed?

And who was this kid named Brad who claimed to be Julian's nephew? Maybe he had gained control over Julian and was spending his money. There had to be a record of spending.

And then Tenley remembered.

She drove straight to the Citizens Bank in the heart of Boston's business district, where both Julian and she held accounts. When Julian feared that he was regressing into dementia, he had asked her, without Carolyn's knowledge, to be his lasting power of attorney. She had access to his several accounts and investment portfolios, and it would be easy to see if large sums had been withdrawn recently.

Ms. Craven at the bank took Tenley to her desk and there they both sat staring at the computer screen as the Assistant Manager scrolled first through his money market accounts, then his savings and checking accounts.

"As you can see," she said, "Professor Landon keeps a rather large sum in his checking, for which he has a debit card. I see he's made several large withdrawals recently." She stopped scrolling and squinted at the screen. "Well, it looks like he bought himself a nice watch, just over $10,000. And an iPhone from Verizon. Oh, I remember...on that purchase the store called, I assume, to verify his identity. He might have forgotten his driver's license...in any regard, the purchase was approved. In fact, I called Professor Landon back on this private phone just to double check.

"You verified that it was him?"

Craven looked over at Tenley. "I called him on his phone and it sounded like the Professor, although I recall that his voice was fading a bit."

"Fading?" Tenley said.

"You know, like a bad connection, a brief cell drop perhaps. Why, is there a problem?"

Tenley looked back at the screen. "Any foreign purchases or any plane tickets to France?

Craven assured her that as far as she could tell the Professor had not made purchases abroad. "But he did make a large purchase a few weeks ago, after transferring $40,000 from one of the money market accounts."

Tenley couldn't believe her ears. "Forty thousand?! Oh my God!" she gasped. She stood up. "I want all of his accounts and assets frozen immediately. There is a possibility that Professor Landon has disappeared...under suspicious circumstances."

"Oh," Craven said. "But I would need the Professor's approval."

"Did you hear what I said? His life may be in danger. Am I not his power of attorney?"

"Yes, you are..."

"Then do it," Tenley said. "Just give me the papers to sign."

On the way back to her apartment, Tenley felt she had done the right thing. Whoever had taken over the apartment was hardly a person of order, his habits suggesting a messy kid who possessed little respect for tidiness and the decor of the exclusive apartment. The logical deduction was that this little imposter was keeping Julian locked up in his own apartment, using his debit card for ATM withdrawals and the purchase of an expensive Rolex. That had nailed the mystery right away: Julian didn't wear wristwatches. And now she knew he wasn't in France as Leighton had told her.

She considered stopping by the police station and filing a missing person report. But they would surely talk with Leighton, who would attest to the fact that Julian was in Paris. And that would probably be the end of their search. She would have to conduct her own investigation. With new determination, Tenley thought, *No, it's up to me now. No one else cares as much as I do.*

"Julian," she said out loud. "I am going to save you!"

◆

Two weeks had gone by since the sailing mishap and although Heather had called several times wanting to see him, Julian felt he was sinking fast. He felt remote and depressed and increasingly guilty for putting on a show for Heather. He should never have purchased the boat, much less led her on they way he had. She obviously loved him and trusted him. He soon found himself drowning in a sea of fiction and deception.

Matters had worsened. It was obvious that he was growing younger. The mirror revealed it: he no longer could grow a beard and now had only soft patches of facial hair as sideburns and just a fuzzy stubble on his chin; he'd developed a swath of pale freckles on his forehead and cheeks; and his face was rounder, cheeks fuller, and it was obvious that he'd lost even more weight.

He felt a sudden compulsion to the tell the truth to someone, a third party, perhaps a confessional priest. But how could they possibly understand? It was inexplicable even to himself.

Unable to sleep, Julian lay awake one night, his small hands clasped behind his head, now tormented by the counterfeit story he'd given to Carolyn, his own flesh and blood. He burst into tears at the horrible lies he'd told her and pounded his fists into the pillow. He sat up again, his face red as if from a tantrum, and wiped the clinging mucus from his nose.

"I never bargained for this," he said in a whiny voice.

He knew he would have to tell Heather, Tenley and Carolyn the truth. He would have to come clean.

He waited until ten the following morning and then called Heather, clearing his throat and making small grunting sounds to make sure his voice hadn't dramatically changed. She had obviously slept in this Saturday morning and her voice sounded slow and monotone.

"Brad, is that you?"

Julian exploded with his confession. "I lied to you...I'm not who you think I am...I mislead you...I'm an impersonator...I'm so sorry!"

"What's wrong, Brad? Has something happened. Are you alright?"

"No, I'm not alright," Julian said in a deflated voice.

"What exactly did you lie about, Brad? It can't be that bad. We've had such a great time together."

"My name isn't Brad and I am not living with my rich uncle."

She took her time to respond. "Who are you then? What's your real name?"

An incredible wave of relief swept over Julian when at last he said, "My name is Julian. Julian Landon."

"Julian," Heather said, pronouncing his name almost the way the kiosk girl had. "I love it. You never looked like a Brad to me. Whatever other lies you told me, it doesn't matter, Brad...I mean, Julian. We've had special times together. And I know you're not twenty-one."

"You do?"

She laughed. "That was the worst fake ID I've ever seen."

"Oh God," Julian said, "no, that's not the point. The ID was fake but not in the way you think."

Heather paused. Julian could hear her take a deep breath. Finally she said, "Julian, I don't care about the lies or the fake name. The person I know is someone genuine, loving and tender. That's all that matters. We have feelings for each other, and I want to see you again. If we talk face-to-face maybe it'll be easier..."

"No," Julian interrupted. "Don't you see? That can't happen. It would be a lie."

He hung up on Heather in mid-sentence and closed his eyes, his throat constricting as if he had just swallowed his tongue. Within ten seconds, Heather called, her number appearing on the phone. He fumbled with it and turned it off.

Again she called, the phone vibrating on the table. Julian grabbed it and hid it in the top drawer of his bedroom chest, underneath his undershirts and shorts. He slammed the drawer shut, angry at himself for having screwed-up the conversation and then hanging up the phone like that. Heather didn't deserve that.

Frantically, Julian shut all the blinds and curtains in the apartment, threw the deadbolt on the door and fell back against it, sliding to the floor, his face in his hands.

"What have I done...what have I become?" he mumbled between sobs. He feared the worst, that he would progressively grow younger and younger until he was a boy, a toddler and then an infant without the ability to think, take care of himself, totally vulnerable and helpless. It was how he had felt at first when he feared that dementia had begun and he was surely but slowly losing his faculties. It was the same feeling, yet strangely different, juxtaposed in an awful, ironic way. Life wasn't fair.

For the next week Julian became a hermit, not daring to leave his apartment and be seen by anybody. He arranged for regular deliveries from the deli, where he had long held an account. The delivery boys knocked and he instructed them from behind the door to lay the bags on the floor, where he'd left a small tip.

Leighton had called once to see if Julian was okay and he'd answered in a fake hoarse voice, "Fine, just fine."

He'd stopped taking his medication, along with the vitamins, in hopes that it would halt the regression. He'd resorted to using a box to stand at the mirror when he brushed his teeth. He couldn't help but notice that his two upper front teeth appeared large and slightly buck-toothed.

Fed up with the television and its repetitive commercials, Julian began ordering e-books online, especially history books, starting with a Gibbon biography. The thought of not having a leather-bound book in his hands and instead reading line after line on a monitor had once been offensive, in fact, repugnant, but Julian soon grew accustomed to it. Books were cheap and electronic libraries comprehensive.

Reading helped pass the day. He found foreign news channels on the Internet and began to rely on them to be presented with unbiased accounts of what was going on in the world. They reminded him of the early formats of news reporting, unfettered and to the point, unlike the entertainment format of domestic channels on cable TV.

Soon he could hardly tell whether it was day or night, a slither of light only visible through the east window and a faint glow at the tops of the curtains. It rained hard one afternoon, accompanied by rumbling thunder and the occasional burst of lightening. He liked the rain for it had a smoothing effect on him and felt old-fashioned and protective in an indescribable way.

Heather and their conversation were always in the back of his mind, nudging forward into thoughts when he was trying to fall asleep. He missed her as he did that part of his life that seemed so recently innocent and uncomplicated.

Julian felt alone in the worst sort of way, ostracized from colleagues, friends, his daughter and young man amours. It had happened so fast, so unplanned. Just months ago he was a fumbling old professor and now this...how could you name it? A transformation, a metamorphosis? A cruel twist of fate?

In the shadowy darkness Julian Landon sat, depressed, alone, held hostage by his own guilt and sense of banishment.

◆

It had been a week since Julian had hung up the phone on her. Heather had been angered at first but soon let that emotion go. She wondered curiously about Julian's confession. It had been so explosive, and most of it didn't really sound like a confession. It wasn't like he had done something terribly wrong, like robbing a bank or killing someone. He had falsified his name and had made up a story of a rich uncle...but that was it. It sounded ever more innocuous to Heather. Whoever he was, the person she knew and had come to love was more genuine than anyone she had known in her life. She knew that he was probably a year or two younger than she, but that was okay. He was handsome and mature and so genuine with his feelings. And there was a touch of mystery to it all.

She had found Julian Landon's name, street address and number on the Internet. Apparently he lived at the posh Garrison Square Apartments. If he didn't have a rich uncle then he was certainly well-off for a kid; he probably lived there with his parents.

This coming Friday Heather planned to get off work early and go to Julian's place to see if she could talk with him. She had to hear the entire story and why he had been so abrupt with her on the phone. Perhaps he needed her and was just embarrassed to call her. She would be there for him. Once they talked Heather knew everything would be okay, and they might even date again.

She called him several times during that week but each time the call went to his answering message, a voice that hardly sounded like him but was probably meant as humor. Even though the voice sounded like that of an old man, there was a hint of Julian's accent in it. *He must have had a bad cold when he recorded that*, she thought.

At lunch on Friday, Heather bought a half-dozen red roses arranged with baby's-breath in a handsome clear-glass vase. She was adventuresome and had given some of her past boyfriends flowers because she earnestly felt that flowers were not only for women and because she liked to see their reactions.

Before leaving for Julian's place, she stopped by her apartment to take a quick shower and to put on a pair of casual slacks and a white lace blouse. She rubbed Miss Dior on her wrist, smelled it and then lightly patted her earlobes, neck and her modest cleavage.

She stopped by Walgreen's and picked out a friendship card, wrote a touching note and sealed the envelope. She thought about buying him a small present, something to lighten his spirits, but decided the card and flowers were enough, at least for this visit.

The Friday afternoon rush-hour wasn't at gridlock yet, but nevertheless it took Heather nearly half an hour to reach the Garrison Square Apartment complex. She stood back and admired the elegant brownstone buildings. Entering one building, she asked the desk clerk if a Julian Landon lived there. She was told that this building housed the rentals, that she thought the Professor lived in the condo building.

Making her way to the next building, which had a much more elegant entrance, she was even more perplexed by the professional title used by the clerk. Professor? Julian had to be the youngest professor in history, but then she considered that he might be a genius. This was getting really intriguing.

There was a man in the huge lobby who said he was the concierge for the apartments. He sounded very formal and had a dubious way of looking at her. He seemed offended by the vase of roses. Heather just assumed he wasn't comfortable around young women.

"I'm looking for Julian Landon," she said, adding, "Professor Landon."

"And I suppose you are one of his nieces?" the man said tartly.

It didn't seem to be any of his business but nevertheless Heather answered, "I'm a friend. We know each other. Is he in?"

Almost with relish, the man said, "Well, that seems to be a questionable matter. Purportedly, the Professor is abroad and his nephew is home-sitting during his absence. I say purportedly because I don't know that as fact. All I do know is that a fellow named Brad is up there ravaging the place."

"Brad? You're kidding"?

The telephone rang on the desk and the man went to answer. Before he did, he gave Heather the floor and apartment number. "Good luck. I don't think you'll get him to answer the door."

Finding the apartment, Heather rapped lightly on the door and when several seconds went by she knocked again, much more firmly. She rose to her tiptoes and tried to peer into the viewing hole but only saw her own reflected eyeball.

"Brad...or Julian, are you in there? It's Heather. I have to see you."

Twenty minutes had gone by and still Julian wouldn't open the door. Heather continued talking to him, telling him that everything was going to be okay, that she had an idea of what was going on, that he could trust her. Eventually she started crying in soft sobs, her shoulders heaving slightly as she tried to catch her breath.

Finally, she said, "Julian, I'm leaving," and placed the vase and card on the carpet. She was walking back to the elevator when she heard Julian's door open. She stopped without turning around, and then heard his voice. Turning around, she saw that Julian and the flowers weren't there but the door was ajar.

She stepped inside, deciding for prudent measures to leave the door ajar, and went into the foyer. She heard Julian's voice asking her to come to the living room. He sat at one end of the long couch, his hands in his lap, looking a bit worse for the weather, gaunt, frail and vulnerable. And there was something about his face.

Heather rushed to sit beside him. She took hold of one cold hand and began rubbing it as if she sensed some vital life force had escaped him. But for the loss of weight and his infirmed appearance, he looked like the Brad she knew...but strangely younger.

He asked Heather if she wanted some tea and rose to make them each a cup, saying only from the kitchen that something horrible had happened to him, was happening to him, and he had to tell her the whole truth.

Sipping her tea, she listened intently to what Julian was telling her. When he picked up a photo of an old bearded man and a middle-age woman he said was his daughter, and let Heather hold it in her lap, she looked at the man and then at Julian and again at photograph.

He explained something about dementia and regressing in time after being given medication.

It didn't sound incredible as much as it did the fantasy of someone with obvious mental issues. Heather kept herself composed, sharing a compassionate look.

"Are you still on your medications?" Heather asked, somewhat tentatively.

"No, I went off them two weeks ago," Julian said.

"That's not good, Julian," she said. "You should never stop your meds just like that. It might be why you are experiencing these..."

"No, Heather, it's the truth," Julian said, standing up abruptly, splashing his tea on the cushion.

She made haste for the door, realizing she might be in danger, that Julian might fly into an uncontrollable rage.

She had just reached the foyer, Julian approaching from behind, when the door opened suddenly and a woman stepped inside, holding a tennis racket in a menacing way.

"Who the hell are you?!" the woman said and then, almost pushing her aside, barged into the foyer.

Thoroughly astonished, Heather followed her into the living room, where Julian had quickly retreated, now sitting on the sofa.

"You little shit!" the woman shrieked as she raised the racket over Julian's head. "Where is he? Where is Julian?!"

Julian looked white in the face as he attempted to stand up. He began mumbling something and that's when the woman went for his throat. "If you don't tell me the truth," she screamed, "I'm going to literally kill you. What have you done with Julian...where is he?!"

Heather looked over in horror. The woman seemed crazier than Julian. She was going to run out the door for some help but decided there wouldn't be time. This maniac was going to kill Julian. Hearing little gasps escape from his throat, she began pleading for the woman to stop.

"He stopped taking his medications," she tried to explain.

The woman had a tight stranglehold. Julian's eyelids began to flutter and a deathly blueness filled his face.

"You're killing him!" Heather screamed and began tugging at the woman's grasp. The racket had fallen to the floor and she briefly considered bashing the crazed woman on the head. She wasn't going to let Julian, for all of his madness, die just like that.

The woman finally released her death-grip. Julian gasped, and then the woman fell into his lap, sobbing heavily. "Please tell me what you have done with the Professor. Please tell me the truth. Are you holding him for ransom? Is he hidden away somewhere? Is he dead?!"

Julian appeared crushed by her weight, sobbing himself, strangely attempting to massage the woman's neck. They lay crumpled together like that, and Heather thought it was the weirdest scene she had ever witnessed. She began backing out of the room again when Julian suddenly spoke.

"Tenley," he said. "I am going to tell you the truth, all of it!"

PART II
"Change always comes bearing gifts."
--Price Pritchett

Chapter Thirteen

Winter came early to Boston. The first overnight snowstorm in early October left the city draped in a cottony whiteness. Now, as the morning grew, sunlight sluiced through portions of the leaden sky, pouring a visible warmth onto the blanketed buildings and streets below. The temperature was expected to rise into the lower forties, but by nightfall it would plummet again.

The transformation from gray and brown to a stunning coat of white was at once comforting and a glimpse of a harsher winter to come. It was a cautionary reminder that the forces of change were both cyclical and inescapable. In most cases, they made for renewable moods and attitudes, although in some people temperaments were destined to match the season.

Not so for Julian, who sat by the window looking down at the charitable whiteness, reminded of his youth and sledding adventures on the hill at Boston Common. The scene brought hope and renewal to an already brightening future.

The telephone rang and Julian answered it immediately. It was Golf, the kid from the hospital.

"Sir, I want to thank you for what you done for me. I'm a free man because of you, and I aim to stay that way. I'll always be in your debt."

"I take it the jury sided with you and your claim of having Tourette's syndrome?"

"No, I was let out on good behavior after our plea deal. It was my first offense." Golf paused. "And I don't have Tourette's. I lied to you, Professor. I lied to a lot of people. But I learnt my lesson."

Julian shook his head. "You were quite convincing in the hospital. I even had my lawyer believing your claim. But that's alright, Mr. Golf. I wanted to help you and I did."

"I aim to pay you back, every cent."

"No," Julian said. "It's a lesson learned for both of us."

"I got a job and plan to send you a payment every month, if that's okay with you. But sorry, sir, I could never replace that Healey."

Julian didn't want to argue with the young man and said that that arrangement would be fine but not to worry if he couldn't pay all of it back.

The call ended with Golf saying, "I'm living proof that anybody can change."

Julian hung up and smiled at Golf's wise, ironic words.

Stopping the medication had worked for Julian. He'd ceased growing younger and a natural reversal was in progress. He'd figured by his looks that he was somewhere in his early thirties now. His hair was still thick but had faded to a grayish brown. His nose was prominent, his earlobes slightly elongated, and he had to shave daily. He was about the age when he first married Elizabeth, handsome, he thought, and still far enough from midlife crisis to enjoy the eagerness and confidence of mature youth.

Heather had sold the sailboat against his wishes and had returned most of the original investment. They hadn't spoken for several months but Julian had sent her a long letter, sharing his joy in their relationship, their love and their wonderful experiences together. She'd accepted his strange account as she had the passing of the storm, as probable fact, still mysterious but, like the weather, something not to argue about. He'd thrown away the withered roses but had kept the sweet card, which lay on his nightstand.

Now as he returned to the window and looked out at the building-tops coiffed in whiteness, Heather seemed a part of a long-ago youth, a dulcet but evermore-fading memory.

With his age reversal came a growing confidence that all that had happened served a purpose in his life, a *raison d'être* not to be analyzed or further challenged. The future meant growing old again. At least he was on the right track this time around.

But now, at this revisited age, Julian found the confidence and stamina of manhood. He ran five miles every morning, weather permitting, and worked out at Mel's place once a week. He dreamed of running the marathon. He no longer liked pizza and hamburgers, intuitively realizing that fat-laden meat was not a healthy choice. But he couldn't give up his craving for sirloin steaks and potatoes, and a good lager beer. Although not a vegan yet, he loved vegetables and salads, intrinsically relating to their wholesome effect.

He had smoked a pipe when he married Elizabeth, but now he had no interest in tobacco, knowing its harmful influence. He couldn't, though, shake the habit of chewing at the erasers of pencils when he was writing. And he wrote almost daily. He had resuscitated his novel, *Odessa's Feud*, and was intent on completing it before his interest and confidence escaped him again.

As much as one could under these strange circumstances, Julian felt in control of his life. His sense of direction to revisit a future he already knew made him feel confident and a bit privileged, as if he knew the ending to a book. Despite that inevitable direction, he was satisfied to live in the moment, to relish in the vibrancy of life, unconcerned by fate or the cold face of the unknown. He knew he would remember these days as the best times of his life.

Later that morning Julian put on his thick jogging suit, a snug wool cap and laced his new pair of Nikes, a size twelve. He put his wallet and keys in a fanny-pack, adjusting the strap around his narrow waist.

Julian wondered how Leighton had processed the strange transformation and gathered, by the look on his face, that the man, still skeptical, regarded Julian as some form of freak, as if in a sudden phantasmal instant he might metamorphose again. He was always polite when he spoke but there was a slight hesitancy in his voice.

"Morning, Mr. Leighton," Julian said cheerfully. "A great day for exercise."

Julian jogged the short distance to Boston Commons and seeing a group of young people sledding down the hill, some using old fashioned toboggans, ski boards and plastic sliders, all excited at Boston's first snowfall, he made his way to the top of the hill.

Two gangly teenagers were attempting to slide down the hill together on a slider, almost making it to the bottom, rolling off in counter directions as they hit a bump. Julian grabbed a slider himself and tried to do a handstand as he shot down the hill. At the bottom, laughing, two kids piled on him, shouting, "Do it again...do it again!"

The second attempt wasn't quite as successful and he rolled in the snow almost to the bottom. A girl pleaded with him to give her a hard push on her sled, which he did, increasing her speed enough for her to go airborne as she hit one of the larger bumps. She wiggled her way up the hill, begging for another push. Several other kids joined in and soon Julian found himself out of breath for all of the sprinting. But it was invigorating and made him feel like a kid once again.

He continued his jog along Beacon Street, past the frog pond and on toward Long Wharf, using the wider streets that had already been plowed. He made several loops around Waterfront Park and then headed back toward the apartments, almost a five-mile run round trip.

Coming around the front of his apartment, he saw Tenley's yellow Beetle squeezed between two utility vehicles on a side street. He glanced at his watch to make sure he wasn't late, and ran past Leighton, who was talking spiritedly to a plow crew. He turned toward Julian, who told him, "I know, Professor Harrington is in."

Inside, he found Tenley fumbling with the keys at the apartment door. Instantly, she looked her beautiful self, her hair fanned out over the collar of a dark winter coat, a wool scarf wrapped loosely around her neck, her cheeks flushed by the cold, looking youthful and elegant.

"Hey, kiddo," Julian said.

Tenley smiled and handed him the keys. She kissed him on the lips. "You're a gorgeous sight, Professor Landon."

Inside the foyer, they embraced each other and kissed again. Julian helped her with her coat and scarf, and then followed her into the living room. She went straight to the window.

"Isn't it beautiful, Julian?"

"A perfect day. We should forgo our plans and kick around in the snow, maybe go sledding."

With a protesting look, Tenley said, "I don't think so. Remember that you're still younger than I am, by a few years I'd guess."

Julian laughed. "You act like you're at least forty."

"I don't *look* forty, do I?"

"Of course not, not a day over twenty...well, maybe twenty-one."

"Oh tell me again, Julian. Tell me again," Tenley whispered and snuggled close at the window.

They saw each other several days a week, either at lunches or at quiet dinners at favorite restaurants. On weekends she would stay at his place for more romantic interludes.

Tenley had ended her lesbian affair to be with Julian. One day she said, "I've changed colors, Julian. I want to be with you." They both knew that his time was limited. Julian had calculated that he had a few months left to remain within her generation. They planned to make best of the time they had left.

They had at one time considered visiting Dr. Farley to explain the curious effects the medication had had on Julian, but they'd quickly realized that there was no credible way to explain those transformational experiences. Perhaps it was the combination of the medication and vitamins, a strange synergistic effect that acted on the body in a rejuvenating way. What did it matter? Julian was enjoying a second go at life in a most amazing way. His memory was as good as ever, his creativity, intelligence and sexual prowess at their peaks. He hoped to retain many of those assets as he rapidly advanced through the decades.

While Julian showered, Tenley called the theater to make sure the show times were correct. They were going to see Steve McQueen in "The Sand Pebbles" at the Brattle, a theater they both loved and often frequented to see old classic movies. Afterward they planned to have an early dinner at an Italian restaurant on Hanover Street.

Julian emerged from the bedroom wearing casual tan pants and red sweater, a black leather flight jacket swung over his shoulder. He looked dashing, stylish and full of manly inertia.

"Julian, what am I going to do with you? You look more handsome every day I see you," Tenley said, catching his arm as they headed down to the hallway.

"You'd better take a picture for old times' sake," Julian said. "Who knows what I'll look like next week."

◆

Over dinner at Giacomo's they were discussing the movie and McQueen's dramatic role with Candice Bergen, when Julian was startled by a familiar face now whispering in Tenley's ear. It was Claudia from the beach, and she had her eye on Julian as if he was a gleaming gem in the rough.

"So good to see you," she said, kissing Tenley on the cheek. Sliding into the empty chair on Julian's left, she introduced herself, obviously oblivious of their prior meeting.

Tenley had prepared for such an occasion, agreeing with Julian that it would not be   prudent to identify himself to previous acquaintances using his real name. The consequences would be disadvantageous and perhaps a bit dangerous.

"Brad Hartwood. Good to meet you." he said.

She kept a long eye on Julian and then turned toward Tenley. "Where in the world have you been? We haven't talked in months."

"First semester is keeping me busy. They don't pay me enough to have all those classes. But it's what I do."

Claudia began spilling out the details of her present-day life. She was engaged to get married to a man she'd met on a Bermuda cruise, that he was much older and very rich, and that she looked forward to a great deal of traveling. He had houses in Sicily, Palm Beach and on Ambergris Caye in Belize. Admiringly, she showed them the large diamond on her finger.

"By the way, what ever happened to that old professor you were taking care of?"

Tenley tried to conceal her smile. "I still do...that is, take care of Professor Landon."

"How's the old man doing? Julian...that was his name." Not waiting for an answer, Claudia turned to Julian and shared their beach experience with him. "It was so pathetic...this poor old man almost drowning and losing his shorts and all of us trying to get him up the beach."

Julian forced a laugh. He wanted to reach over and throttle the woman. He felt curiously protective of his old self.

"You guys just meet?" Claudia asked.

"Old friends," Tenley said. "We haven't seen each other in years. Brad and I met in graduate school."

"From around here?" Claudia said, turning to Julian.

Tenley and Julian looked at each other.

"Actually," Julian said, "I've spent the last five years in Ossining."

"Ossining? As in New York?"

Julian nodded.

"What did you do there?"

"Hard time at Sing Sing. Armed robbery. But I've straightened my ways. I'm totally reformed." He was thinking of Golf and their conversation, trying to keep a straight face.

"Why did you have to rob a bank? You must have been desperate," Claudia persisted.

"Only way I could pay off graduate loans," Julian said, certain by now that she would see that he wasn't serious.

But she didn't. "You must owe a lot of money, Brad. I'm sorry you had to go through all that."

Julian couldn't go on with the pathetic story and just shook his head.

Finally she burst into laughter, reaching over for Julian's arm. "You're no more a thief than I am a nun. So, you're keeping your past a secret. That's okay, Brad. I'm intrigued by secretive men," she said, winking.

After chatting on about her wedding plans, Claudia left them with a pretentious swirl of her body, her diamond hand up, in a pirouette of arrogance and flaunter, Julian thought. On her way out she must have recognized another friend and they embraced with a flair.

"She used to be fun to be around," Tenley said. "Now she's a nutcase swept up in herself."

"More like a modern-day tramp, if you ask me."

After dinner they took a walk to a waterfront park, Julian's arm draped around her shoulders, Tenley holding his arm, occasionally laying her head against his shoulder. As they walked, their breath mingled in the frosty air. Overlooking the water, Julian pointed out the Port of Boston, its lights shimmering just across the Harbor in the waning twilight, making puddles of light quiver around the wharves like strange firelight.

Later at home, in a firelight of their own, they made passionate love.

◆

The next day after Tenley left for work Julian walked to the Catholic Church on Isabella Street. He had been brought up as a catholic but had left the church before he turned twenty. But today he needed to make his confession.

Inside the old brownstone church he took a seat in a pew next to the confessional booths. He was several minutes early and took the time to reflect on what he would say, what sins required immediate admission and which he would delicately omit, should they lead to unexplainable inquiry.

In the booth Julian was asked whether he wanted an anonymous confession, replying that he did, assuming that the other choice would mean giving out his name.

The priest spoke in a low but hurried voice, as if he knew there were many confessions to hear that day. He said a prayer that was unfamiliar to Julian but set a clear tone of a sinner and sin.

"Bless me, Father, for I have sinned," Julian began and then fell silent, not recalling what should come next.

"How long has it been since your last confession?"

Julian said that he'd not made one since he was in his teens, that it was a very long time ago.

The priest sighed heavily. "You should have made a private appointment...but go on. Just confess your most important sins."

"I have lied, Father, and my lies have hurt others. I have lived in deception for many months now. I have had, well, several affairs with young ladies. I have taken the Lord's name in vain. I have made false impressions on others for reasons that weren't exactly my fault. And, Father, I have doubted my faith in God."

In a cold tone the priest said, "I cannot help you if you do not believe in God."

"I don't mean that I that I don't believe in God. It's just a matter of slight doubt. I believe the Apostle Thomas doubted, Father."

Obviously challenged but in no mood to argue, the priest said, "He was doubting the wounds of Christ, not doubting his faith in God. Now, have you committed any crimes?"

"Only the crime of self-indulgence and lust," Julian said, sensing that the priest disliked him. The modern Church was not what he remembered from his early years as a Catholic and seemed, based on the tone of this priest, both unfamiliar and uncongenial.

"Are you a practicing Catholic?" the priest asked.

Julian said that he probably wasn't if that meant regularly attending mass. This confrontational approach was not what he needed right now. And he hadn't yet told the priest the main reason for confession.

"It appears you have strayed far from the flock and that your lifestyle hasn't included God. I will accept your confession, for that is my duty, but I would strongly suggest that you begin reading the New Testament on a daily basis, especially the Gospels. You should plan to attend Mass every week and make regular confession. You should recommit yourself to the teachings of the Catholic Church and make peace with God before..."

It was a very pregnant pause and Julian sensed that the priest had caught himself just in time. *Before what?* he thought ominously and was tempted to ask the priest to complete his sentence.

"Fifty *Hail Marys* and fifty *Our Fathers*," the priest said after a hasty blessing.

Julian left the church feeling more of a sinner than he had entering it. He felt expelled, as if from school by a principal, and he walked away, stooped, head slightly bowed, and full of contrition. He shouldn't have mentioned the bit about doubt. He had been misinterpreted. And he had failed his mission.

He drove to the finest jeweler in town, larger than the one where he'd purchased the Rolex. The glass counters were expansive and reflected the overhead fluorescent lighting like sparkling jewels themselves.

"May I help you, sir?" a pretty blonde asked, instantly reminding Julian of Claudia. That she had a low, soft voice and obvious manners put him at ease. The physical similarity was significant, though.

He told her he was looking for an engagement ring and wedding bands.

"What kind...I mean the engagement ring?" She smiled warmly at Julian.

He told her that he really didn't know and that size wasn't all that important, that he'd know the ring when he saw it. Inadvertently, he added that he hadn't purchased one in decades.

"To a woman size is important, if you don't mind my advice. Perhaps a 3/4 karat or a full karat. Shall we start there?"

Julian said that would be fine and watched intently as the young woman pulled one black velvet display tray on top of the counter. He shook his head slowly. She replaced it and pulled out another. And then another.

"Perhaps if you brought your fiancée in to help you?"

"No, it's a surprise. Aren't all engagement rings meant to be surprises? he asked rhetorically.

Julian noticed that her fingers were long, exaggerated, he realized, by exceedingly long fingernails. They were a soft green and each had a tiny white symbol on it. He realized that he was staring.

She laughed. "Oh, they're scorpions. I'm a Scorpio, of course."

Irony upon irony, Julian thought, and then looked at several other counters, where some very large diamonds with intricate facets glittered under the showcase lighting. They were obviously exceedingly expensive.

"May I ask you a question? Can you describe what your girlfriend looks like? I mean, compared to me."

Julian thought for a moment. "Well, she has blonde hair but shorter than yours. She's about 5 - 7, weighs around 120 pounds and has very blue eyes."

"Perfect," the girl said. "I know I don't look like her but there's probably a resemblance."

"Actually, you resemble someone else I know," Julian said, then wondered why he'd even mentioned it.

The girl was wearing some sort of friendship ring on her wedding finger and she tugged at it, turning it slowly to remove it. "If I were to pick out a ring, this would be it," she said, sweeping her hand over the displays and pulling out a rather large diamond. She wiggled it out of its case and put it on.

"Yes," Julian said, impressed by the style and size of the diamond.

"It's a full karat solitaire set in a serpentine pavé of beautiful smaller diamonds. Total karat weight is almost two. Isn't it gorgeous?"

"Yes it is. In fact, it's perfect. I can see it on my fiancée's hand right now," Julian said, addding that they would pick out the wedding bands together.

"I can't wait to meet her," she said, ringing up the sale.

Julian drove home, now and then glancing at the small jewelry bag on the passenger seat. It was going to be a perfect surprise, the ring, of course, but also the banquet dinner he'd ordered from a fancy caterer. They would be served lobster tail and filet mignon steak, with rice pilaf and roasted asparagus, along with an apetizer of shrimp and then a cheesecake dessert. He didn't want to propose to her in a restaurant, with all the noise and attention, and had planned it the old fashioned way, kneeling at her feet. The feast would be brought to them in familiar and quiet surroundings. *A Movable Feast*, he thought, smiling at the allusion.

In fact, he had once considered Paris as a proposal venue but realizing that he had no current passport and that it would be somewhat of a challenge to get one, he'd given up on that idea. Boston was the perfect place. They had both grown up in the city and had taken their careers here. When the time came, Julian was prepared to die in the *City on a Hill*.

Arriving in his apartment, Julian threw his jacket on the sofa, put the ring box in his chest of drawer and went to check the answering machine. There was one message.

Carolyn was arriving in Boston tomorrow.

Chapter Fourteen

Tenley had received the call while she was lecturing and had called Julian back to hear him frantic and unwilling to discuss whatever it was on the phone. "It's bad," he had said.

Now she was imagining the very worst, that perhaps he'd advanced in age while she was gone or, worse yet, regressed again. The possibilities ballooned in her mind and made her shudder at the thought of who might appear when she opened the door.

Boston traffic was at a snarl and either a bad day at the office or contagious temperaments were having their effects on drivers. One cut in front of her, causing her to brake, and the truck behind her, a large black pickup, its driver wearing a white Stetson, slammed at his horn. Ordinarily Tenley would have gestured at him because it wasn't her fault and because men without manners offended her to no end. This time she didn't. She was too worried at what the immediate future would reveal.

She couldn't find a parking space in front of the apartments and had to go around several times before she spotted a car pulling out of a space on Garrison Street. She walked hurriedly across the street and made her way to the entrance.

Leighton was inside behind the desk. He said, "Good evening, Dr. Harrington." Tenley was somewhat amused that he no longer called her by her first name. She could feel his eyes on her back as she walked briskly to the elevators.

She found Julian sitting pensively on the dining room chair and quickly sat beside him, the chair legs scraping as she pulled closer.

"Honey, what's wrong?" she said, eyeing him carefully for any discernible change in his appearance. He appeared normal except for his hair, which looked tussled, as if he'd been pulling at it.

"Carolyn's coming tomorrow," he said fatefully. "And I can't lie to her anymore."

Relieved that nothing had happened to Julian, Tenley tried to lessen the impact of his statement. "It was bound to happen, Julian," she said. "We'll work it out somehow."

"In less than twenty-four hours my daughter is going to find out that I am her age, and know that I'm an imposter. How could she believe me?"

"We'll just tell her the truth, all of it."

"I can't," Julian said, running his hand through his hair. "Don't you see that I can't?"

"Then I'll hide you somewhere." She noticed that Julian's hands were trembling.

"It is an impossibility. It can't happen. It will ruin everything. Don't you understand?"

The edge of panic in his voice made Tenley uneasy. There was something, she thought, that he wasn't sharing with her. He hadn't acted rationally and certainly not his normal self. He was overreacting. Julian had told her all of the truth and she had believed him. So, too, Carolyn would have to come to terms with inevitable reality of her father's situation.

We'll come up with something. I promise," she told Julian, not having even an idea of what they could do besides telling the truth.

She fixed them a comfortable dinner of leftover roast, mashed potatoes and garlic beans with walnuts. She poured them glassfuls of red burgundy. She lit a candle on the dining room table. Seating herself, she raised a glass and assured Julian that they would have to trust in tomorrow, whatever fate lay ahead. It immediately sounded clichéd and inappropriate given the cataclysmic look on Julian's face.

◆

Tenley had driven to Boston's Logan Airport not entirely agreeing with Julian's desperate plan. Now she sat at a café table in Terminal E with a clear view of passengers disembarking at gate E2A.

The British Airways flight from Paris had been delayed by twenty minutes but Tenley hadn't known why. She assumed heavy winds and turbulence over the Atlantic might have been the reason. The delay had given her extra time to rehearse her lines.

One of the last passengers to exit was Carolyn, who was dressed in a chic gray-tweed pantsuit and green blouse, her hair pulled back into a tight pigtail. She looked very business-like as she walked Tenley's way, a short fur jacket in one hand and an attaché case in the other.

"Carolyn, over here!" Tenley called out, waving her arm.

They hugged and then Carolyn said, "An abominable flight. Delay at de Gaulle, turbulence and traffic coming into Logan. I should have taken a ship."

"Well, you're here safe and sound and that's all that counts."

"My father...I thought he would meet me. Is he alright?"

"Of course," Tenley said, settling into the subterfuge that would follow. "I'm afraid William has taken a turn for the worse. He is with him now in California."

"His brother?" Carolyn said, startled. "What has happened to Uncle William?"

"A stroke, but luckily not a bad one. Julian is with him in the hospital in San Francisco."

"I should go there."

"No, Julian wants you to stay at the apartment. He will phone you tonight. Everything's going to be alright."

"Please, fill me in on the details," Carolyn said as they hurried toward the baggage claim.

Back at the apartment, Carolyn made a comment about Julian's new furniture, referring to it as *man cave-ish*, and then told Tenley that she wanted to take a shower and put on some decent clothes.

It gave Tenley some time to think about the ruse. Julian, of course, was not in California but in a room at the Renaissance, a waterfront hotel in town. He had called an old friend in San Francisco and asked for his help in a *grave* matter. Tenley didn't know the details of their conversation, only that his friend was willing to go along with his plan. He was going to pretend he was William and call Carolyn this evening. Julian knew that she would believe that she was talking with his brother because she hadn't seen him in decades and wouldn't remember his voice. Arthur, his friend, said that he would ad lib the rest of the story.

It still was a puzzle that Julian would go to such limits to deceive his daughter and why he had acted so desperately at the prospect of seeing Carolyn. It contradicted the essence of his personality: his new commitment to honesty. Tenley sensed a genuine trepidation in Julian.

Julian's friend called at seven as promised. Carolyn's phone rang twice before she answered it, looking once at the number on the display. "Yes, it is," she said, and listened intently to the voice on the other end.

"Is he going to make it? I mean, he hasn't lost his faculties, has he? Ah, thank God. Yes, drugs can do wonders these days. May I speak to my father?"

For almost a full minute Tenley watched as Carolyn's face changed expressions, a subtle but visible wrinkling of her brow, almost a frown, then her lips thinning as she stared vaguely into space, nodding once every so often.

She hung up the phone and just sat there looking confused and distant.

"Was that William?" Tenley asked.

Carolyn looked up from the floor. "No," she said, "it was a nurse from the hospital."

"What did he say?" Tenley said, wondering why the plan had changed.

"She. It was a female nurse, of course. She said that William was asleep but would recover, that he'd suffered only a minor stroke. I am glad of that. It's what she said about my father that has me perplexed."

"Oh?" Tenley said.

"The nurse said she didn't know the details but that Daddy had been in a fender bender in the rental as he was leaving the airport and was going to be very late due to paperwork he had to complete for the rental company and that he was still waiting for the next available car." Carolyn looked at Tenley with vague consternation.

"He hasn't been injured, I hope," Tenley said, wondering herself about the account. Julian, for whatever reason, had changed his plans, or at least his friend had.

"You know," Carolyn said, "I haven't seen my father in many months. I feel like he's avoiding me. The escape to Ireland from Paris with that woman, the unanswered calls, and now this, an accident in San Francisco. The whole thing's a bit mysterious, don't you think?"

"Julian's life has changed quite dramatically since his memory-loss recovery. I can't emphasize that enough," Tenley said. "To be honest, I don't think I would recognize the man had I not been there through all the positive changes. I mean, he hasn't changed physically, of course, but his personality has, as his thirst for adventure. I wouldn't worry about your father, Carolyn. He's going to be okay. Don't take his apparent avoidance personally."

"Memory loss?" Carolyn said. "He never told me about that. "I think it's quite normal for a man my father's age to occasionally forget things. That comes with the aging process. But you say he's recovered?"

Not wanting to get into the details, Tenley said that Julian had seen a neurologist and had been prescribed medication that had produced beneficial effects.

Carolyn sighed. "I suppose you're right. He *has* been through a lot for an older man. I just hope he doesn't give out while enjoying these adventures. I'll try not to worry about him. But I do wonder if I shall ever see him again."

Tenley assured her that she would eventually. "Just give him time," she said.

There was a knock at the door and Tenley went to answer it. A man dressed in a waiter's suit announced that he was from *Above and Beyond Catering*. He looked Italian and had the easy smile of someone who was about to perform, confident and entertaining. He pulled two metal carts through the doorway and asked where they planned to eat.

"There must be a mistake," Tenley said as the man went to work in the dining room, laying dinner plates, silverware and wine glasses on the table. Without delay, he brandished a candelabrum, set it on the table and lit the candles.

Finished and ready to serve the meals, the man said, "I am Giuseppe and I am at your service."

"But we didn't order..."

"Wonderful" Carolyn said as she came into the room. "This sounds *just* like Daddy."

◆

Julian sat in a striped lounge chair in front of the large window in the upscale hotel. He gazed down at the lights of the traffic moving slowly on the street below, the red glow of taillights crawling against the gauze of headlights in the late evening. He'd ordered a dry martini following a sudden urge to imbibe; he hadn't had one in years and the cool sting on his tongue reawakened the enjoyment of cocktails, and instantly produced a calming effect.

Halfway through the drink the realization that this was the evening for the catered dinner came to Julian with a rush of panic. He looked at his watch, realizing then that the meal had already been delivered. He thought of the ring and what would have been a momentous evening, and sank down heavily in his seat. He called the desk and ordered another drink.

As planned, Tenley called at eleven. Before she could say anything Julian blurted, "Oh, Tenley, forgive me...it was supposed to be a surprise...I totally forgot."

"It was a surprise and I knew that the dinner was meant to be ours. You're so sweet. I love you."

"What...about...Carolyn?"

"Julian, you've been drinking."

"My...my nerves," he said, realizing that his words were a bit slurred.

"Well, Carolyn is fine and in her usual shape. I'm afraid Arthur didn't call. But a woman who pretended to be a hospital nurse did speak with her. You had an accident on your way out of the airport and are being delayed by paperwork at the rental company. Your brother is fine, only a mild stroke."

Julian yawned deeply and then cleared his throat. "It must have been...Arthur's wife. He must have backed down...at least someone called...did Carolyn believe it?"

"She thinks you are trying to avoid her. I believe she feels hurt by it all, not just the trip but your fling in Paris. I still think we should tell her the truth, Julian."

"No! Never." There was a long pause, and for a moment Julian thought that Tenley had hung up. "I'm sorry, I didn't mean to snap at you. Forgive me."

"Of course I forgive you, sweetheart. I shouldn't have said that. I know it's important to you."

"Where is Carolyn? I mean right now."

"In your comfy bed, probably sound asleep. She was exhausted by her trip. And then that wonderful champagne. I'll tell her in the morning that you called but didn't want to awaken her. Is that okay?"

"Yes, and tell her I love her...and miss her and that we'll definitely meet up. Make it sound like a certainty."

"A certainty?"

"That you feel that I am not being disingenuous. You will call me tomorrow?"

"Of course, as soon as I know what Carolyn has decided. Now, get to bed. I don't think you'll have trouble sleeping tonight. I love you."

After hanging up the phone, Julian sank down in his seat again, his mind now awash with subterfuge and falseness and guilt. He realized that this mendacity would have to be continued as long as Carolyn was here, and he hoped that her business commitments would soon distract her.

The second dry martini was delivered, and Julian gave the young man a ten-dollar tip. He drank it slowly this time, pausing as the slight hint of vermouth tingled his palate. He turned on the television and watched the news on CNN, distracted from his own conflict by those more violent in Middle East and Egypt. Every nation in that region seemed to be at war, either with themselves or with other warring countries. The new terrorism frightened Julian, not as a personal threat but as a growing danger to peaceful nations and civilization in general. Even the former Iron Curtain and the looming threat of nuclear war paled in comparison to what despotic leaders were doing to their people today. A human life no longer had worth, and bloody, horrific massacres were a clear signal that the human race, save for the honest, good people in the world, was regressing at an alarming rate.

Julian's growing cynicism reminded him of his later years, just before the memory loss had taken a sudden turn for the worse, and it frightened him. He was not ready for it again.

He dozed lightly, feeling the weight of the world and his own fate mingled in, awoke, took another sip and finally began to feel himself again. He turned the channel and watched a rerun of last Sunday's game with the Panthers.

It wasn't long before he was thinking, somewhat groggily, about Tenley and his plans to propose to her. Suddenly he missed her, wanting to collapse in her arms against her feminine warmth and look up at her face, soft and luminous in the bedroom light.

He got up and stumbled his way to the bathroom, stood there weaving slightly forward and back, missing the toilet several times, then chuckling to himself. *Now this is sweet anesthesia*, he thought, feeling an urge to dance about the room until dawn-break. Zipping his pants, he caught himself and cursed loudly.

He fumbled his way to the window, looked out at the blurry cityscape lights, and sighed, relieved of something he couldn't quite put his finger on. He stood there, holding himself upright with both hands on the glass, looking like someone who was about to leap.

He fell back in the chair, only half-listening to the game, allowing the absence of thought, the booze and the late hour to have their somnolent effects. He didn't want any of it to end.

Soon he ordered another martini but was fast asleep, dead to the world, when, well past midnight, there was a knocking at the door.

Chapter Fifteen

The threat was gone. Carolyn had taken a flight back to her home in Chicago, had called Tenley twice to check on Julian and announced that she was off to Europe again, that she had four shows before the end of the year.

One evening Julian took Tenley to a quiet, largely unpopulated restaurant in South Boston. It was a weekday, Wednesday, he would remember later. Over drinks, before the meals had been served, he took to his knees and, holding her hand, said, "Tenley, will you marry me?"

She must have known it was coming because there was a wet sparkle in her eyes when she'd sat down still holding his hand. They brightened now, almost glowing.

"Julian," she said, "you're so sweet. Yes, of course, I will marry you. I've been waiting for this day." She lifted Julian to his feet with one hand, and they kissed. He opened the ring case and slipped the ring on her wedding finger. It was a perfect fit. She looked at it and soon broke into tears, and they kissed again.

A loose applause broke out from a table nearby, and then their waitress came over and congratulated them both. She said the drinks were on the house.

Over dinner, Julian told Tenley about his hapless efforts to get back into the Church and plan for a catholic wedding. He told her about the fifty *Hail Marys* and fifty *Our Fathers* the priest had given him as penance.

"My God," Tenley said, "what sins did you confess?"

"None that you don't already know," Julian said. "Are you disappointed that we can't marry in the Church?"

"Of course not. I would have to go to confession and God knows what kind a penance I would receive. We'll have an unceremonious one, private, just to ourselves. The setting means nothing to me, Julian, just that we become husband and wife."

"I love you," Julian said, enjoying the happiest Wednesday in his life.

After dinner they strolled along the Harborwalk, holding hands, swinging their arms as if they were teenagers. Their engagement felt like a strange baptism to Julian, a cleansing of spirit and mind, an innocence he had never experienced before. The sensation made him feel secure, impervious to challenges past and the encroaching unknowns of the future.

They walked as far as Carson Beach and stopped, looking out across the calm waters of Old Harbor Bay at the twinkling lights of the islands. There was a full moon and Tenley used the light to admire her diamond ring.

"I feel an urge to travel," Julian said wistfully.

"Where would we go?"

"I'm not sure. But I am seriously thinking of selling the condo and looking for coastal property."

"Do you mean leaving Boston?"

Julian thought about it for a moment. "Possibly," he said.

"But my job..."

He looked over at Tenley's worried face and then kissed her hand. "I guess we don't have to go. It's just a wistful thought. You know that I wouldn't have the heart to take you away from your teaching career."

"Well, don't completely abandon the thought," Tenley said, obviously intrigued by Julian's idea.

"Or we could buy a sailboat and sail off into the sunset..."

"No more sailboats," Tenley said, squeezing his hand.

As they walked back to the car they encountered a small figure ahead sitting on a bench. Approaching, Julian realized that it was a little boy, perhaps no older than ten or eleven, his head cradled in his hands, sobbing softly to himself.

Tenley rushed to his side and put her arm around his shoulders. "Honey, what's wrong? Are you lost? Don't be afraid."

With sudden cynicism, Julian stopped, looked around, expecting that this was some sort of ruse, that a group of thugs was nearby about to rob them. He had read of such things, even here in Boston. Seeing no one, now embarrassed by his rush to judgment, Julian went to the boy's side.

Tenley was wiping the boy's face with a tissue, letting him blow his nose and now rubbing his back. He was of Latino or Puerto Rican descent, with dark, closely cropped hair and heavy eyebrows, a slight boy, looking fragile and vulnerable.

"What's wrong?" Julian said, parroting what Tenley had said seconds ago. He, too, put his arm around the boy. "Estás perdido?" He looked over at Tenley. "Perhaps we should call the police."

The boy shook his head as if he understood and then pulled away from them, leaning forward, burying his face in his hands. The sobbing intensified.

Despite the chilly air, the boy was dressed in low cutoff jeans, black sneakers and what appeared to be a gray sweatshirt. Julian noticed a crumpled Red Sox cap on the ground.

"I'm not sure he understands us," Tenley said, a look of maternal concern on her face.

Julian asked him, in Spanish, if he needed money to get a taxi. He went for his wallet and in that instant the boy sprang upright, as if he were a snake, uncoiled and ready to strike. "You think I'm stupid, man!" he said, startling Tenley.

"Sorry," Julian said. "We were just trying to help."

"Don't need no help from you or the lady," the boy said, wiping his nose with his sleeve, standing almost in a boxer's stance, leaning toward them as if ready to go a round. "I'm not a spic. I'm an American, born here, so don't have any green card. You insult me, man."

"Sorry," Julian said earnestly. "I didn't mean to offend you. We were concerned and wanted to help. Why were you crying? Do you feel like talking?"

The boy shook his head, his expression hardening, putting on a brave face. "It's personal and has nothing to do with you, man."

"I know it doesn't." Julian said, standing up, accepting the boy's need for privacy. In the moonlight he noticed that the boy's right knuckles were swollen and crusted with dried blood. A hint of black darkened his right eye. And he appeared larger than he had clutched forward on the bench.

Tenley, too, must have noticed the injuries. She stood up, appearing to get a better look at his hand. "You're injured. Were you in a fight?"

"Looks like you've got a good shiner there," Julian said. "Perhaps we should call an ambulance," he added, meaning to be jocular.

"Don't need no ambulance, man," the boy said. "Nothing that a drink won't heal."

"A drink?" Julian said. "How old are you?"

"Old enough," the boy said, wiping at his nose again.

Julian offered him a ride home, no more questions asked. He told the boy that if he didn't want to go with them he would gladly give him some cash for a taxi ride.

"How much?" the boy said.

"Ten, twenty. Would that be enough?"

The boy relaxed and then, after a few seconds, smiled wisely and nodded at Julian. "You people are good...I mean you're honest. I think you really care."

"Of course we do," Tenley said.

"I got more than double that money in my pocket right now but I 'preciate your offer." The boy took a seat again on the bench, and Julian and Tenley followed suit. "Name is Dino and I'm older than you think. I'm sixteen, not no kid anymore but people say I could pass for ten."

"You certainly could," Julian said and then introduced himself and Tenley. They all shook hands.

"You guys lovers. I can tell," Dino said.

"Yes, we are," Tenley said, nodding slowly. "We're engaged to be married."

Julian looked over and smiled at her.

"My girl dumped me for another guy," Dino said. "And I beat up on him. Bastard paid for what he did. Serena and me were close, in love, hardcore, if you know what I mean."

"Yes, we do," Tenley said.

"It really hurts, man. It's like the whole world's coming down on me. This week's been shitty. My old man kicks me out of the house...lose my girl and my honor..."

"Things will get better, I promise," Tenley said.

"They always do. There's always a silver lining," Julian added. "Believe me, Dino. I know that from experience. You'll meet someone else, someone who won't dishonor you and will appreciate and love you for who you are. You'll see."

"Damn right," Dino said. "I aim to get back at Serena. She'll pay for this."

"That's not exactly what I mean," Julian said.

"I ain't no coward. She thinks she can hurt Dino like that...I'll show her and all her bad boys."

Dino's sudden anger startled Julian. He had never been jilted before and tried to imagine what emotions were at combat in the boy's head. Perhaps he had a right to be angry, even *that* angry, he thought, as the boy stood up again and resumed a threatening stance.

"Dino, you were crying," Julian said. "That's only human. And being angry too. But you've got to put it into perspective. Serena was not the one for you. Don't you see that now? You've got your whole life ahead of you."

The boy relaxed and stared solemnly out across the bay, either reconciliation or murder in his thoughts. He reminded Julian of a character in long ago movie, unremembered now, but he thought the actor might be Robert Blake. Whatever his age, Dino was obviously streetwise, bullheaded and proud, half-child and the rest a mixture of adolescent rebellion and reckless conviction. He imagined that the boy had endured a rough upbringing, perhaps at the hands of an overbearing father. He wondered if he lived on the streets.

"I ain't a bad person," Dino said.

"Of course you're not," Tenley said.

"We all have our dark sides," Julian said, realizing it wasn't exactly what he had meant to say.

"I got tough skin and a strong head," Dino said. "Also a good heart."

"Listen, do you have a place to stay tonight...and mean, because your father kicked you out?" Julian said.

"Yes, you're welcome to stay with us for a few days," Tenley said, looking over at Julian.

"Nah, I got things to do. My mission."

Afraid to ask about the *mission*, Julian said, "I have a comfy bed in my study and...a glass of beer waiting for you."

Dino turned to face his benefactors, smiled broadly and reached out to shake Julian's hand. "You're the salt of the earth and more," he said.

Julian led the way to the car, Tenley and Dino bringing up the rear.

◆

"Man, you must be rich," Dino said as they pulled up to the apartment complex. He had been admiring the BMW, fiddling with radio and the GPS monitor all the way home. Julian's Rolex had also caught his eye.

It was late and Leighton was nowhere to be seen. Inside the apartment, Julian showed Dino where he would sleep. He said he had extra pillows and blankets. He watched as the boy went about the room touching the old typewriter, the computer, the desk.

"Man, is that a book you're writing?" he said, eyeing the thick manuscript. He turned a few pages over. "*Odessa's Feud*...now that's a good title. What's it about?"

"It's unlucky for an author to discuss a work before it's finished," Julian said.

"It's a place in Russia."

Surprised, Julian said, "You know your geography. But the book is about a woman named Odessa."

"Bet she's a bitch, a ball-breaker like Serena."

Tenley handed Dino a wet washcloth to clean his hands and then put ice in another and held it lightly between his nose and right eye. He held his head back, blinking the other eye and guiding Tenley's hand with his own to where the swelling had begun to close the lids. "You took a hard one," Tenley said.

"Got sucker-punched, that's all. He's gonna pay for it."

After a midnight snack of leftover casserole, tossed salad and a full glass of water, Dino was finishing his plate, filling his mouth with too much food, occasionally stopping and coughing, then resuming as if he were trying to beat the clock. When his plate was empty, he asked Tenley for more. Julian noticed that he hadn't touched the opened bottle of beer, gulping from the water glass instead.

Scraping the last of the casserole onto his plate, Tenley said, "There's a hot bath whenever you want it, and I think I have some clothes that might fit you."

Dino nodded without looking up from his plate, which was now almost empty. He took another drink of water and pushed back from the table.

"We can order a pizza if you're still hungry. It's early enough, Julian said, amazed at the boy's voracious appetite.

"Nah, man. I had enough," Dino said, swiping up the beer bottle and taking it into the living room. He looked back at Julian who was following close behind. "Got any cigars?"

"I don't smoke anymore," Julian said.

"Man, you don't smoke? That's a shame."

"It's bad for your lungs and I'm told it stunts your growth." The irony of his statement made Julian smile at himself as he considered Dino's small stature.

As Tenley finished the dishes and came in to join them, a gust of wind could be heard outside, rattling the old window with a faint howl.

Julian and Tenley shared a beer and watched as Dino poured his beer into a glass, sipping from it as if the contents were that of a fine wine.

Asked if he was still in school, Dino said, "Nah, I'm taking a leave of absence. Probably get my GED. You don't need education these days; street knowledge is what it's about. I seen college boys that have as much sense as a flea. But books I like."

"What have you read lately," Julian asked, encouraged by the boy's interest.

"Shakespeare, for one, especially *Romeo and Juliet* and *Macbeth*. I like history too, Gibbon's *Decline and Fall of the Roman Empire*."

"That's remarkable," Julian said, to which Dino frowned.

"You think I'm just some stupid shit boy, don't you?"

"No, of course not. I meant it as a compliment. Where do you keep your books?"

Dino didn't answer; he just shook his head and took another sip from his glass.

"I had to get rid of a lot of my books but I still have Gibbon and some other treasures. You're welcome to take some home if you like."

Dino's face brightened. "Serious?"

"Yes, I mean it. They're there to be read and I want you to have them. They're in the study when you want to take a look. Just don't take *Odessa's Feud*. That's private stock."

Loosening up, Dino shared with them the problems he had at home, with his mother gone and his father working two jobs. He said he had an older sister nearly twice his age and that she lived in Norfolk, Virginia, married to a Seaman, and that she'd already had her second kid. He said that he didn't hate his father but that the man was a hard disciplinarian with old-fashioned ideas about raising a kid. Asked what he wanted to do with his life, he said, "I'm open to adventure. I'm thinking of speaking with Joe, my brother-in-law, and seeing if he could get me in. I want to travel, to meet girls all over the world."

He asked Tenley where they had met, seemed comfortable with the abbreviated account, and then asked Julian if he liked teaching. He seemed very interested in their personal lives.

Julian told him the truth, that he had recently retired, adding, "I decided to write novels while I still have the imagination and the stamina. I might return to teaching if things don't work out with writing."

It was half past one in the morning when, after several deep yawns, Tenley said, "I'm ready to crash."

Julian said he was too. While Tenley made up the bed with new sheets and a jacquard blanket, he showed Dino the books on the shelves, pulling out another book by Gibbon. "This one he wrote before he achieved literary success. It's about his love for Switzerland. Not exactly a best seller back then."

Dino instead chose *Love's Labour's Lost* by Shakespeare, which he said he would start reading tonight after taking a shower. He said that he didn't need much sleep and not to worry if they heard him up.

Tenley found some of Julian's jeans from younger days, a Lacoste sweatshirt and boxer shorts, which she laid out on the bed while he showered.

Finally in bed, Tenley said, "I feel good about Dino."

"He's not as dumb as he looks," Julian said, realizing immediately that wasn't what he'd meant to say. "I mean that there's potential for that boy. I can see him succeeding at whatever he chooses to do with his life."

Within five minutes, Tenley was snoring softly. Julian found himself unable to sleep and listened to their guest's footsteps in the den and into the kitchen and then the squeak of the springs of the old study bed. It almost sounded like Dino was playing sports on the bed, perhaps throwing a ball into the hoop or doing calisthenics. The sounds stopped after several minutes, and Julian felt his face flush with embarrassment and stupidity.

He waited until he felt Dino was finally asleep and opened the bedroom door and walked light-footed down the hallway towards the den.

He planned to check on the boy, to make sure he was alright. But the door was locked.

◆

Late the next morning, Julian rose from his bed and saw that Tenley was already up and about. He could smell coffee and hot buns, a fragrance which made his taste buds water and his stomach rumble with hunger. Dressed, his hair combed, he went into the kitchen.

Tenley met him and they kissed. "I guess our visitor has vanished," she said. "But he left us this." She held up a sheet of paper with handwriting on it. Julian took it to the table and sat down. It was a letter from Dino:

Dear Sir, it's Dino here. I want to thank you for all you done. I took three books, the one by Shakespeare and two others...novels by dead authors. I left you $40 for your hospitality. I don't think I'll ever meet people like you again. I called Serena this morning and she wants to see me, so it's good news for now. Stay young. Respectfully, Dino (mite) Delgado.

P.S. I put my number in your iPhone 'case you want to call me. Let me know about the wedding.

Chapter Sixteen

They were married at a Justice of the Peace in downtown Boston. Dino was best man. He had called and asked to be, and Julian had no reason to refuse him. Tenley thought it was a wonderful idea. When he handed the rings to Julian, he'd said, "Man, you're gonna remember this for the rest of your life."

After the service they'd gone to a restaurant in the Wharf area, where they served the best fried shrimp, Dino's favorite. He'd been unusually quiet during the dinner and had not mentioned anything about Serena or any other love escapades. He'd said only that he'd moved back with his father and was working at a local grocery store to save up money.

It would be weeks before they heard from Dino again. On occasions, Julian was tempted to call the boy to see how he was doing but decided that would be an intrusion.

They honeymooned at Martha's Vineyard in a quaint Victorian hotel near the water in Oak Bluffs. After a languorous day in bed, they went to stroll along the beach. It was quite cold for this time in late October, and the forecast was for snow, heavy at times.

Bundled in a light blue, fur-lined winter coat, Tenley snuggled close to Julian against the windless cold.

"I love you so much, Julian," she said.

"I wish we could freeze it for all time," he said, feeling an odd, unsettling feeling as he spoke.

"Love has no time limits. You know that, Julian."

He pulled her close and kissed her, the warmth of their kiss resounding deep in his heart. He had always loved Tenley, even as an old man, and this moment was the fruition of that long-unrequited love. Now, in this instant, it didn't matter about old age and even death. The dream had come true, although in a convoluted way, and Julian was as happy as any man could be, in love with the most beautiful woman in the world who loved him equally and was willing to spend the rest of her life at his side, for better or worse.

He hadn't noticed any noticeable change in his looks over the past weeks and he'd fantasized that perhaps the aging had stopped, or at least slowed down dramatically. Against that reverie, though, was the logic of reality, like a mathematical equation already solved, its result checked and rechecked. It was always there, looming and unforgiving and immutable, like death itself. *But maybe...*, Julian would think while looking in the mirror.

They walked about a hundred yards down the beach and Tenley found a piece of driftwood in the shape of a wave, its smooth wood lightened where the crest of a wave would be. It was so realistic, she could easily imagine the sound it would make crashing ashore.

"It's almost as though someone carved it to look like that," Tenley said.

"It's a sign of good luck," Julian said. "A once-in-a-lifetime find."

"And I know just where to put it."

He carried it back, so that Tenley could keep her hands in her pockets. It seemed to be growing colder by the minute, and now, under a dark swollen sky, there was the smell of snow in the stilled wintry air.

On the way to the hotel they found a small restaurant that served the best New England clam chowder Julian had ever tasted. Still in their jackets, they warmed their numbed fingers around the ample-sized bowls. The meal came with thickly-sliced homemade Irish bread and slabs of real butter. It was nourishing and filling, and settled in Julian's stomach like a three-course meal.

They went to Edgartown, driving slowly down North Water Street and then out the causeway to Lighthouse Beach. Julian had heard that the structure was decorated with lights during the holidays but they found none, for it was obviously too early in the season.

Back at the hotel, they took a bath together in a huge tub meant for two. Julian washed Tenley's hair, gently massaging her scalp and wiping the dripping suds from her face. He washed her back, admiring the perfect bend of her spine and the way her small breasts stood out, pointed and firm.

Tenley then bathed Julian, starting with his hair, down his back and then his chest and below until she found his toes, lifting and tickling them. Julian went under water and came up suddenly between her thighs, making grunting sounds and spurting sudsy water from his mouth. Tenley pulled him up and they kissed until neither could contain themselves any longer. And they ran like drenched children into the bedroom, giggling with urgency.

The night was long and passionate, and at last they fell asleep in each other's arms, wet and warm and exhausted.

Sometime during the night, Julian got up to use the bathroom and then looked out the window. A crust of snow mantled the windowpanes. Heavy wet snow was falling beyond, looking like a barrage of swirling moth-like creatures in the cold heavy darkness.

◆

It was still snowing when they awoke the next morning, the windowpanes now heavily laden, each small pane fogged by the cold. Tenley had to use her sweater sleeve to clear a view of the street below.

The radio said that nearly ten inches had fallen in Edgartown, a record for snow so early in the season. More snow was forecast for the evening.

"It's so romantic," Tenley said as Julian came up from behind and wrapped his arms around her.

"You're shivering," Julian said, concerned that she might have caught a cold in the damp bed.

"Hold me. I'll warm up fast. What's on the agenda today, Professor?"

"Nothing, absolutely nothing. The day is ours."

"We could go to a movie," Tenley said, her voice sounding hoarse.

"I think you need some tea with lemon."

"A hot toddy will do just fine. There's a new Woody Allen movie out and I'd love to see it."

While Tenley checked the show times Julian went out to the nearest grocery store and bought some herbal tea, a lemon and a bag of honey cough drops. When he returned Tenley met him at the door. She was already dressed in her ski jacket and muffler. "We've only got ten minutes to get there," she said.

Fortunately the small theater was within walking distance of the hotel. The street had been plowed, as was the sidewalk, but the snow heaped on either side made passage difficult. Walking single-file, Tenley leading, Julian thought about the car, surely buried to its fenders on the side street where they'd parked it. He didn't have a snow shovel or even a brush, so he made a mental note to purchase both before attempting to head home.

Inside the theater as the movie began, Tenley reached for his hand. Julian wrapped his arm around her shoulders. They watched as the romantic comedy unfolded, Julian laughing out loud several times at the characters' lines, admiring the way the director deftly presented the story. He was engrossed in the screenplay and it wasn't until the movie was ending that he noticed that Tenley had dozed off, snuggled against the armrest.

After they'd exited the theater, Tenley said she had to use the lady's room. Julian said nothing about her sleeping through the movie but his concern was elevated. He couldn't remember her ever calling in sick at the University and she had never complained of being under the weather. He felt guilty for having taken her to bed, soaked to the bones like that.

He watched as the crowd moved toward the exit doors. They were mostly young people in their twenties and thirties, and they seemed underdressed for the weather, some wearing only sweatshirts and jeans, and two young boys in baggy shorts and tee-shirts. One tall young man, talking spiritedly about the movie with his red-headed wife or girlfriend, bumped into Julian, causing him to steady himself against the wall. The man passed by without apology or showing any sign that he was aware of their physical encounter. For a moment, Julian wanted to tap the man on his shoulder to get his attention, not necessarily to get his apology but to let him know that he'd almost been knocked to the floor. Being respectful was not the hallmark of youth these days, but maybe it never had been.

Over ten minutes went by and there was no sign of Tenley. More concerned than ever, Julian went to the restroom door, knocked on it and called out her name. He repeated this when Tenley failed to appear.

"Can I help?" a concerned teenage girl said.

Julian explained that his wife had been in there too long, that she wasn't feeling well and would the girl mind checking on her. He gave the young good Samaritan a description of what Tenley looked like and what she was wearing.

Several minutes later they emerged, Tenley being supported by the girl, her face ashen, her legs appearing wobbly as she reached for Julian.

"Oh no...what's wrong, honey? You look terrible."

"I vomited twice. It must be something we ate."

Julian thanked the girl and then felt Tenley's forehead. "I think you've got the flu. We've got to get you home."

"I...I don't think I can make it." Tenley's voice was shallow. She coughed heavily. She braced herself full weight against Julian's shoulder.

"I'll call a cab. Just hang in there. He fumbled with his smartphone and hurriedly tried to Google cab companies in Edgartown. Unable to do so under Tenley's weight, he found a bench near the restrooms and dragged Tenley to it, letting her fall back against the wall while he rubbed her cold hands.

A couple approached and asked if they could help. The man said he was a nurse and asked if he could take her pulse, which he did, saying only that it was very shallow. "Has she had heart problems?"

"No," Julian said. "Not that I know of. Couldn't it be the flu?"

"That's possible," the man said, feeling her forehead and then pulling down her lower eyelid.

Tenley mumbled something and Julian put his ear to her mouth in time to hear her say, "Oh Julian...I'm going..."

Panic set in, and Julian fumbled with his phone again. His hands were shaking and he asked the man to help. "I've got to get her home. I need a taxi."

The woman was already on her phone, in brisk conversation with the person on the other end. She hung up and told Julian that EMS would be here in five minutes.

It was the longest five minutes in Julian's life.

Martha's Vineyard Hospital was a small but efficient treatment facility, a far cry from the large hospitals in Boston. It was well-staffed, and inside the small emergency ward the nurses were friendly and compassionate. They'd initially asked Julian to wait in the lounge but after a few minutes he'd demanded to be with his wife.

He stood by her bed as a nurse checked her vitals. Afterwards, she slipped an oxygen tube under Tenley's nose and then adjusted the saline line the paramedic had started in the ambulance.

Tenley had come to in the ambulance after smelling salts had been applied, and now, groggily, she attempted to answer the nurse' questions.

"Cancer? Diabetes? Stroke? Kidney or liver problems?"

Tenley shook her head.

"Heart disease?"

Tenley looked over at Julian before nodding yes. She told the nurse that she had a heart murmur diagnosed when she was a teenager. Asked if she had seen a cardiologist recently, she nodded again.

Julian was both startled and confused. She had never mentioned the condition to him, much less told him that she had a cardiologist. He felt guilty again for having taken her to the beach in the cold and having her sleep in a damp bed. He rebuked himself for the sex and for being so selfish.

The doctor came in and read the notes the nurse had made, then examined Tenley, listening to her heart and chest and shining a light down her throat with the aid of a tongue blade. He told her that they would do an EKG and, if necessary, have the staff cardiologist check her out just to be sure it wasn't something more serious than the flu.

After the EKG, as they were left alone in the room, Tenley reached for Julian's hand. "I'm sorry," she said.

"About what? You have nothing to feel sorry about."

"I never confided in you about my heart problem. I should have. But I didn't want you to worry."

Julian's lips were dry. "How bad is it?"

"They say it's a leaking mitral valve. This has happened before but not quite as bad. I've always managed to revive myself by sitting down and resting. Oh, Julian, I'm so sorry. This isn't fair to you. I should have told you before we got married."

Julian leaned forward and kissed her on the forehead and then gently rubbed at her cheek. He apologized for having her outside in the cold and for not changing the damp sheets and for being so selfish.

Tenley smiled. "If what happened last night was a result of you being selfish then please concentrate on being more selfish." She kissed his hand.

Julian lay down next to her on the narrow bed, on his side, propping his feet against a stool, more out than in the bed. She felt warm and awfully fragile as if she'd lost weight from the fever. "We're going to fix you up, I promise. I won't let anything happen to you."

Tenley was asleep by the time he stopped talking. He listened to her breathing and soon a light snoring, interrupted by a few coughs. It was the first time Julian had ever experienced the feeling before, a trepidation that harm had come to Tenley, that she was vulnerable and maybe seriously ill. He couldn't live without her, of course, much less live with the thought that she might suffer. That this was happening on their honeymoon seemed a cruel twist of fate, another unforeseen irony.

After almost an hour, the cardiologist came in, a short balding man in his forties with a permanently serious face. His nose was long and braced his glasses a full inch from his eyes.

"Ah," he said, peering over the rims. "The patient's asleep. Are you a relative?"

"Julian Landon. I'm Tenley's husband." His tone was unequivocal and a sign that he would be involved directly in every course of Tenley's treatment.

"Your wife has mitral valve prolapse...but I am not concerned so much about that. It is quite common and some patients don't even know they have the condition. She does have, though, a pronounced arrhythmia, bradycardia to be specific. This would explain the syncope at the theater. I am recommending that she have an echocardiogram and would like your wife to be kept overnight for further observation."

Julian felt instantly lightheaded and thought for a second that his own heart had skipped a few beats.

"Are you okay?" the doctor asked and had Julian sit down on the chair.

"Yes, yes...I'm fine," Julian said and then asked why Tenley had a fever.

"That, I'm afraid, is the beginning of a bad cold or perhaps the flu. It's another reason we need to keep an eye on her overnight." He scribbled notes in Tenley's chart and then wrote out two prescriptions, handing them to Julian. "One is for your wife when she goes home. The other is for you."

Julian looked down and read the prescription for Xanax.

"In case you can't sleep tonight," the doctor said before leaving the examining room.

More certain than ever now that he had exacerbated Tenley's condition and caused her to come down with a cold, Julian felt a new wave of anxiety sweep over him. What if she worsened? He thought about transferring her to larger hospital in Boston where she'd receive top-notch care for her heart problem. If he had to, he'd hire a helicopter to transport her, if not that, at least a quality ambulance service.

A nurse arrived and took Tenley's vitals again and then cranked her bed up slightly. She was about to inject a syringe full of medication into the line when Julian stopped her. "What are you giving my wife?"

"Atropine and an antibiotic," the nurse said politely. "It will speed up her heart. There's nothing to worry about, Mr. Landon. You wife is in good hands."

Tenley was awake now and had been listening to the nurse. "I am in good hands," she said. When the nurse left she asked if Julian would do her a favor.

"Anything, anything at all," Julian said, holding her hand.

"It's probably going to be a while before they get me to a room. Would you mind terribly if I asked you to bring over some essentials from the hotel?"

"But I can't just leave you here," Julian protested.

Tenley assured him that she would be fine, that she promised not to get any worse. She asked for paper and pen and then scribbled down what he needed to retrieve. She told him to be careful in the snow, that he should call a cab. She kissed his hand.

At the door Julian adjusted his jacket and scarf and turned to face the bed.

"Are you sure?"

"Yes, Julian. I'm sure. I promise to be okay. You have my word."

Julian left the room and the hospital with a burdensome sense that he had made a mistake leaving Tenley alone. *Anything can happen in an hour*, he thought ominously and soon scolded himself for being such a pessimist. He realized then, in that moment of conflict, that nothing he could do would affect whatever fate lay in the future, Tenley's and his own.

Chapter Seventeen

It had been almost a week since the second snow storm, and the roads had been cleared for safe travel. The latter storm had dumped another nine inches, and the snow was piled in five-foot drifts in places where the plows had come through.

Tenley had spent an extra night in the hospital and was released in good condition but with a recommendation to see her own cardiologist when she got back to Boston. She had been convivial on the way back, joking and acting her old self.

Julian had strained his back while shoveling the BMW out of a drift and had been forced to see his doctor for a prescription of Baclofen, a muscle relaxer.

It was good to be back in their home and the first time they'd lived there as a married couple. Tenley became quite the devoted wife, taking care of Julian, washing and ironing his clothes, giving him a haircut when the hair began to curl over his collar, and otherwise pampering him as though he could do nothing for himself. She served him breakfasts in bed and was constantly asking him if there was anything he needed. Even after his back pain had subsided, she wouldn't let him lift anything or stretch too high when he was arranging books on the shelves in his office. And she insisted on drawing his baths, which she said he *had* to take instead of showers.

One day when bringing Julian a cup of tea, he said, "Tenley, I can't take any more of this. You're making me an invalid."

"I enjoy taking care of you," she protested.

"But you're killing me, damn it! I can't even breathe without you interfering. I need some space." As soon as he said it, Julian realized the anger in his tone.

Tenley froze as if an arrow had struck her heart, and then a tear crept from her right eye down her cheek. Her horribly wounded look made Julian get up from his chair and approach her. She turned and walked briskly to the bathroom, locking the door.

Ten minutes later, with Tenley still in the bathroom, the telephone rang. Julian recognized the voice immediately. It was Dino.

"Good to hear from you, but I can't talk to you right now," he said.

"Man...man...it's bad," Dino said in a shaky voice.

"Can I call you back?"

"She's dead, man...she's dead..."

"Who's dead, Dino?"

"Serena...Serena, the love of my life...she's dead...and they think I did it."

"Oh my God," Julian said. "What happened?"

Dino was sobbing and his words were almost unintelligible. "Stabbed...I didn't do it...man, I didn't do it..."

"Where are you?"

In a halting voice Dino told him he was at the Suffolk County Jail but he thought he might be transferred after the arraignment. And then the phone went dead.

Tenley finally emerged from the bathroom, her face a turmoil of hurt and resentment, nose and eyes reddened, her cheeks moist from crying.

"I'm going back to work," she said. "And I'll be out of your way."

Julian went to her but she pulled away stiffly. "Honey, I'm sorry. I didn't mean it to sound that way," he said.

Tenley was about to say something but instead squared her jaw and walked away, making it obvious that she no longer wished to talk about it.

He tried several times to engage her, apologizing for his words and his behavior, telling her that it wasn't her fault but his, that he needed to go back to work himself or find something to occupy his time. "Married couples go through this all the time," he said in desperation.

"I guess you would know," Tenley said acerbically, breaking her silence. She went to the closet and put on her jacket and scarf and then in the foyer she swiped her keys from the marble table, opened the door, slamming it behind her.

Julian went to the living room and sank into the sofa. He had never seen Tenley act like this and, in fact, had never seen her angry. And it was his fault, his own stupid fault. Feeling miserable for it, he went to the kitchen and opened a bottle of Heineken.

In the living room again, he set the bottle down on the glass coffee table and watched solemnly as the little rivulets of condensation drooled over the label and down the sides, swelling into a puddle on the table.

He thought about his first marriage to Elizabeth and tried to recall arguments they'd had, but he could only remember his love and respect for her and the look in her eyes when Carolyn had been born. Perhaps they had never argued. Maybe marriage was to blame, the constraining legality of a relationship, the commitments, the obligation, the roles.

They should never have married, Julian thought with dramatic pessimism. And then it all piled on. She would have to see him grow old, suffer from senility and she would probably end up as a relatively young widow. If he had just let things be in the beginning, if he had not taken the medication, if he had not responded to his love for Tenley, if he had never let this happen...

His pitiful rationalizing made Julian sick to his stomach. He snapped himself out of it. There were things he had to do, people who needed his help.

He called the Suffolk County Jail and spoke with a sergeant named Roberts. He was told that a young man named Bernadino Delgado was being detained pending an arraignment tomorrow.

"What is the charge?"

"First degree murder. I doubt that the judge will allow him a bond."

"Can I visit with Mr. Delgado?"

The sergeant said no, that he would have to wait until Delgado was properly incarcerated following arraignment. Asked if an attorney had been assigned to the case, Sergeant Roberts said he didn't know and was there anything else?

Julian hung up the phone. He felt as though he had been talking to someone in a different world, a place estranged from society and its deferential tones, a place both clandestine and off limits to the rest of the normal world. He felt helpless and angry. He wanted to hear Dino's side of the story.

He immediately called Jacob Pearson. He was out for the day but his secretary said she would gladly forward a message. He provided the pertinent information, asking that Pearson look into the case just to provide Julian the details of the offense. He said not to worry, that he was not asking Pearson to take the case.

Afterward, Julian sat down and began drinking his beer.

◆

Tenley called later that evening. She was spending the night with a friend and she would try to call him tomorrow.

"Please, Tenley, don't do this," Julian pleaded. He apologized again, for his behavior, for his wretched life, for what shouldn't be happening.

"I just need time to think," Tenley said. "You can respect that, can't you?"

"I love you, more than you'll ever know."

There was a long pause and then the phone went dead. He thought at first that the cell had dropped, that some interference had ended the call, but then he felt the silence elongate like a tunnel, with gaining clarity and finality.

The next morning, after a bad sleep, Julian ran to the phone when it rang, hoping it was Tenley.

"Julian, are you alright? You sound winded," Jacob Pearson said.

"No, I'm fine. I was expecting someone else."

"I can call back later."

"No, Jacob. Please fill me in on Delgado."

Pearson sighed. "Well, I have an insider who was able to pluck out some details about the case. Apparently, Delgado, who is technically a minor, has been charged with first degree murder in the death of one Serena Mendoza, who died of a single stab wound to the upper chest. The police feel Delgado is responsible as he was spotted by a witness at the scene of the crime. He has asked for a public defender. That will take time, so the arraignment might be postponed."

"Oh God. It's that bad," Julian said. "Is there anything I can do to help at this point?"

"Short of hiring a defense lawyer, I would say not. You'll probably be able to speak with the boy after the arraignment. Julian, who is he to you?"

"Dino was my best man."

"What? You married again? That's wonderful. By the way, you sound robust, a little different than the last time we spoke. It must be married life and all that...*amour*."

After a lengthy pause Julian said, "Jacob, do you know anyone who will take the case?"

"Pro bono? I doubt it. Law firms tend to limit those kinds of cases and many prohibit it."

"Then find me a cheap lawyer. I need to help the boy."

Pearson laughed. "Cheap? In Boston?"

"Do what you can and have the attorney call me," Julian said.

Pearson said he would, reminding Julian that there would be a hefty retainer in a case of first degree murder. When he hung up, Julian tried to imagine Dino as a murderer. It didn't seem possible and certainly not in character with what he remembered of the boy, a proud, sensitive kid who liked Shakespeare and Gibbon. But then there was the matter of his temper, but even that didn't suggest he could commit something as serious as this offense. He would know more after he spoke with Dino himself.

After lunch Julian drove to the University, for the first time having to park in an unreserved parking space. He knew no one would recognize him. He walked tentatively down the hall toward Tenley's office and knocked on the door. A male voice said, "Come in." It was Harvey, his replacement, and for a few moments he just stared at the man, feeling at once resentful and confused as to why he had taken over Tenley's office.

"May I help you?"

"Actually, I was looking for Professor Harrington."

Harvey smiled, his teeth large and white and perfect, suggesting a recent makeover. "Oh, Tenley is still on her leave of absence. An extended honeymoon, I believe. Is there something *I* can help you with? You're not a student, are you?"

"Hardly," Julian said. "By the way, why are you in her office?"

Harvey's smile vanished as did his friendly composure, and he stood up from the desk, leaning forward slightly, his hands planted firmly on the desktop. "I hardly think that's any of your business, is it? I'd like to see your security ID."

Julian turned, slamming the door behind him. He heard Harvey call after him as he walked down the hallway toward the exit. In his car he was tempted to call one of Tenley's friends. Abruptly, as if an old fog had revisited, he couldn't remember any of their names.

Resigned to the fact that he would have to wait for Tenley to call him, Julian made sure the phone was set at it's highest volume and then drove blindly around town, not paying attention to street signs or direction. He soon found himself on the Massachusetts Turnpike, heading west toward Auburn. The noise of the tires and the passing traffic had a lulling effect on him, calming his nerves some but having no consequence on the sobering notion that he might not see his wife again.

He passed Auburn and then took an exit for Nipmuck State Forest, where he used the restroom and then strolled along one of the hiking paths, it's banks still swollen with snow. There were many hikers, some with backpacks and others with ski suits and walking sticks, all taking advantage of the brisk, sunlit afternoon. Julian sat down on one of the benches leading to a pond and watched as a young couple advanced. The young man was tall and well-built and the girl, wearing an unzipped yellow ski jacket was talking animatedly with her partner. As she passed she slowed down and then looked back at Julian, either as if she pitied the sight of him or perhaps had falsely recognized him. She smiled and went on.

Julian went through the phone's address listings but found no friends belonging to Tenley. He called her cell just to make sure but the call went straight to the recorded greeting. He was too depressed to leave another message and slipped the smartphone back in his pocket.

Had it come to this? Had some frivolous contretemps resulted in a breakup of their marriage? How could Tenley suddenly not love him? It didn't seem possible. He realized that he was overreacting and that his depressive mood was likely the contributor.

Back in his car heading home, Julian suddenly realized, with panicked epiphany, that he didn't have any pictures of Tenley, nor of their wedding.

◆

That evening he hurriedly went through the remaining boxes in his office, pulling out old photos from their clear plastic bags, searching frantically for what seemed like crucial evidence in Julian's mind. He went to his computer and looked through the few photos there. He had never enjoyed taking pictures and, in fact, possessed no camera, but certainly Tenley had taken photos, perhaps with her smartphone. He could not remember her having a regular camera.

The improbable was becoming plausible, settling in Julian's stomach like a cold weight. He went to the bedroom and found Heather's card on the table. He fell back on the bed. At least that part of his life had happened; the proof was there. He fumbled with Tenley's chest of drawers and found her clothing, underwear, socks, pantyhose and a drawer full of sweaters. He almost wept with relief. The closet revealed blouses, jackets, pant suits and coats. He looked at his wedding band, turning it slowly, and breathed a long sigh of relief.

Why had he even doubted? Angered by his overreaction and his ridiculous suspicion, Julian went to his desk in the den. He had to give Tenley her space and trust in the strong love they had for one another. He had to occupy himself. Tired as he was, he placed the old typewriter on the desk, rolled in a fresh sheet of paper, ready to continue with his novel. His hands felt huge for the antiquated machine and he wondered how he had ever managed before.

Over the next two hours, Julian was able to produce two new pages for the story but when he reread them, the dialogue seemed stale and his main character's narrative non-descriptive and rote.

It was almost eleven o'clock. Julian grabbed a fresh beer from the kitchen and, still dressed, lay down in bed. For lack of any other reading material, he'd found an old copy of an AARP magazine featuring an attractive actress who had just turned sixty-five. He read the article, interested in a special diet the actress had been on for the past twenty years. She looked hardly a day over forty.

In Julian's mind the telephone rang and before he realized that it was actually real and coming from his jacket pocket in the living room, four rings had elapsed. He took a deep breath and answered the call.

"Julian?"

"Thank God it's you, Tenley!"

She was sobbing lightly. "I love you, sweetheart, and I'm sorry I behaved in that way. I've had the worst cramps and I guess my hormones were raging."

"I love you too," Julian said. "Please forgive me for doubting you."

"Doubting me?" she said, perplexed.

"I mean, doubting our love."

"You doubted our love?" Tenley said. Her sniffling had stopped.

"No, that's not exactly what I mean. I suppose I doubted that fate would bring us back together again."

"I love you, Julian. I'm your wife, and this has nothing to do with fate. Why are you acting that way?"

"Please forget what I said. It's been an exhausting day. I've been worrying about you and when you didn't answer my calls, I thought that maybe something had happened to you."

"I know, darling. I should have known it would upset you and make you worry. Forgive me. I promise that I won't ever coddle you again, I mean, crowd you in, telling you what you should or should not do."

"No," Julian said. "Please coddle me all you want. I love when you do it. I really do. When are you coming home?"

Tenley said that it was too late for her to leave now, that she was in bed at her friend Susan's apartment. She would return home the next morning. She said she planned to cook Julian a very special dinner, that they had to celebrate their reunion and the end of their foolishness.

They ended with more expressions of love and promises that neither would get upset again. Afterward Julian sat there with his beer, realizing how foolish he had been to entertain such a notion. How could he have let himself believe that Tenley wasn't real, that their relationship had never happened? It had been such a strange feeling, like he'd awakened from a long dream and realized people in that dream were not real, that the drama in the dream had never happened.

It had not been the best of days, beginning with the news about Dino, who would probably be incarcerated for the rest of his life, and then his escape from the city and the absurd reaction about Tenley.

The beer soon relaxed him. He finished reading the article and decided to shave and take a bath, in case Tenley arrived early next morning. He turned on the bathwater, took the shaving cream and razor from the medicine cabinet. When he saw his face in the mirror he froze. Without taking the next breath, he grabbed a hand towel and rubbed at the glass. The face looking back at him had changed. His temples had grayed, his hair had thinned and had turned somewhat coarse, and his gaze lacked the sharpness of his earlier youth. Not realizing that he had been holding his breath, Julian finally exhaled deeply. He continued to stare.

The bathwater was still running fifteen minutes later, water cascading over the edge of the tub, encroaching Julian's feet, creeping across the beige tile floor like a menacing tide.

Chapter Eighteen

It felt like he'd contracted a fatal disease, and the feeling only grew worse when Tenley saw him the next morning. She wasn't as startled as he thought she might be. She kissed him, her hands cupping the back of his head, and then they sat down on the bed.

"You look distinguished," Tenley said. "You're not really that much older."

"How much older am I?" Julian asked, already guessing that he'd aged about ten years.

"Just a few years, sweetheart. You're actually more attractive than ever. Men get away with that sort of thing while we girls have to spend our time covering up the years. You're not seventy, that's for sure."

"Thanks a lot," Julian said, seeing no humor in the statement.

Tenley snuggled close. "We both knew this was coming and we're just going to have to deal with it. Julian, we love each other, we're married and will spend the rest of our lives together, *for better or for worse*, remember?"

"I suppose I'll have to get another driver's license and then update it the next time around."

Tenley smiled, rubbing at his back. "You're handsome, sexy and the person I passionately love."

Soon she was unbuttoning Julian's shirt and then slipping out of her blouse with a playful but determined look her eyes. They hugged and Julian was instantly aroused by her fragrance, a medley of perfume, body heat and urgent passion. When they made love, all practical matters left Julian, all worries and circumstances of fate, all doubts. Afterward he lay there, his head upon her breast, listening to her runaway heart, which could have been a fluttering bird or the awakening of a powerful presence that would soon leap into his own heart.

◆

The afternoon brought a profound sense of acceptance to Julian. He returned to the mirror several times and decided that the changes weren't that obtrusive, that indeed he had overreacted. Their passionate lovemaking had underscored his remaining vitality and the deep, unshakable love he had for Tenley.

He wrote several pages of his novel and then, feeling successful, made out of list of things he wanted to share with Tenley, a *bucket list* of places he wanted to visit, small adventures to experience, all he had been either too young or too old to enjoy during the past six months.

Julian's passport was still valid and the photo had been taken when he was sixty-two. They decided that, with some senior charm, he would pass customs with little problem. Tenley's passport had expired, but they could expedite the application by paying additional government fees.

They planned to start with Paris, *the City of Light*, where they would spend a long, formal honeymoon and then travel on to Rome and Greece. Although Tenley wasn't exactly enthusiastic about the idea, Julian talked about hiring a sailboat and its captain and sailing along the coastal Mediterranean.

Within a few days, Tenley's passport arrived. They booked a flight on Air France, reserving two seats in business class. They made reservations at the Hôtel Le Bristol in Saint-Honoré, which Julian knew to be one of the best hotels in Paris. Together they shopped for new travel clothing, purchasing suitcases and some good jewelry for Tenley.

It was early November and would be cold in Paris, so they bought new overcoats, scarves and shoes. Tenley had her hair done, toning it with darker shades of blonde and having it cut in a short pixie style. She looked beautiful, Julian thought, and a bit French.

Julian bought a new digital camera, certain to document all their experiences and to take many shots of Tenley. They would probably be gone for a month, and Julian informed Leighton about their leave and asked if he would be so kind as to keep his mail for the duration. He tipped the man handsomely.

Julian called his financial advisor and told him he would need approximately $50,000 in extra cash. His assets were fine and he wouldn't require selling stocks or dipping into liquid cash. Above that amount, Julian deposited $10,000 in Tenley's personal checking. They hadn't yet ordered new checks with both names on the account. Julian had amended his will to include Tenley, who he wished to receive two-thirds of his holdings, the rest going to Carolyn.

Tenley extended her leave of absence at work, saying she would be back at the University after the holidays. She seemed more excited than Julian had ever known her to be, parading in front of him in her new attire, putting on newly-purchased hats and shawls, looking ever more the *belle-fille* who would capture Paris. She checked out places in the city she wanted to visit: the Eiffel Tower, the Left Bank, the *Champs-Élysées*, *Notre-Dame* and the Louvre, where she couldn't wait to see the Mona Lisa and Venus de Milo. She wanted to stroll along the Seine River and watch the artists at work.

The evening before they were set to leave, Dino's attorney called and explained the retainer fee and how he planned to handle the defense case. His name was Trout and he talked with a pronounced Bostonian accent. Julian asked how he planned to enter a plea.

"Dino, your boy, says he's innocent, that he knows who killed the girl," Trout said. "But I advised him take a plea if the DA offered one in exchange for a lesser offense, perhaps manslaughter, a crime of passion. But who am I? Just his lawyer, his best chance for a shorter prison term..."

"I gather Dino didn't accept your legal advice."

"Thick head, that's what he is," Trout said. "He's costing you plenty if we go not guilty...you know that, don't you?"

"I trust that you have won more cases than you've lost and that you will hire an investigator to extract the real facts of the crime. Mr. Trout, I trust that you will win freedom for Dino."

The conversation was cut short when Trout said he had another incoming call and that he would get back to Julian, who immediately wondered whether Pearson had made the right choice in recommending him.

"You're doing everything you can for Dino," Tenley said as they ate their evening meal in the kitchen. "No one would do that for someone they hardly knew. I am so proud of your dedication and your selfless concern for others. Do you think Dino's telling the truth?"

"I think Dino is telling the truth as he knows it. I also believe he has a rough edge to his character." Julian said, recalling the fight the boy had had over Serena. "But he's a tough, intelligent kid...and he likes Shakespeare."

There was some more last-minute packing and as they lay in bed while Tenley was practicing her rudimentary French, Julian read the instruction book to his new Nikon and then took some practice shots of the end of the bed and several of Tenley with her glasses on, looking quite professorial as she practiced some essential French phrases.

"*Voulez-vous coucher avec moi?*" Julian said, remembering the old Rod Stewart song.

Tenley flipped through her book and said, "*Pas en ce moment, mon amour.*" She then laughed and gave Julian the longest hug. "Julian, you have made me so happy. I feel like a princess who's about to visit her kingdom. I don't think I'll sleep a wink tonight."

Thirty minutes later, Julian gently lifted off her glasses and closed the open book, pulling the covers to her head. He got out of bed and went to the other side with his camera. He wanted to capture her face as she slept and he took several shots, looking at them in the LCD screen. They were perfect and all the evidence he would ever need.

◆

The flight early the next morning was a good one, although Julian felt a little cramped even in their business-class seats. Tenley had a window seat and stared intently outside the new 747 even as it cruised at 41,000 feet. This was her first transcontinental flight, and Julian could tell she was a bit apprehensive about flying over the ocean. She had listened attentively to the steward as he described how to use the life vests in case of a water landing, an improbable situation, Julian knew, that any enlightened person knew would prove disastrous.

They arrived at Charles de Gaulle at a little past two in the afternoon under a cold and cindery sky. Tenley had not slept aboard and was tired from the flight. She told Julian that she wanted to take a nap before they went out to dinner that night.

The junior suite at the Hôtel Le Bristol was grandiose. The rooms were spacious and elegantly furnished with mahogany and cherry wood furniture, an easy blend of Louis Quatorze and contemporary styles. There was a sectioned-off sitting room with couch, table lamps and an ivory-painted coffee table, a huge gilded mirror above the settee. The bedroom was enormous, with a king bed, elegant dressers and an antique-white dressing table for Tenley. There was light gray carpet throughout the suite, and large floral drapes hung from two large windows, one that opened onto a shallow balcony overlooking *Rue du Faubourg Saint-Honoré*.

Tenley sank back into one of the Louis XIV wingback chairs,

obviously exhausted from the trip, and closed her eyes.

"Oh Julian," she said, "I don't feel like a princess but rather a queen." She looked over at Julian who was standing at the window. "And I have my prince charming and my king all in one."

"It's perfect," Julian said. "Everything I ever imagined." He walked by the settee and glanced in the mirror, not with conceit but with hope that the trip had not aged him further. It hadn't.

Tenley was obviously suffering from jet lag. Julian worried that it might be her heart and asked if it would be better to have dinner delivered to their suite. She agreed and while Julian looked over the menu and then ordered, she drew a hot bath.

They ate challandais duck for two with creamy polenta with fresh corn and roasted figs with cinnamon sticks. Julian had picked out a Montes Alpha Pinot Noir, a perfect pair with the duck, he thought. For dessert they had caramel flan with cookie sticks. The meal was served on Pillivuyt Porcelain plates, with fine silverware and crystal wine glasses. The man from the hotel restaurant who served them had brought a single red rose in a silver-fluted vase. Julian looked across the small round dining table as the single candle flame flickered faintly in Tenley's eyes. She had eaten most of the meal but she looked weary, her face a bit pale and her eyes not quite as bright as when she'd boarded the flight in Boston.

After dinner, they watched an old *All In the Family* episode dubbed in French on television. Archie Bunker had an odd nasal voice, which seemed to falsify the true character. Tenley groaned every time he spoke. Julian said it sounded like Archie had changed his sexual orientation.

It stormed later that night, first with heat lightning that caused stuttered images to dance in the living room, elongating the furniture with spectral shadows, which made it look like the furniture was creeping along the floor. Rain and thunder followed and then a rousting wind that made the window frames creak.

Tenley went to bed early, fatigued by the flight and late dinner. Julian peeked in on her fifteen minutes later and saw that she was fast asleep. Standing by the balcony window, he opened the sheers and looked out at the Parisian landscape, across the dark jagged tops of buildings, the domes, the irregular stove pipes, the towering spires and the lights of the stretching avenues. He could just make out the Seine and beyond that the brightly-lit structure of the Eiffel Tower.

The nightlife was palpable, and he could imagine the cafés along the Champs-Élysées, young men and women sitting at tables under red and pinstripe awnings, chattering about the passing storm, their feelings and aspirations yet to be realized. He wanted to be among them, their youth and their dreams and to linger forever in the inveigling Parisian *joie de vivre.*

Julian had once visited Paris to attend a mathematics conference decades ago. He'd brought Carolyn to brighten her mood following the recent death of her mother. He recalled how enchanted she had been with the city and how, indeed, it had lifted her spirits. She was eleven then, moody and starting her road to the autonomy that would shape the rest of her life. It was no surprise to Julian that she traveled to this city as often as she did now during her bustling career. He remembered how they'd walked through the Tuileries Garden and watched the young boys sailing their toy boats in the pond. She'd asked, quite out of the blue, "Daddy, how old are you?"

Silly, Julian thought now, that he would recall such a trivial event. He missed those days as a single parent, a stuffy professor trying to be part mother and part fatherly disciplinarian. He wondered how he'd managed it, working full time hours but always managing to be home and have supper with Carolyn. The part-time nanny had been his saving grace, taking over when he left for his office, making sure she caught the bus to school each morning, cleaning the house and preparing dinner by the time Julian returned. He tried to recall the au pair's name, a young woman from Bolivia, but couldn't.

In spite of his new life with Tenley, he now missed those ordinary days, the routine and the parenting. Carolyn had grown up to be a head-strong woman with all the beauty of her mother. She was intelligent, obviously independent but always on the go. He'd often thought he wouldn't live to be a grandfather, and sometimes he blamed her for her indecisions about marriage.

For a few moments he missed her terribly, not what she had become in her career but her days as a bright, inquisitive young girl. He did not look forward to seeing her anytime soon. But he didn't know why.

◆

Early the next morning there was a rap at the door and before Julian could reach it, a plump woman wearing a loose flowery dress and white Victorian maid hat let herself in.

"Bonjour, Monsieur et Madame," she said with a broad smile, entering the bedroom, surprising Tenley, who pulled the covers up to her chin, and set down in the middle of the bed a large wicker breakfast platter. The aroma of coffee and bacon and a faint hint of parsley and onions wafted about her. She handed Julian a copy of *Le Figaro,* the latest morning newspaper. Turning for the door, the woman said, "Bonne journée."

Still sleepy, Tenley opened the platter's cover. There were two omelets filled with melted cheese and asparagus, thick slices of bacon and fresh scalloped tomatoes filled with hollandaise sauce and parsley. Fresh coffee and two buttery croissants with slabs of butter were on separate small plates. Small glasses of orange and tomato juice, the latter with celery sticks, sat next to them.

Tenley seemed famished as she sunk her teeth into the warm sweet flakes of the croissant. "Julian," she said, "now this is pure French and such a lovely way to start the day."

Julian agreed and added, "I've never been in a hotel where a concierge lets herself in like that."

"Only in Paris. I think it's charming," Tenley said.

◆

They visited the Louvre, the Eiffel Tower, Notre Dame, Sainte-Chapelle, the Tuileries, and strolled in the Bois de Boulogne. The days were perfect: bright sun, cool temperatures and the autumnal air of a city alive with the fragrances of food, human toil and people in love. They ate at the best restaurants, and one evening took a horse-drawn carriage through the winding cobblestone streets of Montmartre. Tenley wanted to visit the great Palace of Versailles. Julian rented a car and they drove through parts of the wine country on back roads to get there. After visiting the palace they walked through the expansive gardens with their towering chestnut trees, colorful flower beds, sculptures and fountains. They remained there the entire day, eating a late dinner back at a café in Montmartre.

"I don't want this to end," Tenley said, after biting into her omelet baguette and wiping her lips with the red linen napkin.

"We could buy a place here or at least a pied–à–terre in the city," Julian said. He could imagine living here, among the French people and their lively culture. Boston seemed so far away now, and the thought of them living in the dreary apartment, especially in the winter snow, seemed a dismal alternative.

"Seriously?" Tenley said.

"Well, you'd have to give up your post at the University..."

"I could teach here, Julian. There are plenty of established universities in Paris. I'm sure it wouldn't be hard for me to find a position. I'd do it in a heartbeat if that's what you want. But what would you do?"

"Finish my novel and then buy a beret and paint along the Seine."

"I think you *are* serious," Tenley said, taking a sip of the fine table wine.

"Any and everything is possible."

They would never talk about it again. They spent two weeks in the City of Light and then boarded a flight for Rome. Tenley thought she had spotted Carolyn at the airport and Julian had acted like a juvenile, dashing into a nearby restroom until the coast was clear.

Rome was attractive in a different sort of way. The city seemed old, untidy and depleted. The weather was not good, which added to the drabness. Everything seemed ancient and crumbling, especially the Coliseum, which appeared to have deteriorated even more during its long ancient history.

They visited all the tourist spots and then took to the road, driving through small towns and villas and eating great food at small roadside restaurants. Tenley's health was now robust, and she seemed to have the energy of a teenager, at times pulling Julian along when he felt the need to sleep in for the day. It was unlike him, and he attributed his fatigue to the hustle and bustle of traveling.

Spending two days in bed, Julian felt rejuvenated and ready to explore again. He felt cossetted by Tenley, who made sure he was getting plenty of rest before each jaunt through the ancient city. She made sure that they ate three meals a day and took time to relax in a café or park bench following long walks. Although Julian felt overly coddled, he didn't complain, even when Tenley seemed to be giving him unnecessary orders. He was scared that if he spoke up, she would leave him again.

They rented another car and drove to Ostia on the Mediterranean coast. They bought swimsuits and sat in the sun on the beach, which was largely vacant because of the season. The temperature was in the mid-sixties and the water still warm enough for a hasty dip. Tenley looked stunning in her white bikini, her curved shape and smooth skin that of a woman half her age, Julian thought. They dove into the clear blue-green water and swam out a ways, splashing at each other on the swim back. Afterward, they sat on the beach blanket, huddled under a massive Turkish towel, feeling the combined warmth of their bodies.

They ate at Don Pepe, a small but quaint eatery with Moroccan arches and beamed ceilings. They shared a huge platter of fresh paella, drank sangria, and felt pot-bellied when they finished. Tenley said she'd lost her figure after one meal and that she would have to starve herself for a week. Julian had drank too much of the sweet wine and felt tired and wondered if he would manage the drive back. Tenley must have noticed.

"I'll drive," she said and then held the door open for Julian, making sure his seatbelt was secure.

"Thank you, Miss Nightingale," Julian quipped and reached across the console and held Tenley's hand.

Soon the sound of the tires and the gentle rumble of the car lulled him to sleep. He awoke several times, only to fall asleep again. He had a dream about Tenley. They were back at the beach, and it was a stilled night, the light of the moon laying a lustrous footpath across the surface of the water. Tenley rose slowly from the blanket and turned her ear to the sea as if she had heard a curious sound. Julian watched as she made her way down to the water, moving effortlessly, as if gliding on a cushion of air. She stopped and looked back him and then stepped onto the shimmering trail of moonlight, slowly walking out on its surface. Once she stopped and called out to Julian. "It beckons...it beckons," she said. He ran down to the water's edge, plunged in and began swimming desperately to reach her. It appeared that Tenley had stopped to wait for him, and when he arrived he tread water, looking up at her towering and gossamer presence. Out of nowhere, lightning struck the water and in that instant Tenley slipped down, disappearing beneath the surface. He dove down to reach her again and again but each time his hands felt nothing in the dark, frigid water. He let out a long anguished scream and abruptly awoke from the dream.

Tenley had pulled over to the shoulder of the road and was looking over at Julian as if he were a stranger or a ghost.

"God, it was horrible," he gasped.

"You were flailing your arms and one time grabbed at the steering wheel," she said. "And that torturous howl... I thought you were possessed."

"I'm sorry. It was such a real nightmare." Julian looked down and saw that his hands were trembling. "I could use a drink," he said.

"Do you want to talk about it?"

Julian closed his eyes, trying to will the memory away. "No," he said, still trembling, wondering whether even a shot of bourbon would begin to have an effect on his composure.

They drove on, Julian's eyes wide open as he feared that closing them, even for a second, would plunge him back into the nightmare. Tenley glanced over several times and reached over to rub his hand.

They arrived back at the hotel past midnight. In bed, Tenley asked him again whether he wanted to talk and he shook his head. She kissed him, rolled over and was asleep in short time.

Julian allowed himself to think about the dream, to revisit the horror of losing Tenley to the dark, hungry sea. He'd had bad dreams before nothing as portentous as this. He felt certain that it was sign that something terrible was going to happen. And then, feeling childish about it, he picked up the camera manual, flipping through its pages. He was overreacting, he thought, opening to a page with the camera's diagram.

It occurred to him suddenly that he had failed to bring the Nikon along on their trip.

Chapter Nineteen

Julian's aging was much more pronounced by the end of their stay in Rome. He could see how his hands were swollen at the knuckles. The skin sagged under his arms and he was slightly pot-bellied, with wrinkles under his eyes and more pronounced jowls. His hair had thinned even more, balding slightly at the top of his head. His eyes looked distant and pale.

Tenley had noticed the changes long before Julian had, but said nothing, trying not to worry him. But the transformation became more evident as each day passed. She would never tell him that he looked almost as old as when he'd retired from the University. He'd lost his broad shoulders and some of his height, and showed a slight stoop when he walked. He refused to go out, feeling guilty for having ruined their adventures, and preferred to stand at the tall window overlooking the fountained piazza.

They forewent further travels abroad and in the first week of December took the first flight back to Boston. Tenley pretended that she was no longer interested in traveling, that she missed the city.

A depressed mood descended on Julian a few days after they were back in the apartment. He shut himself in the den, refusing to come out for meals and sleep, forcing Tenley to knock frequently at the locked door. She would leave plates of food and drink in front of the door and watched, relieved, when it opened long enough for Julian to scoop up the meals and take them inside.

There seemed to be no middle age for Julian. He had gone from a manly youth to a decrepit form of himself. It seemed unfair and almost cruel that all this had happened. He had known the time would come but never imagined how accelerated age would feel, on the cusp of such magnificent youth.

Without telling Tenley, he restarted the medication and vitamins, and tried to exercise in the den, performing pull-ups and leg stretches. He took a mirror into his office and constantly looked for signs that his aging had slowed. He rubbed cream on his face and his arms. He worked the muscles of his cheeks and grimaced repeatedly to exercise his jowls and his neck muscles.

When he saw Tenley he would cast his eyes down, as if to avoid her eyes and the stark truth he would see in them. She gave him his space and kept her conversation restrained, not wanting to upset him.

She'd taken another leave of absence from work, fearing Julian might do something rash in her absence. She took over the bills and performed the necessary chores of the day, allowing Julian his privacy.

Julian spent his days ruminating about his erstwhile youth and the various identities and lifestyles he'd enjoyed. He thought about Claudia and, of course, Heather, with whom he'd felt the most intense infatuation and carefreeness. Selfishly, he missed those days and longed for the impossible again.

He began to think about his relationship with Tenley. His marriage seemed fake, altered by a cruel fate, and he wanted her to enjoy her youth without wasting her time with an aging old professor. He loved her but didn't want to tie her down anymore. She had a life to live, people to meet, experiences to enjoy and perhaps a more suitable relationship to look forward to. He wondered if she would agree to a divorce, perhaps an annulment. He thought about escaping in the middle of the night, taking only a suitcase and formally leaving her the apartment and his Beemer, along with a sizable amount of his investments. He would live in cheap motels and take on a new identity. He would wile away his remaining years alone and incognito.

He tried to read but couldn't concentrate. His attempt to return to his novel was a fiasco and he found himself tearing up sheets of failed writing, stuffing them into the wastebasket with disgust.

He had no grandchildren to cheer him up, no real friends other than Tenley, whom he still loved but felt was a part of a generation that he was no longer privy to anymore. He no longer feared Carolyn's presence in his life. He longed for her childhood days, their walks, the hockey games, her soccer meets, their travels and mostly their talks. Back then, father and daughter were the best of friends.

He thought of his own childhood growing up in the huge house on Franklin Street in Waterfront. His father was a very successful banker and property investor, and the two boys had lived privileged childhoods and had attended the best of schools. His mother had been an alcoholic and had abandoned her maternal duties in favor of nights on the town, drunken parties and social affairs, where she often made a fool of herself, eventually staining the family name. His parents divorced when Julian was ten, and when he was old enough to seek reconciliation with his mother, news came of her death in an institute in California. He vaguely remembered one bright period during his boyhood when the family was a true family, his mother and father in love, and he close to his brother. As an adolescent Julian drew away from his father, and on one rebellious occasion blamed him for his mother's alcoholism. They were not close after that and only corresponded by mail and postcards. His father died in his early forties of a brain aneurysm, a distant but wealthy man. Julian had shared his sizable inheritance with his brother, investing most of it in mutual funds and stocks. He had done well financially and had achieved his aspiration to become a professor and teach mathematics. His only regret during his career was that he had failed to nourish enduring friendships.

Life was not always fair, Julian thought, but why had it come to this: a cruel and suffering fate? He wondered when dementia would set in again and if this time around it would be worse. He couldn't put Tenley through it, not again.

Many people in life had flirted with the notion of suicide, and Julian was no exception. He'd thought of it once when Elizabeth died, in a moment of desperate loneliness, and now again as his depression worsened.

He considered seeing a priest but soon that idea seemed improbable, given his bad experience during confession. All seemed inescapable, cruel and utterly hopeless. His life had become a prison with no possibility of freedom.

One night he had a dream. He could only recall that he was in a squeaky bed in a small room, perhaps in a hospital, and there was someone bending over him. "Julian...Julian?" she said. "Are you there...can you hear me?" Her voice was so insistent and the words so repetitive, Julian could feel a small rage gathering inside him, swelling his throat and flushing his face. He felt paralyzed and unable to speak. He was trying to tell the person something important, something so crucial that his life was at stake.

When he awoke early that morning he felt as if a heavy chainmail had been lifted from his body. "I'm here," he said softly to answer the woman in the dream. All seemed calm and as it should be. There was no anger, no desperation, no guilt, only a pacifying sense that he had reclaimed himself. He noticed that he had been crying, for his eyes and cheeks were moist and he had a salty taste in is mouth. He lay back and clasped his hands behind his head, and only pleasant thoughts filled his mind.

He dressed and opened the door to his den, stepping out as if from a dark dungeon, feeling the sunlight pouring in through crevices of the living room draperies. He pulled the curtains wide and for a few moments luxuriously indulged in the welcoming warmth of the sunlight.

He opened the door to the bedroom and found the bed made and Tenley nowhere in sight. In the foyer he saw that she had left him a note. His heart raced for a moment until he read the familiar cursive handwriting. Tenley said she was shopping for food and would be back by noon.

Julian took a hot bath and then went to shave, pausing as he looked into the mirror, for the first time without apprehension. The image staring back at him was his former self, but he noticed a placid warmth in his eyes and a look of benevolence on his face. He had grown a coarse beard, which he immediately liked. He began shaping it with spots of lather and the razor, and when he had finished he thought he looked a little like Sean Connery in his later years.

His depression had lifted, his mind now free of the dark clouds of uncertainty and apprehension. He forgave himself for having even considered ending his life, a life that now seemed full of new promise and acceptance. He felt terrible, though, for having put Tenley through it all. He was surprised that she hadn't left him. He would make it up to her by moving back into the bedroom, by sharing his time and the new ideas he had for adventure. They would take a cross country trip, visit his brother in California, drive up the Oregon coast and explore British Columbia. He would never again spend his days sequestered in his dingy office, wasting the precious years he had left.

He thought about going to Mel's gym and working out (and made a promise to himself that he would recommit himself to daily workouts) but realized that this wouldn't be fair to Tenley. Perhaps they could exercise together.

In the kitchen Julian sipped his coffee and then decided he would surprise Tenley with a fine lunch. He would cook her a ham omelet with cheese and chives, her favorite, and foie gras on toast, with slices of tomato aspic. He would open a chilled bottle of Riesling, and they would reminisce about their adventures abroad.

By 11:45 that morning everything was ready: the food, the wine and Julian's renewed mien and attitude. He turned on the radio to a classics station that was playing a violin concerto by Brahms. Then he sat down in the living room, facing the foyer, ready to greet Tenley as she came through door.

At a quarter past one the telephone rang. It was Tenley, and she sounded surprised. She told Julian that she hadn't expected him to pick up.

"Are you okay, Julian?

"I fixed you lunch." The words came out suddenly, sounding cross, and they were not what Julian intended. "Yes, I'm fine. I was just worried about you."

"I'm sorry, Julian." Her words seemed abrupt, stated as if they were a prelude to some further admission.

"When are you coming home?" Julian said.

The pause that followed formed a lump in his throat. Finally she began, "I was going to leave you a message that I would be out for the day. Do you remember Harvey? He died this morning of a massive heart attack. They asked me to come back to my post...in fact, they didn't just ask. I think it was a veiled threat that if I didn't return my position would be in jeopardy. In the past month two professors left for more lucrative opportunities, and now with Harvey gone... Julian, I have to go back. I'm there now, looking through the semester's new curricula. We can talk more about it this evening."

"Sure," Julian said, feeling both disappointed and a bit selfish for even considering that she would surrender her career because of him. "I only want what's best for you. I've put you through a lot these past few days, and you deserve a distraction. "We'll work it out."

"You sound much better. Is the depression better?"

Julian said it was and apologized for locking himself away. Tenley told him that she would be home by six and was sorry for missing lunch.

"I love you, Tenley. Very much."

"I love you too."

Julian sat down at the table and ate part of his omelet. He wrapped Tenley's plate and placed it, along with the unopened wine, in the refrigerator. He listened to some Mozart and decided he would go for a workout at the gym, now that he knew Tenley would be out for the day. He had put on weight during their travels in Europe and decided that a good sweat would do him good.

In the bedroom he searched for his navy sweatpants and shirt, rummaging through all the chest of drawers. He opened the closet and checked the shelves. Also missing was the athletic bag with his water bottles and towels.

Maybe Tenley had put them somewhere or perhaps given them away, believing that Julian would no longer have use for them. He would stop by a nearby sporting store and purchase new ones before heading off to Mel's.

The temperature was in the thirties but there was a warm sun. The brightness was almost blinding, the colors more vibrant than he had ever noticed before. Even in winter, Boston looked rejuvenated, as if the last mantel of snow had melted away the season's ashen cloak, bringing an illusion of newness to the streets and glistening brownstones.

After leaving the sporting store, where he also had to purchase new tennis shoes, he drove straight to the gym. He found Mel behind the counter looking at a copy of *Sports Illustrated*.

"May I help you?" Mel said, barely looking up from the magazine.

"Hey, Mel," Julian said, smiling. "I need a good workout today."

The man looked up. "Are you a member?"

"Mel, it's me. Professor Landon. I've been coming here for years. Don't you recognize me?" Julian fumbled through his wallet for his membership ID, but he couldn't find it.

"Let's see," Mel said, turning toward the computer keyboard. "Is that Landon with an *e*? First name?"

"Julian. Julian Landon with an *o*. Mel, I can't believe you don't recognize me. I've grown a beard...maybe that's why."

Mel gave Julian a long, vague look, and then shook his head slowly. "How long since your last visit, Mr. Landon?"

"Well, it's been a few months. Surely you remember my nephew Brad, who spoke with you for certain reasons. He wanted an ID and he paid you a good sum for it."

Mel looked offended, almost confrontational. "Listen, I don't know what you're talking about and I *don't* make IDs. Now if you want to open an account with us, I can help you with that."

Julian wondered whether Mel was suffering from premature dementia or that he'd had an accident and injured his brain. He had known the man for decades. They had become casual friends, Mel often sharing with Julian many of his romantic escapades and his dreams to one day travel the world.

Finally he said to Mel, "I'm sorry. I'm obviously mistaken. But thanks for your time."

Outside, he found himself jumping to strange, improbable conclusions. He began to doubt his own memory and, for a fleeting moment, his own past. And then it seemed all so ridiculous. It wasn't his fault that Mel appeared to have a memory lapse. All that mattered was that he and Tenley were real and that their relationship would endure.

He gave the storefront one long glance and then walked across the street to his car. Inside, he opened up his wallet and looked through his credit cards and his original license. Beside the photo of his daughter there was a picture of Tenley he had taken before their departure for Paris. There, tucked in a slot with his AARP card, was the membership card to Mel's Gym. He was tempted to return to the gym and present it to Mel, but the idea soon felt trivial, serving little purpose.

On a whim, he drove through Waterfront and looked for the house in which he had grown up. He found it, recognizing the large columns outside and the brick steps leading to the portico. He hadn't driven by in years and the sight of it, like the membership card, was an affirmation of past and present circumstances.

He visited Roxbury Latin School, where he'd attended high school, and remembered good times there and the old ways of youth. He recalled a boy named Ashton in the ninth grade who became his best friend and with whom he'd indulged in the benign delinquencies of adolescence. Ashton went on to Harvard, aspiring to be a lawyer, but they'd never kept in touch. And then there were memories of his first love when he was a senior, with a senator's daughter named Mary, who taught him the prudence of manners with the distaff side, as well as the *French kiss*. Where were they now? he thought with a touch of yearning.

It was the old, more formal youth that didn't exist today. It glowed faintly now with fondness and gratitude and lingering detachment. Would he remember his life as Brad in the same manner as he aged?

That evening after dinner, Tenley talked about her plans. Julian was supportive, telling her how important it was to keep her career going and that he needed to be more serious about his writing. He shared with her his plans to finish the novel and then begin work on a textbook. He too needed to keep his mind challenged.

Julian told her about his strange experience at Mel's. She had no explanation for the man's behavior. He asked her about the missing bag and his gym clothes. She said she didn't know but that it was possible she'd discarded them by accident one day while cleaning out the apartment. He apologized again for his depressed stupor and said he knew it would never happen again.

"It's okay, Julian. You don't have to apologize. Look at what you have been through in the past few weeks. The important thing is that you are stable again."

"Yes," Julian said, uncertain as to why she had used the word *stable*. It seemed a term better suited for someone who was ill.

He told her that he was thinking of traveling again and about his plans for driving across country and up the Oregon coast. "We could do it during the summer when the school year is out," he said.

Tenley smiled but said nothing, seeming indifferent about his idea. Julian decided she was probably weary following their travels in Europe and that her concentration now was on the school year and what lay ahead.

In bed later that evening, Julian turned to Tenley and said, "It's so good to be me once again."

"You silly old codfish," she said. "You've always been you."

◆

As the days passed, Tenley returned to her full schedule at the University and Julian resumed work on *Odessa's Feud*, this time with a reinforced determination to finish it. He got up early each morning to have breakfast with Tenley and then would have dinner waiting for her when she returned from work, which was sometimes late in the evening when she attended meetings. He wrote half the day and then went for his daily walk. The exercise helped the growing arthritis in his knee and gave him time to prepare the next chapter in his book. Sometimes he would rest on a park bench and watch the squirrels scurrying across the frozen grass. The cold didn't seem to bother him, and he felt that it was good for his general stamina. He thought a lot about Tenley and how important she was in his life. Although their relationship seemed less passionate, he loved her deeply and shared a genuine friendship with her. He had married the woman of his dreams and, although their age difference was substantial now, he felt secure that their marriage would last and certain that he would live out his life together.

Julian had only a few chapters to complete, which he did so in record time. In less than two weeks the first draft of *Odessa's Feud* lay stacked on his desk. He thought the novel was decent but needed some polishing before earning the title of a completed work. He planned to submit the manuscript to an old editor friend who had helped him publish several articles for the American Mathematical Society.

Tenley was proud of his accomplishment and urged him to continued writing. They celebrated at one of their favorite restaurants, and Julian amused himself with thoughts of literary success. He already had an idea for his second work and had begun to structure the storyline during long walks.

Immersed in her teaching, Tenley worked long days and sometimes on weekends, but always managed to spend dinners with Julian. On days off they went to plays and an occasional movie and often walked along Harborwalk, bundled against the cold with ski jackets, mufflers and gloves. They talked about the more aesthetic qualities of life, its simplicity and privileges, discussing metaphysical points of view. Tenley believed in reincarnation but in a fanciful way, saying she planned to return as a butterfly or some species of bird. Julian told her that he too had considered the idea of reincarnation.

They hardly argued, and on the occasional nights they made love, the passion was subdued for Julian. Tenley liked having her back rubbed and certainly more foreplay. While the old sexuality in Julian seemed dulled, there were infrequent times when he forgot his age and the limits of his libido and was able to bring himself to climax. He would watch Tenley's face during those times, how her neck arched and her spine stiffened and her mouth opened roundly and shut, as if unwilling to release the sexual joy in her body. On those occasions Julian would be the last to fall asleep, choosing instead to gaze at his wife's perfect body in the prime of womanhood, breathing softly, her breasts still swollen and flushed with arousal.

In a peculiar and relative way, it was the best of times in Julian's life. Youth and younger manhood had its frenetic edge, its defiance, its lust and its flaunting sense of eternity, but at this genuine age life for Julian was far more predictable and real. He appreciated that aging had returned him to a more mundane way of living. He enjoyed listening to music, classical reading and times outside where cheerful birds and small creatures reaffirmed his belief that life was a blessing.

If he thought about death, he did so without fear, remorse or regret. He only wished to live a long life, to be with Tenley as long as providence provided him that opportunity. He could not imagine her ever growing old or having to deal with the inequities of aging. If she did live to a ripe old age, she would age gracefully, with dignity and without the spurious notion that youth could be prolonged by artificial means.

Julian's fear of Carolyn's return failed to raise the level of panic it once had only weeks past. He was unable to reconcile whatever lingering discomfort he felt by her impending intrusion, but he knew that it hadn't interfered with his deep love for his daughter. He wanted to see her, despite the vague risk he sensed that might be involved with that inevitable reunion. It had been a month since she had last attempted to call him.

Julian Landon, despite his advancing age, took refuge in the belief that he had lived a long, fulfilling, albeit strange, life.

PART III

"Everything comes to pass, nothing comes to stay."
--Matthew Flickstein

Chapter Twenty

I t was Christmas in Boston. The city was festooned with colorful lights, pageantry and a spirited gaiety seen in the bustling of folks purchasing last minute gifts and cars bearing Christmas trees, whisking by and stirring up images of childhood anticipation.

Heavy snowfall had coated the trees and the parks and parked cars, many of them seemingly wedged in for the season by tall banks of plowed snow. The air smelled of the toasty merriment of crackling fires, of fresh-cut pines and of murky sea odors brought in by a light easterly breeze.

Julian and Tenley had decorated an elegant Douglas-fir set in the living room in front of the main window. Strung with colorful lights, ornaments and loops of gold and silver tinsel, the tree with its star just touched the fifteen foot ceiling. They wrapped gifts and listened to Nat King Cole, warmed by the hissing glow from the fireplace.

Tenley was off for two weeks and Julian had put the manuscript in the drawer until the new year. They spent all of their time together, indulging in Christmas preparations, shopping, attending the Boston Common tree lighting ceremony and listening to carolers. Tenley had talked Julian into attending the faculty party at the University, where Julian reunited with old colleagues and met, for the first time, Tenley's former lover, a tall attractive young woman with haunting eyes who regarded him with a vague look of contempt.

On Christmas Eve they attended midnight mass, in Julian's mind not as much for worship but for the enjoyment of a boyhood tradition. They sat in the back pews and listened to Monsignor O'Brien's masterful work at the organ, beginning with *Adeste Fidelis* and other Christmas renditions and ending with the Handel's triumphant *Hallelujah* chorus. Outside, after the mass ended, Julian kissed Tenley and they wished each other Merry Christmas.

They spent every minute of the holidays together, neither one talking about teaching or writing projects, and entertained themselves by dining out, going to shows and enjoying daily walks about town.

One evening while reading together in front of the hearth, Julian looked up and said, "You know, I was brash and rather selfish in my youth as I look back on it."

"Which one, darling?" Tenley said.

"The second go around. How thoughtless I was to preoccupy myself with such foolish things...young girls, nightclubs, extravagance and notions of self-fulfillment. Looking back on it all, sometimes I wish none of it had happened."

Tenley looked offended. "That would include me, our falling in love and our romantic escapades. How can you mean that?"

"Not that part of it, of course. I have no regrets about our relationship and where it has led us. But I have to be honest with you. I was in love with you long before then, during the last years at the University. You probably didn't even notice."

"I did and in more ways than you might think," Tenley said, laughing. "You always looked at me in a special way...and your eyes traveled. Women know that sort of thing, like an extra sense. And to be honest with you, I was attracted to you, maybe not physically, but on an intellectual level. You seduced me with your worldly knowledge and your professorial ways."

"I am so happy now and so full of love for you. I don't ever want it to end."

"It won't. Not as long as we remember this very moment, right now, in front of the fire, our conversation, our love. The past and the future mean nothing. You know that, Julian. We exist only in the present moment."

"Yes," Julian said, now fully understanding the notion.

"It makes you think of people so caught in the frenzied future of their lives, on what the dollar is going to bring tomorrow, of futile pursuits and illusory rewards. I've known people like that at work, and several friends of that mindset. They appear happy and fulfilled, but you can tell that they always live on the edge of uncertainty and with a hope that the next day will be better, more fulfilling."

"Then." Julian said, "we'll always live in the present and not worry about what tomorrow might bring. No matter what happens in our lives."

Tenley was wearing a pink housecoat and a white shawl Julian had given her for Christmas. Her eyes were so blue in the firelight, they looked like sapphires gleaming under a jewelry light. She sat, one leg over the other, her hands poised on the back of the book she had been reading, and watched Julian silently for several long moments. Slowly, she smiled.

"You look absolutely stunning," Julian said and went to kiss Tenley, who wrapped her arms around him and kissed him back with urgency.

The moment might have led to a more passionate encounter but abruptly there was a series of rapid knocks on the front door. Tenley seemed startled, holding on to Julian as if she sensed danger, and finally let him go to answer the door.

Julian looked through the peephole but saw no one outside. "Who is it?" he said.

A few moments passed and the voice said, "Someone from your past. Please let me in."

Julian had recognized the voice instantly and he opened the door. It was Dino dressed in an orange prisoner's outfit, shaking from the cold, looking apprehensive and quite obviously on the run. He bypassed Julian and went straight for the fireplace.

Tenley was startled by the abrupt entry and stood up.

"Mrs. Landon," Dino said and crouched down by the fire, rubbing his hands together furiously.

"You escaped," Julian said and immediately began to consider the consequences, none more urgent than the legal repercussion for harboring a fugitive.

Dino looked back at Julian and said, "They treat you like shit in there. Couldn't take it anymore. I need a place to get my head straight."

"Well, you can't stay here," Julian said, adding emphatically, "It's out of the question."

"I'm your best man. You're the only person I can trust."

"You committed a crime...murder at that, and if I let you stay here then I'll be committing a crime."

"But I got nowhere else to go, man. You're my only chance."

Ever more aware that he was breaking the law, Julian shook his head. "No. I can't help you this time. Either go or I'll call the police."

Dino began sobbing. "Then call the police."

Tenley covered Dino's shoulders with her shawl and began to rub his neck. It was obvious to Julian that the boy had won an ally. "Let's just listen to what he wants from us. His suit is wet and I think he's got frostbite. Julian, get some dry clothes and something for his feet, and I'll warm up some coffee."

When he emerged from the bathroom in Julian's oversized jeans and sweatshirt, Dino looked like a boy playing grownup in front of his parents. He was still shivering, rubbing at his shoulders, and when Tenley handed him the coffee cup she had to place the cup in his hands. Shaking, he sipped the hot coffee.

"Professor," he said, examining Julian's face, "what happened? You look ancient."

Julian came right to the point. "Did you kill Serena?"

Tears came to the boy's eyes. "No, man. How could I kill the love of my life?"

"It's called a crime of passion. It happens all the time, especially as a result of unrequited love."

"Julian," Tenley said. "Give Dino a chance to explain himself."

"Serena was seeing this guy named Benny ever since we broke up. They were talking about getting hitched, and I wanted to talk to her one last time. We met at the park where you found me. Serena started crying when I told her how much I still loved her but that I wanted her to be happy. Things happen, I guess. We were having a last kiss when her fiancé Benny showed up. Man, he was furious, cursing at Serena, not treating her like a lady. He accused her of shacking up with me. Then he began slapping her, hard I mean, almost knocking her out. I went to save her, and Benny threw a punch, hard enough for me to see stars. I got up and went after him, trying to protect Serena. She got up and started yelling at Benny...I mean words I'd never heard her say before. And then he had her by the throat. Man, I thought he was going to kill her, so I grabbed him by the neck and was trying to pull him off...and that's when it happened."

"What?" Julian said, already feeling skeptical about Dino's account.

"That's when he stabbed her in the chest and seeing what he did, ran away cursing. I held her in my arms and tried to put pressure on her wound, trying to stop her from bleeding to death, but I think that bastard nicked an artery. I watched her die, man!"

"Oh Dino, I'm so sorry," Tenley said, gently rubbing his back.

"I hope you called the police," Julian said.

"I did," Dino said, "and that's how I landed in jail, accused of Serena's murder."

"Did you tell them what happened, that Benny was responsible?" Tenley said.

"They said I had a motive, that I was a shunned lover and that no jury would believe me because of the knife."

"But the other guy had the knife and I'm sure that his prints were all over it," Julian said, now beginning to entertain the possibility that Dino might be telling the truth."

Dino looked up from his coffee cup. "But it was my knife," he said, explaining that he had pulled it on Benny to try to scare him away.

Julian didn't want to hear anymore. He didn't know whether he believed Dino or not. For a moment, selfishly, he thought of the boy's presence as an intrusion at a time when all seemed right in his and Tenley's lives. He didn't need this now, and he cursed himself for ever opening the door.

Dino said he just wanted to stay the night and borrow a few dollars from Julian. He would be gone in the morning. He said that he wanted to track down Benny and bring him to the police and that it would be the only way he could prove his innocence.

"You're not going to kill him?" Tenley said nervously.

"Nah, I ain't no murderer and you know that, Mrs. Landon. It's something personal. I need to look him in the eyes for what he's done to the love of my life."

"You know he's not going to go willingly," Julian said.

"Yeah he will. I have a plan."

◆

Dino left very early that morning and this time left no note. On occasion Julian would check the papers to see if there was a story about his re-arrest, or worse, that he had been accused of another murder.

One day before the new year Julian panicked when he couldn't find his car keys. Tenley was out, and he ransacked the apartment, throwing open drawers, looking inside vases, pulling books off shelves and then sinking into a chair in the living room, his palms pressed over his eyes. He didn't tell Tenley when she returned home.

The next day was worse. He was disoriented, and a numbness had crept into his mind as if he'd had too many martinis the night before.

He tried to concentrate on a book and soon found himself not being able to recall the previous paragraph. More panic set in. He took his novel from the drawer and attempted to read the first chapter. None of it seemed familiar save for the title.

At least he could remember the past. Names and experiences came to him with little effort. But the present was another matter altogether. He eventually resorted to writing himself little notes, which he stuffed in his pockets for fear Tenley might discover them. He could still recall mathematical formulas and he used them again to associate planned necessities and tasks in his mind.

Dementia had returned; he was sure of that. The onset had been so rapid this time, he feared that its progression might soon leave him totally feeble-minded, unable to perform simple routines like brushing his teeth, dressing or even going outside.

By the third day the panic had left him. As he had done before when he first came to grips with his failing memory just before retiring, Julian began to accept the inevitability of his deteriorating condition. He grew weary and sad and tried to avoid Tenley for fear she would notice what was happening.

Finally he couldn't take it anymore. He went to Tenley and confessed the horrible truth of the matter in a flood of emotions and clipped sentences. He wanted to fall into her arms and cry his heart out.

Tenley rushed to his side and kissed him on the forehead. "Don't you think I knew?" she said. "This morning I found the notes in your pockets. And I've noticed your moods lately." Sitting on the floor beside his chair, she now looked up into Julian's face as if searching for some clue in his eyes. "We both knew this would eventually happen."

"You're not going to leave me?" Julian said pathetically.

Tenley grabbed for his hands. "Of course not. You're my husband. I love you, darling."

"I suppose I could see Dr. Farley and go back on the medication. I could start the journey all over again."

"Is that really what you *want* to do?"

Tenley's question set a tone of resignation in Julian's mind, as if a dying patient were being asked if they wanted to go through painful treatment again. *Would it be worthwhile?* he asked himself. Where he was now in his convoluted life would be exactly where he would return, no matter the postponement. It was inescapable.

"If you do," Tenley said, "I'll wait for you."

"I couldn't stand weighing you down. You're still young."

"For better or for worse, remember?" Tenley said, now rising and kissing him on the lips. "I am never going to leave you, darling."

"One day at a time. I'll live in the present moment and not worry about tomorrow."

"That's the way it must be," Tenley said. "I've researched dementia. Some of it is normal at your age. The more serious symptoms are more gradual. We can work with it, Julian. We'll do word puzzles together, exercise and take vitamins known to improve memory and brain function. Nothing is hopeless. You of all people know that."

"I do...I do," Julian said, a new hope brightening in his heart.

◆

Julian gave it his all. He took the vitamins, went for daily walks with Tenley, became ever more proficient at word puzzles and began reading again. Tenley engaged his mind by constantly asking questions about the date and time, who the President was, where he had placed items. They talked about current events and reminisced about old adventures.

Confidence returned and soon Julian started spending short periods at work on his novel.

Though memory issues still plagued him, Julian took these impediments in stride. He still employed the use of personal notes, especially during more challenging bouts of amnesia. He made a game of it, using both formulas and strange mental images to remember names and words he had forgotten. Sometimes they worked.

The past, though, was as clear and as real as if it had happened yesterday. He remembered conversations he'd had with Tenley, Heather and Dorothy and the experiences of youth as a cocky, self-absorbing young man named Brad. These memories became prized possessions, and he only looked upon them with fondness.

There were infrequent days when he awoke in the mornings and couldn't recall what day it was, much less what routine to follow. Tenley didn't allow him to fall back to sleep and helped him get dressed, eat breakfast and settle into a simple routine of sitting by the window, pointing out streets and familiar buildings. When he couldn't read, she read to him, most of it Shakespeare and occasional passages from his beloved history books. She would pause now and then, asking him questions and answering them when the distant look on his face made it obvious that it was all incomprehensible to him.

But there was an abundance of days when his mind returned and he acted his old self, not aware of his regression. They both cherished these times, spending every moment together, talking, reading and sharing their feelings. Each experience was evermore precious, whether they were making salads together, taking walks and observing the perfect order of nature. Tenley taught Julian how to practice living in the moment by letting his mind's focus go, allowing thoughts to pass and becoming a distant observer. They would do this together in a quiet park or bundled in front of a nearby beach.

It could be said that they were more in love than ever, more passionate about small experiences and more aware of the simple graces of life. Although Tenley was still half his age, sometimes Julian imagined that they were both very old and had been married for decades. Each day became a blessing, with little regrets to remember and vast opportunities for daily growth and sharing.

Julian became well enough for Tenley to consider going back to work. She said that she would carry her cell phone on her at all times and that he was to call at the slightest notice that things were regressing. She made it clear that her department chair understood that she might have to leave suddenly at any given moment and that her return to work was only a trial.

Julian was jubilant about the idea and did everything he could for her to understand that he would be just fine, that he was feeling great, reminding her that he hadn't had a relapse in weeks.

Though he missed her that first day she returned to work, Julian was confident that he could manage alone. He had his notes and his quirky reminders and now a deep trust that nothing would further disrupt his life.

The telephone call he received one frigid afternoon in March would change all that.

Chapter Twenty One

The day was very cold but clear, with the sun shimmering through a rarefied and transient overcast. The moderate snowfall the night before had turned into a crusty coat of ice and refrozen snow, making walking difficult and driving hazardous for some. Despite the inclement conditions, Boston was Boston, with its rugged denizens almost unaware of the impediments of treacherous weather, accustomed as they were to long harsh winters.

People were out and about, going about their routines, seemingly unfazed by traffic backups due to unplowed side streets and getting stuck behind the slow-moving yellow plows. The noise of the city was no different than on a bright spring day. Workmen were plying their trades, people were shopping and even the ducks on the half-frozen Charles River had a busy air about them as they waddled around looking for morsels of food.

The red BMW sportster driving down Storrow Drive was traveling more slowly than the passing traffic, at times causing impatient drivers behind him to sound their horns. It might be said that the driver inside was headed to a funeral at a processional crawl or that he was a novice driver experiencing his initial encounter with inclement weather.

But Julian was just being careful. He'd had a bad night. His thoughts were murky and filled with a wary apprehension that things might get worse. He watched carefully for landmarks, even though hospital signs clearly marked the route.

He drove around Massachusetts General Hospital several times trying to find an empty parking space. On his third unsuccessful attempt, exasperated, he found a Doctor's Only space and pulled into it. *Well, he was a doctor*, he thought with vague contempt.

Inside, Julian remembered the floor but couldn't recall the room number. He pulled a wad of crumpled note paper from his pocket and held the number written on it up as he passed several rooms. Finally it matched a door number across from the nurse's station. He opened it and found the vaguely familiar face of a nurse adjusting a fluid drip from an overhanging bag.

"Professor Landon," she said cheerfully. "I thought with the weather you might not make it out today."

"I'm here."

"I think Tenley's feeling a bit better today," the nurse said and moved away so that Julian could approach.

Perhaps Julian thought that the person he was about to see was not his wife and instead an impostor, someone he would not recognize. When he saw Tenley's face his knees buckled and tears flooded his eyes. She reached for his hand and urged him to come closer so that she could kiss him.

"Darling, I think I'm improving," she said, wiping the tears from Julian's cheeks.

"What happened? Tell me again why you are here."

"I had you write it down. Don't you remember? It's probably on one of those notes stuffed in your pockets. I had a stroke, Julian, while I was at work. An ambulance took me here. I've been here for five days."

"Are you getting better? When will you come home?"

"I still have some motor problems on my left side but otherwise I'm okay. I might have to have some physical therapy, but Dr. Huxley says I can attend those sessions on an out-patient basis. Julian, I was very lucky. It could have been a lot worse." Though it was obvious, she asked him how he was doing.

"I do better when you're with me. I miss our talks and our reading. I miss everything about you," Julian said, a rim of new tears welling in his eyes. "Leighton was rude to me today."

"I'm sure he didn't mean to be."

"He said that it wasn't a good idea for me to drive today. I told him off."

"He only had your best interest at heart. It was because of the weather, I'm sure."

"It's because he thinks I'm too feeble-minded to drive."

"Oh Julian, you can't let yourself think that. You're having an emotional day and it's probably because of what happened to me. As soon as I get home you'll be feeling much better. I promise."

"I forgot the flowers...I forgot the flowers, damn it!" Julian said, giving himself a hard thump to the forehead.

"Stop that right now," Tenley said, raising her voice. "If you plan to beat yourself up, you can do it somewhere else."

"I'm sorry," Julian said, reaching for her hands. "Hold me like you used to do," he added, trying to maneuver Tenley's other arm around him. It fell limply to the side of the bed.

A faint look of horror filled Julian's face as if realizing, without really understanding it, that part of Tenley was dead. He shouted for the nurse through the open door. She came right away and Julian showed her Tenley's arm. The nurse looked into Tenley's face, nodding, and then led Julian away, out the door and into a small lounge across the hallway. She fixed him a cup of black coffee and then sat down next to him on the small couch.

"Professor, it's alright," she said, gently massaging his free hand. "This has all been very traumatic for you. You wife is going to be fine. She has some paralysis, but the stroke didn't affect her speech, her ability to think and feel normal feelings. With proper therapy she'll probably make a good recovery. Trust me, Professor. I wouldn't lie to you."

"Yes," Julian said, regaining his composure. "Of course she will. When can she come home?"

"That will depend on how she progresses each day. The final decision is up to her neurologist and the nursing staff. I know you miss your wife and that you need her to be at home with you, but you must let her heal first. Perhaps you could arrange for a friend or relative to be with you in the meantime. You have a daughter, don't you?"

"Carolyn," Julian said with vague reminiscence.

"Have you spoken with her?"

"No."

"I'm sure she would want to know, don't you think?"

"No," Julian said emphatically and stood up. "I want to be with my wife now."

With a concerned look on her face, the nurse watched Julian exit the room and then looked down at the spreading puddle of black coffee on the white linoleum floor. It looked as dark as she imagined the future would be for the professor.

◆

When he left the hospital, still troubled by Tenley's condition, Julian couldn't remember where he had parked his car. In fact, the memory of ever parking it was gone.

He called for a taxi and then made the driver wait until he'd located the piece of paper with his address on it. He gave the cabby a $100 bill and told him to keep the change, for fear of not knowing how much change to expect.

Leighton must have seen the taxi and he followed Julian to the elevator, holding the door until he saw the professor had pushed the right button to his floor. Julian glowered at the man but said nothing.

Inside the apartment Julian went straight to the liquor cabinet and poured himself a tall glass of bourbon. Seemingly in deep thought he watched the amber fluid settle in the glass. Most of his visit with Tenley had fragmented into slivers of remembered emotion, soon blurring into insignificance the harder he tried to hold onto them. He was puzzled by the glassful of bourbon, having only a vague recollection of pouring it. He knew only that he had to do something, and when the dim notion of having to escape finally came to him, he raised the glass and took a long drink. And then another.

Soon a vague sense of control came to Julian. He hadn't forgotten to imbibe his favorite bourbon and to anticipate the strange sensation of escape it produced. It made him forget about his condition. Strangely, forgotten memories became clear to him. He began to recall why Tenley was in the hospital, that she had suffered a stroke while at work. Suddenly he remembered where he had parked his car and realized that it had probably been towed. He felt his heart ache for Tenley and even remembered the last time they'd made love. These revelations assuaged the fears, the uncertainties and the tedious hold of amnesia that had plagued him for the last several days.

He took yet another swallow of bourbon, feeling its edifying effects, and was illuminated by the rush of sudden knowledge, memories, sensations and there in the distance a curious luster of hope.

There were repeated telephone rings, but Julian was oblivious to it all. He had collapsed on the sofa, his head forward, breathing deeply, his hands loosely clutching the bourbon glass. He might have been dreaming of wonderful things, for there was a look of deep calm on his face and an occasional wince of delight as his lips thinned into a barely noticeable smile. Soon he settled into a fathomless snore, each breath causing his chest to rise briefly and then fall, stilled and seemingly permanent, until the next breath erupted with a deep nasal tremor.

He did not notice the repeated knocks at the door or the voice calling out to him. He did not see the man enter and stand over him, watching him sleep. The visitor took the glass from his hands, left to prepare the bed and returned, lifting Julian into a half-standing position. He did not feel the strong arms of his benefactor carry him gently into the bedroom, cradling him as if he were a child exhausted from play, before lowering him onto the bed and raising the covers to his chin.

The man went to the kitchen and poured a glass of ice water from the refrigerator and then went to the medicine cabinet in the bathroom. He dropped several aspirins into his palm and went back to the bedroom, where he placed the medicine and glass of water on the bedside table. He saw the card and began to read it, puzzled by the youthful love note and the unfamiliar name at the end. He carefully sat down next to Julian and took his wrist, making sure the pulse was strong and regular. He placed Julian's hand atop the other on his chest and then held his own hand there for several moments, as a parent would feeling the peaceful slumber of his child.

The telephone rang and the man answered it in the living room. He tried to calm the anxious voice on the other end and then told the caller that there was no reason to send someone over, that Julian was in good hands. He promised to write the message down and place the note on the night table. He said he would check on Julian the next morning.

Back in the bedroom, he saw that Julian had turned on his side, now barely awake, fumbling for the glass of water on the table. He placed the note on the table, and then lifted Julian's head slightly and assisted him with the water. Dreamily, Julian blinked his eyes several times and then turned over, mumbling the name *Leighton* before falling asleep again.

"Sleep well, Professor," Leighton said and then quickly let himself out of the apartment.

◆

Julian managed to sleep through his hangover the next morning. It was eleven when he awoke, feeling both refreshed and clear-minded. He remembered Leighton's face and was soon swept up by the generosity of the man. He had obviously helped him to bed and made sure he was alright.

He read the note on the table and smiled. Tenley had called during the night and she had left him her number at the hospital. He took a deep breath, resolved that this day would be better than yesterday. Before returning Tenley's call, he looked up Dr. Farley's number and dialed it, hoping to make an appointment with the neurologist. Following a lengthy pause, he was told by a kindly-mannered man that she was no longer there but that another neurologist had an opening that afternoon.

"But I just saw Dr. Farley a few months ago," Julian said, puzzled.

The man was silent at first and then said, "That's okay. I think you'll find that Dr. Riley is highly qualified. He is friendly and very professional. This afternoon at four. Is that a convenient time for you?"

Julian called Tenley and apologized for having scared her. He told her that he loved her and couldn't wait for her release from the hospital.

"Oh Julian, I'm so glad you're having a better day. I love you too, darling. But promise me you'll never get drunk like that again."

He told her that he had made an appointment with a new neurologist, adding that Dr. Farley was no longer at the medical group. "It's strange, don't you think?"

"You can't let things like that bother you, Julian."

Julian told her about not being able to find the BMW and having resorted to taking a cab back home. He felt as though his independence had been snatched away and that he had lost the last residual of personal freedom. He feared the car had been towed to a police storage lot.

"Don't worry about it, Julian. There comes a time in everyone's life when things must be accepted as they are. The car isn't important anymore. You can call a taxi anytime."

"I could hire a driver, I suppose."

"They're exceedingly expensive and often times unreliable," Tenley said.

"Well, I am going to hire one when you are ready to leave the hospital," Julian said adamantly, adding, "I'm not going to have you crammed inside of a cab."

Tenley reminded him to write down the address of the doctor's office and suggested he take notes on what he planned to ask. Julian told her he would come to the hospital after the appointment and that he couldn't wait to see her.

"Me too, darling," Tenley said before hanging up the phone.

After their conversation, Julian shaved, took a shower and dressed in casual attire. He ate a brunch of Swiss cheese and ham sandwich and a glass of cold milk. His vegan predilection no longer seemed important as it was when he was this age the first time around. Longevity seemed an unsettling pursuit considering his condition.

He went to the den and pulled out the manuscript, reading unimpeded through the first several chapters. The plot and the characters came back to him with clarity, a rare experience he wasn't about to squander. He looked at the time and began to continue where he left off on *Chapter Forty*. Odessa, his heroine, had just admitted her affair with Charles to her sulking husband, *whose sweltering ire glowed in his eyes like a wildfire on a cold distant beach.*

Julian worked until three thirty and then called for a cab. He had the address in hand, although he had failed to write down questions he planned to ask the new doctor. Those queries would come naturally, he thought, when he felt comfortable with the doctor.

◆

"Julian," a man with a round face and balding pate called out as soon as Julian had taken a seat in the waiting room of the clinic. He was holding the hallway door open, gesturing for him to enter. "Dr. Riley," the man said, patting the back of Julian's shoulder. "So good to see you again."

Julian had no recollection of the doctor and thought it strange that the man had recognized him and inferred that they had met before. He was going to correct the neurologist but thought it best that he not say anything. There was a possibility that Dr. Riley was right, and Julian just didn't remember.

Dr. Riley led him not to an examining room but straight to his office, a large room with an oak desk set against a wall with a huge chart of the human brain. Bookshelves lined the rest of the walls. An oak drop leaf serving table sat next to the desk. A tall pitcher of water and several glasses rested upon the table. In the center of the room was a small conference table with chairs.

"Please have a seat, Julian," Dr. Riley said, pulling back one of the conference chairs. He then took a seat across from Julian. "How have you been feeling?"

"Today's a pretty good day. Yesterday was horrible." Trusting the doctor, Julian went into greater detail about not being able to find his car and now being resigned to having a taxi take him everywhere. He decided not to say anything about his binge for fear that his intentions might be misunderstood. He did tell Dr. Riley about Tenley's stroke and how he was trying to spend as much time with her at the hospital as he could.

"What else do you do during the course of an average day?"

Julian told him that he read when he could and that he was slowly progressing on his novel.

"That's wonderful," the doctor said. "Keeping the mind challenged is so important during the early stages of the disease."

Confused, Julian said, "Disease? No one told me that I have a disease. Is it a brain illness?"

Dr. Riley sat back in his chair. He had a kind face with tired, sensitive eyes. His demeanor projected trust, honesty and compassion. "Julian," he said, "what do you remember from our last visit?

Julian was stunned by the question and then he thought about it, searching his mind for even the slightest recognition. He couldn't answer the man.

"We ran quite a few tests. Do you remember any of them?"

"No," Julian said. "I don't recall ever meeting you before."

"That's okay. It was not one of your best days and given the diagnosis, it's understandable that you would repress that memory."

"I know I have dementia," Julian said. "Please don't tell me I also have a brain tumor?"

"You have been diagnosed with Alzheimer's Disease, Julian. I know it sounds like a fatal diagnosis but people live many years, most of them independent and fulfilling years. The progression is different for everyone. If you take care of yourself diet-wise, exercise regularly and continue to stimulate your mind you may delay the onset of the more serious symptoms of the disease."

"How bad is it, Dr. Riley?"

"You are probably entering stage four."

"How many are there?"

"They range from stage one to stage seven."

"Oh God!" Julian said. "Why didn't someone tell me this before?"

Dr. Riley said nothing at first. He looked at Julian with such compassionate eyes it made Julian think that the doctor had intimate knowledge of what was going through his mind. Finally he spoke.

"Alzheimer's is still a largely unknown disease. Researchers have made incredible leaps during the past decade but we still don't have all the answers. Much is a mystery. There may be genetic predispositions, correlations with diet and exercise and even clinical depression. And then there is the manner in which the mind, our thinking process, adapts and even protects an individual through amnesia."

Julian sat up straight in his chair. "I don't understand," he said.

"Well, for example, you say that you don't recall meeting me before and all the testing procedures, but in fact I have been seeing you for almost a year now."

"That's impossible. I only saw Dr. Farley once."

"Julian, you only saw me. There is no Dr. Farley."

Julian sat there, frozen with incredulity and a swallowing sense of gloom so dark that all but Dr. Riley's face was lost to obscurity. He was barely aware that the doctor had poured him a glassful of water, urging him to drink. And when the light returned and the room became familiar, Julian said nothing more, watching as the doctor wrote out several prescriptions, telling him that he would call them in to his pharmacy and arrange for the medication to be delivered.

"I want to see you again in two weeks," Dr. Riley said, escorting Julian back to the waiting room, where the receptionist wrote out an appointment card and asked him to take a seat until the taxi arrived.

At home Julian stretched out on his bed and allowed his mind to process the events of the afternoon. He had suspected some form of dementia a year before he retired but no one had ever mentioned Alzheimer's. While the possibility may have resided in a far corner of his mind, he had never considered that the disease had been causing his memory loss and confusion. If Dr. Riley had been right and for whatever reason Julian's subconscious had swallowed up all of the memories of meetings with the doctor, then this implied something Julian had never considered, that his mind was in some strange way protecting Julian from reality. The more he reflected on this notion the more focused his mind became. Awareness blossomed again. He could remember just about everything now: his retirement, taking a mysterious medication that stopped the memory loss and then sent time in reverse, the flings with the girls, falling in love with Tenley, getting married, the trips abroad. The memories were clear and real. Even Tenley would vouch for them. He would ask her if he had really been seeing Dr. Riley for a year. She, of all people in his life, would know.

Julian washed up and then called for a cab. Riding to the hospital, he recalled an old movie in which the main character at the end was faced with the reality that nothing he had experienced in his life had ever occurred, that the evidence had vanished. The memory gripped him as he pulled up to the hospital and soon he began to fear that he would not find Tenley there, that she had never been a patient.

He remembered the floor and the room number and went straight there, almost out of breath. He pushed the door open and when he saw Tenley, such relief overcame him he had to take a seat in one of the chairs for a few moments.

"Oh God, Tenley," he gasped, approaching the bedside.

"Julian, you look like you've seen a ghost. Do I look that bad, darling?"

Tenley was finishing up her dinner: broiled chicken breast, mashed potatoes, carrots and a slice of pumpernickel bread. Julian reached over and pinched a corner of the bread and put it his mouth. It was real.

Tenley moved the tray and motioned for Julian to sit beside her on the bed. "So how did your appointment go?" she asked.

He told her everything but the diagnosis. "Are you aware that I have been seeing Dr. Riley for a year?"

The expression on her face told Julian that indeed she wasn't aware of that fact. "I thought you only saw Dr. Farley," she said.

"Well, Farley has vanished. Dr. Riley seems to think I have been his patient for quite sometime."

"Oh," Tenley said. "Perhaps he's mistaken. But even if it were true, it doesn't change things, does it?"

"What do you mean?" Julian said in a puzzled voice.

"Well, what I mean is that what is real is simply a matter of perception. If you perceive something to be true then it *is* true. What may seem true for Dr. Riley may be only his point of view, his perception. What matters above all is what *you* believe. We can only live through our own perceptions."

"What are you saying? It doesn't make much sense."

"I'm sorry, Julian, I don't mean to confuse you. I can't explain why Dr. Riley said what he did. Now, is it really that important? Our truths and our love for each other are more important than anything or anyone else. These are real things, Julian."

"Yes."

"And we must hold onto them as long as we can."

Julian reached for Tenley's arms, forgetting the palsied one, and hugged her for the longest time, nuzzled in the warmth and fragrance of who could only be the most real person of his life.

Chapter Twenty Two

Julian spent all the time he could find to be with Tenley at the hospital. They had delayed her release due to a serious bladder infection, and put her on antibiotics. Her neurologist had spoken with Julian, assuring him that this condition was nothing to be alarmed about. He had ordered a physical therapist to work with Tenley several times a week and had decided, when she was well enough, to transfer her to the rehabilitation section of the hospital.

Julian brought her flowers every day and received permission to cater meals, which they ate together, sometimes with a glass of wine. He brought her books, all of her favorites and some of his own, word-puzzles, Scrabble and a chess set. He catered to her every whim, lavishing her with attention and notions of future adventures.

Given the reality that she would probably not be able to return to work for some time, if at all, Tenley seemed evermore interested in Julian's plans to travel to the northwest and explore the rugged coastline. They talked about places they wanted to visit. Tenley said she'd never been to San Francisco and wanted to start there and then visit Coos Bay and the Olympic National Forest before traveling to Vancouver.

With the help of the nurse, Julian bathed Tenley every day, washing her hair and her back and letting her sink down to her chin in the bubbly water. He exercised her left arm and leg and encouraged her to resist the motion to measure how much control she could exert. He helped her put on a new nightgown and wheeled her back to the bed, bringing her her favorite perfume and facial powder. Using a hand mirror with her good hand, Tenley watched as he dried her hair and then combed it to her liking. He then helped her with her makeup, putting on her eye shadow, her mascara and the light pink lipstick she favored.

Often times Julian would spend the entire day and part of the evening with Tenley. He had no other commitments in his life but to take care of his wife. One morning he arrived and found her with a sullen pout on her face. It was so uncharacteristic it almost didn't look like Tenley at all, as if some farouche imposter had taken her place.

"Tenley, what's wrong?"

She broke into tears. "It's hopeless. I will never get out of here. I can't do a damn thing for myself. I'm worthless. I just can't go on like this anymore."

Julian went to her and tried to embrace her but she stiffened and pulled away. "Darling, you're not worthless. How can you say that? You are a wonderful person, beautiful and kind-hearted and so full of love. I adore you. You are my life."

"Well, I want my own life back," Tenley retorted and like a child shuffled her back to Julian. "I don't want to be taken care of anymore. You're suffocating me."

Recalling that those were the exact words he'd used when Tenley was lavishing him with too much attention, Julian understood completely. For a while he said nothing, not sure there was anything he could say to make her feel better. "I'll go then," he finally said. "I can appreciate that you may want your space. I love you, Tenley."

"Go then!"

Tenley's muffled words felt to Julian like a dagger in his heart. He nodded and walked toward the door.

"And call that damn daughter of yours!" Tenley said angrily. It's time for you to face the truth!"

Julian left the room but wasn't about the leave the hospital. He asked the attending nurse to call Tenley's doctor, that it was urgent that he meet with him, but was told he was in surgery. The nurse said, "I know your wife is having a bad morning."

"She asked me to leave," Julian said, sounding vanquished.

"Depression often sets in cases of stroke," the nurse explained. "You can't take what she said personally. Hemiplegia is an awful thing to adjust to. Your wife is dealing with the frustration of not being able to take care of herself, of losing part of her independence. It must be devastating for a woman as young as she is and with such intelligence."

"Yes," Julian said. "I understand."

"The best thing you can do at this point is to be supportive but not over-indulge yourself by doing everything for her. It's natural that you want to pamper her. But you must see this from her perspective. It's okay that she experience natural failures during the course of the day. In fact, it may very well motivate her, to get her to fight back against her motor limitations."

"Is she ever going to be well?"

"Your wife is strong and young and that's the good part of the equation. The stroke has traumatized part of her brain, but it could be worse. I'm pretty confident that in time, with proper support and intervention, she will make a good recovery."

"Thank God," Julian said, feeling the tension release.

The nurse leaned forward. "Sometimes caregivers suffer the worst in these cases," she said. "You must look out for yourself and know your limits. When your wife is released you might want to consider finding someone who can assist you, perhaps a close friend or a nurse. Please don't try to do it all alone."

"Yes, I'll do that," Julian said and thanked the nurse for her advice. He stood up as she exited the room and then sat down rather heavily, pondering the arrangements of home care he would have to consider. He decided that some alterations to the apartment would have to be made, perhaps special bathroom railings and a tub with a door, a motorized wheelchair and one of those automatic recliners he had seen in an advertisement that would assist Tenley to a standing position. There might be special exercise equipment she would need, and he would purchase those. Whatever Tenley needed, Julian was prepared to provide it, notwithstanding the cost.

Julian left the hospital late. He spoke with Tenley's physical and occupational therapists and with the new shift nurse. He tried again to see her neurologist but was told that he had left the hospital as soon as his surgery had finished. He would be doing rounds tomorrow and would see Tenley then.

In the cab Julian looked out the window at the slow-falling snow. Although saddened by Tenley's emotional state, he felt newly focused, his memory intact, all sharpened by an important mission in his life: to help his wife fully recover. His own symptoms and his new diagnosis seemed devalued in view of what Tenley was going through. He felt good and charitable and tipped the driver accordingly.

That evening he thought about Tenley's angry comment about Carolyn and her confusing remark that he needed to face the truth. He hadn't seen or talked with his daughter in many months. He rationalized again that she was too busy with her life. He couldn't explain, though, his own reluctance to contact her.

Before bed he went to the window, opening it slightly. The cold air stunned him for a few moments, tearing his eyes and causing him to take a sharp breath. Standing there, looking out over the dark cityscape, he began to shiver. For all of the winters he'd spent in Boston, this was a dark shuddering cold he'd never experienced before. Much of it came from within.

◆

Tenley's mood improved significantly. Now she wanted to be with Julian as much as possible. She had started her therapy and eagerly shared with Julian her improvements. There was a fierce determination in her eyes that left no doubt that she would one day be able to walk again and regain function of her right arm. Her neurologist had started her on a new, experimental medication that had just been approved by the FDA and had shown remarkable potential in cases like Tenley's.

"Well, here we ago," she said to Julian as she swallowed her first dose. "I might be twenty again by the end of the week."

"No more time travel in our lives," Julian quipped, encouraged by Tenley's good humor.

She told him that Dr. Huxley was going to move her to the rehabilitation unit in just a few days and depending on her progress there, he would probably release her from the hospital in the next few weeks.

Julian was ecstatic. He told her about the renovations he was making to the apartment, describing the fancy new tub that had been installed a few days ago. He asked her whether she would like a new bed, the kind that elevated the head and feet.

"Don't you dare," Tenley said. "I like the bed we have and can't wait to be back in it...with you."

A custodial aide, a petite Asian woman with an unsmiling face, entered the room and went about her duties, emptying the wastebasket, refilling the pitcher of water and placing a new packet of toothbrush and paste on the bed tray. She left with the same silent efficiency as when she'd entered the room.

Julian was puzzled by the familiar interruption. He remembered it happening before but long ago. He had never experienced déjà vu like this before and it left him curious but confused. Suddenly, a flood of likewise sensations came to him. Snippets of re-experience cascaded through his thoughts and emotions. He looked over at Tenley, knowing exactly what she was about to say.

"Julian, lie down beside me."

They lay there in the small hospital bed, Julian attempting to assess the strange premonition he'd just experienced, soon abandoning the notion as Tenley snuggled close. He brushed Tenley's hair, fanning it out on the pillow. He rubbed her temples and her forehead and watched the soothed look on her face. He kissed her lips.

"We will always be together...until death do us part," Julian said.

Tenley smiled but said nothing.

◆

Tenley was asleep when he carefully slid out of the bed later that evening. It was past eleven when he finally got home. He felt so uplifted by Tenley's change of attitude and her determination to leave the hospital, he felt exceedingly happy, almost giddy when he went to bed. Even now he missed her and wished that he had remained with her for the duration of the night.

With the clearest of thought he remembered every moment with Tenley, from the early days at the University, through all of his youthful frolicking to their adventures abroad. The images evoked by those memories were clear and real and immovable. In his state of clarity, Julian began to doubt his diagnosis. He wondered if he had managed to heal himself, perhaps through his mission to help Tenley. He realized that, in spite of their love for each other, their relationship would have to weather the hardships that lay ahead. There was a possibility that she'd never walk unassisted again, that she might spend all of her life in a wheelchair. Her moods might change daily, and he would have to be there for her at all times.

Julian fell into a deep, welcoming sleep. He dreamed of Tenley but also, curiously enough, about Leighton, who had taken it upon himself to assist Julian during his evening of drunkenness. It could be said that benevolence was the general theme of his dreaming, as there were also fleeting visions of his efforts to help Golf and Dino. It was the kind of sleep that caressed all that was good and profitable in his life, discarding fears and uncertainties and all inclinations of ill destiny. At one point Julian experienced another vision of flying, this time suspended above all of Boston, beyond the bustle and drama of city life below.

It was well past two in the morning when the telephone rang. Julian vaguely heard it but the sound was quickly absorbed by the soaring pleasures of flight.

Chapter Twenty Three

Tenley did not come home. She was moved to a nursing home in South Boston a week after another, more devastating stroke robbed her of most of her motor function and her ability to speak. Her doctors had no explanation for why she had suffered another thrombosis, given that her progress up to that point was going so well. They had increased and combined several doses of anticoagulant medicine to lessen the chance for another stroke. They had spoken to Julian about her medical fragility and the probability that she would need nursing care for the rest of her life. One of them told him that he should never give up hope and should encourage Tenley to do the same.

Miracles do happen.

Julian visited Tenley every day of the week. Sometimes, when there was a spare bed available, he would sleep in the room with her. At first there were more bad days than good ones as Tenley struggled to communicate with him, making round shapes with her lips and odd whispering sounds that were unrecognizable as words. She would squint with arduous concentration and use her good hand, bent at the wrist, to motion what she wanted. Sometimes she would stiffen her body in utter frustration, her face flushing and her mouth wrenched shut.

It hurt to see her this way, to witness her desperate efforts to communicate simple words and to see her fail time and time again, reconstituting her silent exasperation and rage. Her features changed, her natural expression hardening into a permanent sulkiness. Inside, Julian knew, Tenley's brilliant mind was functioning. Beneath her morose exterior there was the Tenley he had always known, loved and adored. Her love for him resided there, along with the smiles, the gentle touches, the humor and the memories of their lives together.

Remembering her love for poetry, Julian would spend hours reading her verse: Dickinson, Bronte, Keats, Frost and Elizabeth Barrett Browning. These were the only times when she seemed at peace, closing her eyes and moving her lips as if she were reciting the words with him.

One evening Julian was reading her Dickinson and when he'd finished reciting one poem, she nodded her head urgently as if she wanted him to repeat the verse.

ADRIFT! A little boat adrift!
And night is coming down!
Will no one guide a little boat
Unto the nearest town?

So sailors say, on yesterday,
Just as the dusk was brown
One little boat gave up its strife,
And gurgled down and down.

But angels say, on yesterday,
Just as the dawn was red,
One little boat o'erspent with gales
Retrimmed its masts, redecked its sails
Exultant, onward sped!

Julian spent hours memorizing it and would recite it to her at just the right times, when she looked like she was sinking again.

They developed a rudimentary system of communication at the suggestion of Tenley's speech pathologist. One fast blink meant *yes,* two indicated *no,* and a slow blink meant *I love you.* Tenley would make a game of it, throwing in combinations of slow and fast blinks and having Julian guess what they meant. While at first he was frustrated with himself for not guessing the right word she was trying to convey, one day it occurred to him that there were clues hidden in motion of her eyelids, like mathematical notations ready to be solved. She had developed a number system using a combination of blinks with both eyes. The system became much more complex and soon Tenley was teaching him new variations to include words and phrases.

With intrepid determination and daily training with a speech therapist, Tenley eventually regained some of her ability to speak. Her altered voice may not have seemed natural to others who knew her but to Julian it was genuine and a clear sign that she was beginning to return from her paralysis. Sometimes, even before she had formed her words, Julian knew exactly what she wanted simply by reading the expression on her face.

Tenley's physical and occupational therapy began to show remarkable improvement. She regained feeling and movement in her left arm and leg, and eventually learned to maneuver herself about in a wheelchair. Her first encounter with the piled books and then a floor lamp on the far side of the room caused both Julian and Tenley to burst into fits of laughter.

"Excuse me, Miss," Julian said, "but do you have a license to drive that thing?"

And she had responded in a struggling voice, "No…but I plan on taking the driving test."

When Tenley wasn't using the chair Julian would attempt to do wheelies, once falling backwards, his legs sprawled above him. The nurse who had walked in regarded the antics with little humor and reminded Julian that the cost to replace the wheelchair was over two thousand dollars.

"Old...c...codfish!" Tenley said after the nurse left the room, and they both started up again with a laughter so spontaneous and unconfined that tears came to their eyes. Then on, just about everything caused them to burst into maniacal giggling. It was a day for unrestrained enjoyment and laughter and hope.

There were setbacks: TIAs, the doctor explained, little spasms in brain arteries which caused a return of fleeting paralysis, loss of speech function and occasional short term memory loss. But the fire had been lit inside Tenley's mind, and each hindrance brought on a furious battle for recovery. She had faith and indefatigable courage, and like the little boat adrift in Dickinson's poem, the next morning would find her sailing against a profitable wind, evermore determined to regain loss ground.

◆

Julian eventually sold the apartment and moved into the retirement home with Tenley. He rid himself of nearly all of his material possessions and made handsome donations to charity. He gave the BMW to Leighton, who at first refused it and finally said he would keep it "...should the Professor ever decide to move back into the apartments."

He walked into the Engine 9 & Ladder 2 district Firehouse on Sumner Street and meeting the first volunteer firefighter, gave him the Rolex watch, no questions asked. Like many of his chosen beneficiaries, the young man said he couldn't possibly accept it until Julian assured him that any reputable jeweler would give him ten grand for it and that he could share the money with his buddies or donate it to the firehouse.

He gave away clothes to local charity shops and delighted in giving away coins, most of them silver dollars, to children and young adolescents working at their after-school jobs.

With the help of his attorneys Julian started a foundation to reward young achievers with either scholarships or grants for entrepreneurships. He set up a trust for Tenley, making sure that she would never have to concern herself with financial worries. He also changed his will, making sure his wife would receive whatever was left in his holdings and accounts. He considered re-including Carolyn in his will but felt again that she would never need the money due to her very profitable career and her own lucrative investments.

He wanted to leave Heather something but he had long forgotten her address and even her last name. She had refused the boat, and Julian reasoned she would do the same with monetary gifts. Even so, he remembered his young love with great fondness but with little deliberation, as Tenley was now the sole focus in his life.

He made sure that there would remain enough money in his account to settle the eventual bill for Dino's legal expenses. He made a codicil to his will, giving his best man $10,000 but only if he was found not guilty of the murder charges.

The apartment he'd rented was not in the nursing care unit of the retirement home but on a different floor, in the senior living unit, it's window overlooking a small park, where he could watch children at play or young lovers holding hands on benches. Save for his books, a small desk upon which the old typewriter lay along with the nearly-complete *Odessa's Feud*, the room was spartan. The extra space in the room served an important purpose, for Tenley would often visit in her wheelchair and Julian wanted to limit any obstructions that might impede her maneuvering. Often she insisted on making the short trip on her own because it was a daily challenge that improved her coordination and provided her the exercise her doctors had recommended.

On Tenley's 35th birthday Julian surprised her with a catered vegan dinner, red wine and a birthday carrot cake with thirty-five candles on it. They sat at the small table in the middle of the room and Tenley looked down at the tofu and vegetable pot pie as if it was some foreign delicacy, and Julian laughed at her expression. He had returned to his vegan lifestyle, convincing his wife that culinary choices of this kind were both nutritionally and ethically purposeful.

"Delicious," Tenley said, tasting the buttery-like crust and fresh vegetables inside. She reached across the table and squeezed Julian's hand. "Of all the fancy meals we've enjoyed on our travels, this is the very best."

Her face was the brightest Julian had seen in a very long time. They could be sitting in a quaint restaurant in Montmartre or in a café along the Mediterranean coast, and it wouldn't have made any difference. They were together, and that was all the adventure they needed.

Julian gave Tenley two gifts, one a gold heart-shaped locket necklace and a new laptop computer. She had excitedly torn off the red-and-silver wrapping paper and opened the box, eyes-wide as she examined the computer.

"Oh Julian, you shouldn't have. Thank you. I adore you."

Julian helped her remove the wrapping on the small jewelry box and then held up the locket. "It's beautiful!" she said and attempted to put the necklace on.

"No," Julian said. "First you must look inside."

When she saw the small color photo of Julian, tears again flooded her eyes. "I can't believe you found a photo of yourself. It looks like it was taken recently."

"Leighton took it for me and a camera shop reduced it to fit inside. This is the way I want to be remembered."

Tenley looked up. "I will never have to remember you, Julian. You will always be with me."

"I'm seventy and you're 35..."

"There you go," Tenley said. "Worrying about tomorrow when tomorrow isn't here."

"I want you to promise me one thing," Julian said. "If something happens to me, you must live your life and find romance as you meet other people."

"We don't know what tomorrow will bring," Tenley persisted.

"Please promise me."

"No."

"If something were to happen to you, would you want me to wallow in sorrow and never get on with my life?

"That's cruel, Julian."

Tenley said she didn't want to talk about the subject again and that if he ever were to bring up the matter in the future, she wouldn't talk to him for a week.

They ate their cake and then Julian filled up their wine glasses. Tenley read him some of *Browning's Sonnets from the Portuguese*, including her favorite:

> *How do I love thee? Let me count the ways.*
> *I love thee to the depth and breadth and height*
> *My soul can reach, when feeling out of sight*
> *For the ends of Being and ideal Grace.*
> *I love thee to the level of everyday's*
> *Most quiet need, by sun and candle-light.*
> *I love thee freely, as men strive for Right;*
> *I love thee purely, as they turn from Praise.*
> *I love thee with the passion put to use*
> *In my old griefs, and with my childhood's faith.*
> *I love thee with a love I seemed to lose*
> *With my lost saints!---I love thee with the breath,*
> *Smiles, tears, of all my life!---and, if God choose,*
> *I shall but love thee better after death.*

After the wine and the cake and the readings, Julian lifted Tenley from her wheelchair and carried her to his bed. They lay under the covers naked, cradled together, breathing in tandem, their breaths locked in a cadence of love so strong words and voice would have been superfluous, if not ruinous. Soon Julian ran his hand over the curve of her hips, the small of her back, her breasts and her stomach, watching her mouth open when he'd drawn her sensations of unspeakable pleasure.

Spooned together, their breaths mingled, husband and wife, they both fell asleep, bereft of dreams and memories and feared awakenings.

Chapter Twenty-Four

Spring came early that year. Julian could tell because the children wore no coats or sweaters as they played in the park outside his window. Lovers held hands, wearing tee-shirts, shorts and sandals. While he could not hear what they were saying, he imagined conversations about passions, aspirations and hopes. The children were carefree, swinging on swings, climbing multicolored playground structures and swooping down slides, their parents sitting on benches watching them with vigilant eyes.

Julian's mind was like a sponge: on some days it was filled with awareness and recognition, on others it was dried up, little filling the dull, porous spaces of emptiness. He would wake on bad days to a dearth of recognition, feeling confused and lost in foreign surroundings. Other days like this one, Julian was his old self, able to recall important matters and to indulge in logical thinking, anchored at last by full awareness and reasoning.

Sometimes the anchor held for days and weeks, and his thinking was largely unimpeded. Old memories were accessible, although newer ones required deliberation and coaxing. Although they were met with some irritability, Julian learned not to fight off the bad days. Acceptance and patience worked to keep his attitude positive.

Terrible days were the ones devoid of awareness. Everything felt sterile and foreign, even once-familiar surroundings, books, a chair and the annoying sunlight invading his room.

Sudden rage would consume him although he didn't know why. He would throw things across the room and then yell at them, cursing unintelligibly in an anguished tongue. He resorted to slapping himself in the face or hitting the wall behind his bed. It was a rage for survival in a new world of unfamiliarity and closets of darkness so dense he was afraid that if he fell into one he would vanish forever.

One day he awoke and realized that he didn't know himself. He just stared at the ceiling and then examined his hands, turning them slowly from front to back as if they were exquisitely made foreign objects. He wondered vaguely whether he had ever noticed them before. There was no fear, anger or resentment, only a delicate web attaching him to the numb sensations he felt. Curiosity would set him afloat and he felt like a tiny boat on a vast sea, calmly bobbing under a blue sky.

During a long stretch of bad days, Tenley became an intruder, and an unremitting slave-driver. She forced him to repeat simple routines, to remember words and use them in cogent sentences. She taught him simple word recognition and how to label objects in the room and to touch her face and point out facial features she would name. She read to him several times a day: poetry, classical fiction and even chapters of his own book. When there was time she would describe in detail their experiences in Europe, the places they'd visited, the foods and the wines and the colorful people.

One day she arrived in his room with scissors, shaving cream and a razor. "We are going to take years off that handsome face of yours," she said, clipping away at the straggly beard, which had long overgrown its intended boundaries. All of this she did with her good hand, the other limp at her side.

Julian watched in dull puzzlement as the clippings fell on the white towel she'd placed across his chest and neck. She applied the cream, massaging it into the remaining stubble and then shaved it clean.

"My God," she said, "you look a little like Brad."

The name must have registered in a solitary memory cell, for Julian cracked a smile and then began patting his shaven face. Tenley brought him a hand mirror and watched his expression brighten even more.

"Brad," he said cheerfully.

"No, you're Julian, sweetheart. Brad doesn't exist anymore."

"Why?"

"I love you, whoever you are."

Julian made the appropriate sign with his hand, wagging it with a big smile on his face.

◆

Tenley's nearly full recovery was not apparent to Julian. He had lost his memory of her seizures and the long months of rehabilitation. Occasionally, he was aware of her comings and goings. He felt anguished when she was not there by his side but was sustained by the hope of her return. Their times together were precious and meaningful to Julian, and Tenley's arrivals soon became sudden and exciting surprises.

One splendid day in late June, Tenley and Julian visited the park where they had met Dino. She pushed his wheelchair up to the bench where they had found the boy weeping.

"Honey, do you remember Dino?" she said.

Julian's brow was furrowed, a dark empty mood fastened to his face. It was as if she had asked him to solve a very complicated formula. His eyes seem to work the computation, his jaw clenched with the effort.

"It's okay," she said and began to recount how Dino had entered their lives and that he had been best man at their wedding. She then looked about and pointed out scenery items, the squirrels and various species of colorful birds. She noticed the little girl playing with her doll in the nearby grass, her mother or nanny seated at the far bench. The youngster had short black hair with bangs, which took on a silvery hue in the bright sunlight. She was watching them intently.

When the girl approached, Tenley noticed the pale, almost porcelain quality of her skin. She had small round lips that tightened with discernment as if she were about to reveal a long held mystery.

"What's wrong with him?" she said, peering around to look at Julian's face.

"Sweetheart, there's nothing wrong with him," Tenley said.

"He looks lost," the girl said in a cultured English accent.

Julian assumed an expression similar to the one on the young girl's face but it soon became more intense as evidenced by the squinting of his left eye and an overall expression of someone about to curse.

"Piss off!" Julian said with a grunt.

The girl jumped back, obviously not expecting the subject of her inquisition to be able to respond. She looked up at Tenley and then back at Julian as if she suspected this was some sleight of voice.

Tenley apologized, saying that Julian hadn't meant to say that.

"Well," the girl said, sighing, "he was just pretending to be lost."

Tenley pushed Julian around the park, stopping at a small pond where a duck and her six ducklings were wading lazily around the perimeter. She pointed out the small family and told Julian that if she could she really wanted to come back as a duck or swan. She praised him when he said the word *duck* and appeared to understand her comment about reincarnation. She took advantage of this impromptu sign that Julian was struggling to come out of his dreary fog and asked him what he saw when she pointed to an object. He responded correctly half the time and when he didn't she saw in his eyes a sudden blankness, as if a door had suddenly slammed shut in front of him.

Julian was still there, if only for sporadic moments of awareness, as if a candle were burning at the end of a deep cave, flickering against the cold breath of obliteration. Tenley saw it as her mission to keep that flame alight, in spite of what she knew about his poor prognosis. She redoubled her efforts to keep him stimulated by reading him the news, passages from books he'd loved and always her poetry recitations. At least every other day she took him outside to sit in the courtyard or push him along sidewalks to visit familiar surroundings.

One evening when she was reading him the last chapter of *Odessa's Feud*, Tenley stopped, a lump in her throat and unable to proceed to the next page. The story was hauntingly autobiographical, about a woman who had lost her mind to senility and her ultimate bargain with the devil to trade all sensibilities and passions of love in order to regain her functioning mind. At this point in the final chapter Odessa confronts her lover with her decision. It was beautifully written, with romantic scenes she recognized as their own.

She finished reading the chapter to Julian, teary-eyed and sad and full of amazement. "Julian, it's beautiful, absolutely beautiful!" she said and arose from her chair and, leaning forward, kissed him on the lips.

She realized that the manuscript was started sometime when he was at the University, probably when he first began to recognize the signs of his own memory loss. In an odd way it made sense of Julian's life, the almost magical effects of the medication he'd taken and the brief reversal of time, the passionate love affairs, all of his flaunting and his thirst for adventure. Julian had written the story for Tenley but had never asked her to read it. The original dedication page read:

For Tenley, whose brilliance, imagination and beauty belong to a future unknown, and whose kindness and presence supplied the inspiration for this story.

Julian had loved her from his early days teaching. He had kindled that love when she had been one of his students. She returned to those days and now remembered the flirting glances and gentle embraces. They had been discreet and at the time had left no effect upon her. But it was all so clear to her now. Julian had known her destiny and his own and that, in some far future, they would get married and spend the rest of their lives together.

"I...love *you*," Julian said, startling Tenley as she sat there with the book in her lap, tears still in her eyes.

Tenley took his hand and pressed it to her heart. "I will always be with you, no matter what becomes of us."

"Forever." Julian said.

One day Tenley didn't come to visit in the nursing home. Julian was in a more lucid state of mind and the emotion of fear erupted in outbursts of anger and whimpering sadness. He demanded of the nurse that he be taken to her, that he had a right to know, that she was his wife. The nurse told him that she was fine but would not be able to visit today. This only sharpened his awareness and his determination to know the truth.

Early that afternoon, after the nursing attendants had removed the lunch tray and cleaned the room, Julian swung his feet to the floor and forced himself to a standing position. He was immediately horrified that he was wearing a pair of adult diapers. This observation required further investigation and queries for the nurses, but Julian knew he didn't have time. He found a pair of gray slacks, a shirt and shoes in the closet and put them on, using the wall to steady himself when he felt he was losing his balance.

He slipped into the hallway unseen and began retracing his steps in the direction of Tenley's room. It was a long but uncomplicated route and as he walked, Julian felt a jubilant sense that he was again in control of his life. He suddenly became aware of his condition but was not intimidated by the knowledge. What mattered was what he was experiencing now, *in the moment* as Tenley referred to it. This rush of coherence brought him physical strength and a resurge of mental stamina he had not experienced in a long while.

He found Tenley's room and entered it through the open door. She was on her side facing the wall, her head buried in the pillow, her left arm outstretched. She was asleep, breathing deep breaths, her neck and back rising with each inhalation.

"Tenley," he whispered and reached for her arm, which he began to stroke softly. It was warm to the touch and soft and oddly unfamiliar.

The woman turned to face him. He realized at that moment that this was not his wife but an older woman with gray hair and a dark mole aside her nose. She screamed an ugly scream, at a high wavering pitch, which in no time brought in the nursing aides. One went to comfort the woman and the other grabbed hold of Julian wrists and held them with overpowering strength.

"Where is Tenley, my wife?!" he demanded, struggling against the iron grip of the aide.

Within seconds two security men arrived and each took hold of his arms, escorting him out of the room. In his mind he had the strength to break away or to knock down the guards and then leap into the nursing station and start interrogating the head nurse. But the inclination vaporized when he realized that he only had the strength of an old man who had long ago lost his vitality. The men forced him back and placed him in a wheelchair with Velcro straps to restrain his wrists and ankles.

Recognizing the intruder, the charge nurse came out of the station and told the men to release the restraints. "Julian," she said. "I'm sorry...we didn't recognize you."

"My wife," Julian said in a deflated tone. "What have you done with her?"

The nurse rubbed one of his hands. "She's not here now."

Panic flooded Julian's face. "Has she died?"

"No, of course not," the nurse said.

"I don't understand."

Sensing a need not to inquire further, Julian capitulated to the puzzlement and suddenly felt a yearning to be alone.

Back in his room Julian asked if he could visit the courtyard and get some fresh air. Impressed by his improvement that day, the staff agreed and then made him promise that he wouldn't venture beyond the nursing home grounds. He felt the sudden urge to read, so he took his glasses and one of Tenley's poetry books as he left the room, escorted by the aide.

The courtyard was vaguely familiar to Julian. It had two crescent-shaped stone benches facing each other, several lawn chairs, a cherry blossom tree and forsythia shrubs surrounding the area. There were flower beds with crocuses, daffodils and wild roses, all in gathering bloom. A stone statue of Saint Francis holding a bird bath in the shape of a large clam was set among the flower beds. Julian watched as a small squirrel navigated up the statue and perched itself along the rim of the bath, occasionally dipping his nose into the water and then rubbing its paws together as if washing its face.

The observation made Julian even more aware, as if a magnificent dawn were rising before him. What he saw was the present moment in its perfect composition, an instant of perfection far from by the clamor of life, past memory or future thoughts. It was a scene that begged to be experienced, a notion that gave Julian great wonder and peace.

Had Tenley been there he would have pointed out the squirrel, now frozen at the base of the statue, the robin alighting on the rim of the bath, dipping his beak for a drink, and how the clouds drifted across the sky. He would share the fragrance of cherry blossoms and the chatter of birds, and how all of it had an exquisite feel of orderly meaning.

He opened *Sonnets from the Portuguese* and flipped through the pages. All were blank.

A cascade of memories suddenly overflowed his thoughts, of Carolyn when she was a young girl, of her life as a successful business woman and of the deep love he had for his daughter. He couldn't remember when he'd last spoken to her. It seemed odd and remote, as if their relationship wasn't exactly real. Why had he been so reluctant about contacting her and receiving her calls? He realized then that Carolyn didn't know about his condition or that he and Tenley had married and were living in a nursing home. He had so much to share with her.

That evening he found himself tucked into bed with no recollection of having left the courtyard. When the lights were turned off, he lay there staring up at the darkened ceiling. He found himself waiting.

On the very edge of slumber he was vaguely aware of someone opening the door and approaching the bed. The slice of illumination from the hallway that fell upon his closed eyes gave him a faint inclination to open them, but he didn't.

In an instant he was floating in a dream, which became a scenario and a conversation with Tenley. They were discussing Shakespeare and the strange topic of whether Hamlet and Horatio had a platonic relationship or a sexual one. Tenley was so ardently supporting the latter viewpoint Julian finally surrendered to that opinion. The conversation moved to other less literary issues concerning life, its meaning and whether religions had it all wrong about heaven and hell, Tenley insisting that daily life was heaven and hell was a mindful state and what you made it out to be.

Then he took her hand in his own and lifted her effortlessly into an airy estate of blue sky and weightlessness. Her face, he remembered, was bright with wonder. "Oh Julian," she said as they flew together into the phantasmal realm.

Chapter Twenty-Five

July that year was unusually cool for the season and that first Wednesday could have been a day like any in May but for its abundant greenery and the lush growth of ivy on brownstone exteriors. The snowmelt that spring had caused the Charles River to overflow along some of its banks. Channels remained at high-tide levels, prompting officials to post new *low wake* signs near marinas and estuaries. Fishing was bountiful and it looked to be a record catch for the small lobster boats chugging out to their pots during evening hours.

Julian's regression was profound. Except in dreams, he was merely an embodiment of himself. He was bathed, dressed and fed by benevolent presences beyond his comprehension. Sometimes he recognized a face or a voice but they were all but a fleeting cognizance.

One day he was aware of Tenley's presence. It grew on him slowly, a tattered sensation. He noticed her perfume, the sweet fragrance of her breath, the caring touch and soon her familiar voice, all of it in some peculiar suspension of familiarity.

When she kissed him on the forehead, the sensation was clear and real and seemed to pulsate through his body. He suddenly felt alive inside his cumbersome exterior, like a fire had been lit, a dazzling release of warmth.

Tenley, where have you been?

She smiled and pressed her hand on his forehead, pressing it firmly until the silent inquiry dissipated.

He lay there stilled, comfortably vulnerable and vacant. It was as if he were awaiting a new spirit, a fresh persona.

◆

Julian awakened one morning to find Tenley in his room, fiddling with the coffeepot. The aroma of warmed croissants, fried eggs and coffee filled the air.

Julian lifted his head and was startled to discover that he had the strength to sit up.

"Tenley?"

"Ah...Mr. Winkle has come back from the dead," she said. "Do you realize it's almost ten?"

"I don't understand."

Tenley came over and sat on the bed. She leaned over and kissed Julian on his lips. "Good morning, lover-boy."

"But I recognize you. I understand that you are here."

"I should hope so," Tenley said. "We are married. I am your wife."

"I thought I was dead," Julian said, running his hands over his face and then reaching for Tenley.

They hugged and then Julian lowered his ear to her breast. The soft heartbeat he heard brought tears to his eyes. "You're real," he whispered.

Tenley looked into his eyes. "Today is the first and only day of our lives," she said. "Let's not be inquisitive or question our moments. Just let them be and live them."

"But..." Julian began as Tenley cupped her hand over his lips.

She got up and opened the window curtains. The sunlight poured in, bathing Tenley's form with a fantastic aura of brilliance. She looked like an angel, and Julian could almost imagine wings tucked at her side. Her hair was radiant and her skin shone with a purity that was almost blinding.

"You are an angel," Julian said. "I must be in heaven."

Tenley laughed. "Sweetheart," she said, "there are no such things as angels. Heaven only exists in the moment...and it is what you make it."

The old rationality set in and Julian found himself challenging Tenley's nebulous assertions. "One day I'm an old senile man on the verge of dying and then suddenly everything is back to normal...a wonderful normal. Things like this don't happen in real life. Ergo, you must be an angel!"

Tenley said nothing but continued starring at him with her dusty blue eyes.

"If not," he continued, "then this is some strange loop or perhaps a warp in time. There has to be an explanation."

Tenley's stare grew more intense. "Why does there have to be an explanation, a rationality for everything? Just accept how you feel, now, in this moment. Nothing else matters in the least, Julian. Let go of that false rigid mindset of yours. You don't need it anymore."

As he had always done, he trusted Tenley implicitly.

After breakfast they dressed and decided to go for a walk. The sun had taken the early morning chill out of the air but the day was still autumnal-like, low humidity, with an eddying northeasterly breeze. Objects and the facades of buildings appeared curiously new to Julian as if his perception of familiar things had undergone a magical renewal. Or as if he possessed a new set of eyes. He was intrigued by the textures and shades and the way the sunlight glistened off the angles and crevices of surfaces.

They both walked effortlessly, almost as if they were moving on cushions of air, yet their feet were firmly planted on the sidewalks. This unencumbered forward motion felt adventuresome to Julian as if they were embarking on another journey together.

When they arrived at a small park overlooking the Neponset River they walked to the water's edge and sat down on the fresh grass. They held hands.

"I love you so much," Julian said and then became wistfully pensive.

Tenley kissed him and lay her head on his shoulder.

"I only wish we'd had a child," Julian said.

A yellow board boat sailed by, moving through trinkets of sunlit water. A young girl waved at them. The air about them quivered in a slight breeze.

Tenley took his hand and placed it on her stomach.

Startled, Julian felt a slight movement inside. He looked up into Tenley's eyes.

And then all of it ended.

◆

There were voices but none that he could identify.

He was aware of physical contact, sounds, especially music, and powerful fragrances: perfume, the smell of disinfectant, food, spring air, flowers, trees and the mellifluous scents brought in by a breeze. Words did not captivate him as much as his ability to dwell in the redolence of all that stimulated that part of his brain. It became the connection to the outside world. A particular smell would bring a faint recollection, from which fleeting moments of awareness would spring and then fade.

He sensed that he was an infant, which could have been his own infancy so many decades ago. That subtle awareness became comforting and eased his feeling of powerlessness. Voices, touches and odors became affirmations that he was still alive in what seemed like a very compassionate world. But in time the voices became unrecognizable, all inflections of human sound blending into one soothing maternal tone.

Soon the senses of taste and smell left him. Satiation became a dull fullness in his stomach, sustenance not having passed through his mouth and palate but from the external pulsing of a pump. The urgency of hunger failed to exist anymore and so too the rudimentary sense of thirst. He lay in a state of effortless compliance.

One night something extraordinary happened. Julian awoke into a presence of grand illumination. He was able to smell, taste and hear, and his mind bloomed with the luxurious powers of recollection, reason and awareness. He was instantly able to recall the real events of his life: his childhood, his courtship with Elizabeth, the birth of his daughter, his years as a teacher and the enduring friendships he'd nourished.

Although her name was real, Tenley was missing from this experience. He was aware of their relationship as if it had only been a wishful dream, a fancy to suit his aging years. He struggled to reveal that dream, hoping again to enter it and explore this puzzling contradiction, but that seemed unallowable in this fragile venue of presence.

Julian persisted though. The love he had experienced with this person *was* real. He wanted to argue this affirmation with someone, but his connection to the outside world was no longer there. And then it didn't seem to matter anymore.

He imagined that he was dying and that all was reversed. Death was the exterior of a life from which he'd been evicted. He was not afraid but felt pangs of regret and abandonment that he had left loved ones inside.

As if he were slowly suffocating, he poked an imaginary finger into the pliable membrane of life, hoping to puncture it just long enough to get one last gasp of life, a breath that would keep him alive just one moment longer. To his astonishment, one of the pokes was successful and all life gushed into the blackness around him, sweeping him up like a giant wave in a torrent of vivid memories, shades and layers of experience that repeated like video reruns, over and over.

Layer by layer, he relived his first marriage to Elizabeth, the birth of Carolyn and the ensuing happy journey of their marriage. He accepted how he'd changed following his wife's death and had retreated into his teaching. He searched for Tenley and the experiences they'd had, but they eluded him. He repeated his search, slowing down each recollection until it came to a standstill. And then he entered each fragment of remembrance: the fragrances, the tastes, the sensual stirrings and the infinite sensations of love. He experienced the flamboyance of manhood, the carefree sexuality of life, the sadness and the poignant feelings of absolute joy.

Tenley, where are you? I must see you again. He heard his voice as a whispery, wind-swept sound.

He found himself on a tenuous brim confronted by an intellectual choice to linger where he was or to let it all go, with no fear of making the wrong decision. The choice soon became analytical and posed a curious ethical dilemma: if he chose to stay he would infringe on the rights of others waiting to enter this world.

But he had to find Tenley. He wanted to tell her that *this* was the other side, that death just meant entering a different layer of awareness. It seemed so simple a revelation.

Soon an urgency overwhelmed him. The decision to either stay or go became obligatory, compelled by some beneficent presence well beyond his comprehension.

But Julian didn't go. He didn't vanish into a vacuum of darkness as he'd once suspected death would be like. For a brief moment he was inside someone else's awareness, feeling a primitive knowledge of someone with no experiences. It felt pure and innocent and full of ancient joy.

When the final darkness came, he was sitting at a café in Montmartre on a warm Parisian evening. And he was about to say something important.

PART IV

"Reality is merely an illusion, albeit a very persistent one."
--Albert Einstein

Chapter Twenty Six

The attractive middle-aged woman sitting in the back of the bus as it traveled along Glen Ray Road in West Virginia closed her eyes, took a deep breath and then looked back at the facility in which she had been incarcerated for almost five years.

She had lost almost everything: her fortunes, possessions and nearly all of her friends.

She'd murdered no one, nor robbed a bank nor committed a lifetime of crime. But she had broken the law. Avarice had caused her to make a foolish decision when she tried to cover up one occasion of inside trading.

Most of her assets had been used to pay off expensive attorneys, innumerable fines and penalties and the lawsuits brought against her by some of her vengeful former employees. There were some small trusts that escaped mean-spirited lawsuits but their value would hardly sustain her for very long.

She had been provided one hundred dollars and her entering possessions, along with bus fare that would take her as far as Charleston, where there was an airport.

As the bus pushed its way over The New River Gorge National River on I-64, she looked out of the window and stared at the vehicles streaming by on the highway. Once cynical about traffic and the indifference of drivers, she now welcomed what she saw with great optimism and acceptance. Even the ashen sky and the smoke curling up from factory stacks seemed to have their proper place.

At last she had her freedom.

Upon her arrival at the bus terminal in Charleston, she hailed a taxi to take her to the airport. She had only an hour left before her flight was scheduled to be boarded. She gave the cabbie one of the fifty dollar bills in her purse and told him it was a matter of life or death. He tipped his hat and took off in a cloud of blue smoke, navigating through the dense traffic, diverting to back roads when there was a bottleneck ahead. They arrived at Yeager Airport with fifteen minutes to spare.

During her flight to Boston the sadness she had been holding back for over a week overcame her like a tidal wave, colliding with emotions of grief and guilt. Her new-felt joy of freedom vanished. In a confused moment she wished that she had never been released from prison. She felt like the crushed cockroach of her fanciful dreams.

She closed her eyes and tried to feign sleep. She felt the tears escaping from the corners of her eyes.

The passenger in the seat beside her, a pleasant older man with unruly white hair, leaned over and asked if she was okay. She nodded but didn't open her eyes. In her mind she replayed the phone call she had received in prison the week before she was released. The anguish of that experience and the realization that nothing could reverse the sad news was a leaden grief in her heart. She knew she would have to live with that sorrow for the rest of her life.

Laced with that pain was a terrible sense of guilt. Maybe if she had called just once or at least written a letter...but then nothing would have altered the final course of events. She thought about her crime and how through the years she had learned to forgive herself. Forgiving was a healing process.

Now, flying at 31,000 feet over western Pennsylvania, she suddenly felt a magnificent wave of forgiveness. It was not self-forgiveness but from a powerful source, an entity she immediately recognized. Blessed by that reprieve, she soon drifted into sleep.

◆

They approached Logan airport and descended onto runway 33 Left with a 15 mph tailwind. The passenger who had intervened when the woman had been crying turned out to be a retired Pan American pilot who had flown into the airport many times in his long career. Perhaps because he sensed a troubling appointment for the woman after landing he talked nonstop about his flying experiences and then in great detail explained the landing procedure for the Boeing 737.

The discourse was interesting but did not distract the woman from what lay ahead. She thanked him for his concern and for sharing his knowledge of flight.

Exiting the plane, the passenger turned to the woman and said, "All's well in a good landing."

She took a cab to the Marriott at Long Wharf. A parcel was waiting for her at the desk when she registered. She excused herself and sat down in the lounge. Opening the package, she retrieved a debit card and a renewed driver's license, along with several hundred dollars in cash.

There were important people to call. The woman wasted no time and began by calling her uncle in California. He had already been informed and had taken the news well, for he had been expecting his brother's death.

She then called Boston University and asked to speak with Tenley Harrington. She was told that the professor had recently married and that she was on a leave of absence. She was given Tenley's personal number. She informed the operator of Professor Landon's recent death and asked that the sad news be shared with his colleagues there. She then called the funeral home and confirmed the arrangements for the gravesite service on Wednesday. Before calling Tenley she telephoned her friend in California.

"Carolyn! Thank God you're out," Heather said.

"Thank you for everything you have done," Carolyn said. "I would never have survived without your friendship and help. Thank you for the package and for helping arrange things."

"I'm really sorrow about your father," Heather said. "I'm just glad I had a chance to spend time with him when I flew out there last month. He was a kind and generous man."

"Yes," Carolyn said.

"I just wish I could be there for the service. I feel so guilty for not being able to."

"Heather, you've been planning this trip for years. If my father knew I'm sure he would insist that you go. When do you leave?"

"Next Wednesday if the weather holds up."

"Please call me the day you leave, Heather. After then I guess I won't hear from you for many months. You are so brave and I am so proud of you. I know you can accomplish this."

"It's a dream finally come true," Heather said.

Carolyn waited until the afternoon to call Tenley. She was indebted to her friend for having done so much for her father, for arranging the transfer to the nursing home, for taking care of him and for filling the role of a caring daughter. Her friend had honored her request that her father never be told of his daughter's incarceration. Carolyn always believed that she would be granted an early release and be allowed to spend the remaining months with Julian. But the parole board had not granted her that favor, only agreeing to release her should her father die during the remaining six months of her sentence.

She made the call shortly after four in the afternoon. She had anticipated a long conversation, for they had a lot to catch up on. She hoped that Tenley would share the last few days of her father's life. They had to confirm the service arrangements. Last but not least, Carolyn needed to shower her friend with gratitude for all she had done.

The answering machine picked up on the fourth ring. She listened to Tenley's recorded greeting while she assembled an abbreviated message of her own. But when the recording beep sounded she was abruptly at loss for words.

She hung up, planning to call her friend later on that evening.

Chapter Twenty Seven

The husband and wife were seated on the sofa in the small apartment near the University campus. They were cuddled together watching television, the woman's feet propped up by a throw cushion atop the glass inlay coffee table. The husband was gently stroking his wife's swollen belly, occasionally pressing his ear to it to hear the mysterious sounds of the life burgeoning inside.

They were going to have a baby in less than two months, their first after a long period of trying and innumerable visits to a fertility clinic. They knew the sex of the fetus and had already begun furnishing the light blue room that used to be the husband's office. Two recent baby showers had provided just about everything they would need in the first six months of their son's life: baby food, clothing, crib, baby monitor, diapers and innumerable baby toys, including several mobiles to hang above the crib.

It could be said of the couple that they were the happiest people in the world, this despite the recent death of the woman's colleague and dear friend.

She had been there during Julian's final hours and was holding his hand as he took his last breath. He had drifted in and out of a coma for weeks, with only fleeting moments of awareness. She recalled the faint smile on his face and the eased expression of someone who had just arrived at a perfect destination. Julian, she knew, died with peace, liberated from the horrible tangles and shreds of broken memory that had tormented his later years. She only wished that he had stayed around long enough for the impending birth of her child.

Her husband Brad had answered Carolyn's call and handed the phone to Tenley. She and Julian's daughter talked for almost an hour. Carolyn wanted to know about the last months of Julian's life at the nursing home. *Was he in pain? Had he suffered? Had he ever talked about his daughter?* Tenley assured her that despite brief moments of consciousness Julian spent most his time in the cocooned safety of peaceful coma.

They reconfirmed the service plans. Tenley said she and Brad would pick up Carolyn at nine on Wednesday morning. The cemetery wasn't too far from the hotel.

◆

On that misty morning in late October, Tenley, Brad and Carolyn drove to Forest Hills Cemetery. Fall colors had given way to bare branches and mounds of leaves as an early winter set in in Boston. The snow hadn't come yet, but in the chilled air under ashen skies there was the smell of it, a distant storm like a cavalry waiting for the signal to charge. They drove down streets where gaggles of school children stood around waiting for their buses, swaddled in colorful coats and hats, looking all the ready for what the new day had in store for each.

The older section of the cemetery had a worn, gothic look to it, with stone obelisks and headstones of every variety, some in the shapes of beds, cradles and pets. Statues abounded, along with shrines and mausoleums with gargoyles and seraphic sculptures. Fall leaves of rich earthen colors mantled the ground, edging up the base of headstones, cherry trees, sugar and Japanese maples, umbrella pines, and weeping hemlocks.

They were the first ones to arrive at the gravesite, a simple mound of earth with its headstone facing south. The interment had occurred a week past but the fresh-cut flowers on the dirt and laying against the headstone looked as if they had been placed there just hours ago.

They all knelt down in front of the gravestone, a polished gray stone with dark engraving and a small sailboat above Julian's name with an inscription below it. Tenley explained that it was a poem by Emily Dickinson, one of Julian's favorites.

The ceremony took place shortly after eleven that morning. Father Hagel spoke of Julian as a beloved man with strong intellectual faith. He mentioned his dedicated years as a professor of mathematics and said that Julian had never strayed from the flock. He concluded by reminding the attendees that Julian was now with God teaching Him complex mathematical formulas. Tenley and the others smiled faintly.

All of Julian's friends and staff from the nursing home were there. Leighton laid a bouquet of lilies and carnations at the base of the grave. Others brought flowers too. Tenley held a vase of yellow roses, which she placed against the headstone inscription.

Claudia was late for the service but arrived in time to join hands with the others as they recited Dickinson's poem. She had brought two other friends with her. They had all spent time with Julian at various times, volunteering at the nursing home or just visiting with him.

Dino was there. Carolyn turned and asked Tenley who the young man was. She explained that they had befriended Dino once while Tenley had taken Julian to the park. The boy was in trouble and Julian insisted on helping him with various legal problems. Dino repaid him by spending hours at his bedside and helping Julian with grooming needs.

As if he knew they were talking about him, Dino came around from the other side of the grave. He was dressed in a faded green flak jacket, tattered jeans and a black Red Socks cap.

"You must be Carolyn," Dino said, extending his hand. He was not in the least confrontational but spoke his mind matter-of-factly. "Glad they let you out. Guess that's one thing we have in common."

For a second Carolyn looked like she had been struck by an arrow. Slowly she smiled and thanked Dino for taking care of her father.

"Your Dad was like a father to me. He helped me plenty when times were rough. He was a decent man."

◆

The service lasted less than an hour. Those who had come from the nursing home piled into their blue van, waving at the others as the vehicle pulled away down the driveway to the cemetery exit.

Tenley, Carolyn, Dino and Brad stayed by the gravesite. Dino approached the headstone and knelt down, bowing his head. He remained there several minutes and then wiping his nose stood up. There were tears in his eyes. He approached and gave Tenley a long hug and then shook hands with Brad and Carolyn.

Extending the handshake with Carolyn, he said, "I think the professor would want you to know that he asked about you several times when I was with him. Sometimes he pretended that you had visited him, like it was part of a story going on in his mind. Towards the end he just got too mixed up, but I know that he loved you."

Carolyn smiled and thanked the young man.

They watched as Dino walked to his car, an old red Beemer with a rusted rear fender. He honked his horn as he drove off.

Tenley was the last to pay her respects. She placed her hand on the cold earth at the head of the grave. Her husband and Carolyn stood back. A northeast wind blew her shiny blonde hair which rose like a fan at the back of her head, exposing the supple skin on her neck. Her hand made an impression in the loose soil.

"Julian Landon, you will always be with me," she whispered.

Chapter Twenty Eight

Tenley returned to her teaching post at the University. She had used all of her vacation leave to be with Julian during the last two months of his life. She was happy to be back, although, like a missionary having returned from long dedicated work, she missed her time with Julian.

She had taken his old office and would often find herself at the window, looking down at the courtyard. His old desk was still there, along with boxes of reference books. Sometimes she would turn away from the window and imagine him sitting at the desk working on computations and formulas, his glasses on, his gray hair unkempt, occasionally rubbing at the bridge of his nose.

A month after the service Carolyn dropped her a card. She thanked Tenley for all she had done. She reminded her that their mutual friend Heather had just made port in Cabo San Lucas and that the around-the-world trip was going as scheduled. Tenley never heard from Carolyn again.

On a wintry morning a week after Christmas Tenley gave birth to a nine pound baby boy with eyes the color of robin's eggs. Brad had been in the delivery room and had taken it upon himself to video the birth. In the hospital room when the baby was united with his mother, both Tenley and Brad had tears in their eyes. He was a gorgeous baby with a nascent fuzz of blond hair, dimpled appendages and a face that seemed to mimic his mother's expressions.

"Oh my God," Tenley said and turned to kiss her husband. "He's beautiful!"

They made their final decision about the baby's name as he was being washed and checked by the neonatal nurses. It had never been a question in Tenley's mind.

◆

Six months later Tenley was offered a teaching position at the Université Paris-Sorbonne in the Latin Quarter of Paris. She had always wanted to travel abroad and had applied for the position with little hope that it would be offered to her.

At first she wasn't sure she wanted to leave Boston and her friends, and she initially decided not to accept the position. Brad thought it was a great opportunity for her and the family and silently but persistently laid the groundwork for his wife to accept the offer. And when she did they all celebrated by going to a family restaurant, their son sitting in a highchair as Tenley fed him small pieces of her omelet.

That evening they lay in bed, little Julian between them. Brad was watching a football game and appeared to be teaching his son the basics of the game. But Julian kept looking at his mother with adoring eyes and little flinching smiles.

Later that night when Julian was fast asleep in his crib, Tenley watched her husband. His soft snoring lulled her to sleep. At first she thought she was dreaming of him but soon realized that it was a vision of her dear friend Julian, her son's namesake. He wasn't visible in the dream but a strange presence of him became a theme in her dreamy wanderings.

In the dream she was attempting to open the tiny locket Brad had given her when Julian had been born. Urgently she fumbled to open it but couldn't feel the pendant's edge. She pulled too hard and the golden locket fell away.

Suddenly, as if being led away by someone, she found herself flying. She rose from the ground slowly at first, then felt herself being propelled by a powerful buoyancy, as if the ground lines to an air balloon had been suddenly cut.

The dizzying height frightened her at first until she realized she had the freedom to maneuver wherever she pleased. She thought she was flying at an impossible speed but soon realized that all objects below were spinning furiously under her feet. She soared over expanses of blue and green water, over estates of endless meadows, over towering trees, over metropolises and intriguing castles, experiencing an awesome sense of liberation.

She came to rest in a foreign place, at a foreign time, sitting at a café table smiling, ready to answer the gentleman's question.